THE POWER OF MONEY

MARTIN MERCER

MINERVA PRESS
WASHINGTON LONDON MONTREUX

THE POWER OF MONEY

Copyright © Martin Mercer 1994

ISBN 1 85863 047 9

First Published 1994 by
MINERVA PRESS
2, Old Brompton Road,
London SW7 3DQ.

Printed in Great Britain by
Martins Printers Ltd., Berwick upon Tweed

THE POWER OF MONEY

CONTENTS

Chapter	Page
The Keys Of The Kingdom	7
Ebony and Ivory	32
Balling The Jack	39
Sister Golden Hair	46
Four Women	62
Spring in Bavaria	79
The President's Wife	87
Watchers at the Feast	100
Husbands and Lovers	111
Family Ties	117
The Samurai	132
Caribbean Return	157
Voodoo	161
Lady Elizabeth Goes To Hollywood	168
Revenge	175
Executive Action	198
Endings and Beginnings	209

THE KEYS OF THE KINGDOM

It was quiet enough to be the dark side of the moon. Susie Watkins looked round her husband's office for the last time; at the seventeenth-century credenza, at the splendid malachite and ormolu table on which ancient European kings once dined, at the rich tapestries that hung on the east wall of the room.

Those tapestries used to adorn a Norman castle, and in a way they still did. The Duparier Building in LA was almost a kingdom in itself and the private office of Roman Duparier the inner sanctum. And an execution chamber.

Susie lifted the soft leather weekend bag she carried and put it down carefully on the studio president's desk. More by touch than by sight she began to fill the bag with those little items which had so personalised the room as Roman's.

As her hands fell upon one certain piece, the tears that had been so near these last few days came in an unstoppable rush. It was her gift to him the day he became president: a framed photograph of Ernest Hemingway. Under the great man's signature Susie had written: "Grace under pressure, darling. Don't forget."

She touched the silver-framed portrait as if it was an icon. "Did you forget?" she asked aloud, into the emptiness. "Did you?"

The thirteen-year-old girl's head was spinning and her breath seemed to catch on an imaginary fish hook in her throat. Lying down on the bed didn't help. The combined effect of the champagne and the quaalude had robbed her of the willpower to fight the wave of nausea and fatigue that was sweeping over her. Am I going to die? she thought. The last thing she saw before passing out was Brett Sagan, the movie star, gazing down at her with stern disapproval and shaking his head.

Just out of her seventh grade classroom, Natasha Landi had been brought to the house high on Mulholland Drive with the promise of meeting Brett Sagan. She had agreed in the expectation of being able to boast to her friends back in the Valley about what Sagan was really like.

The man who had taken her to the house was Rudy Gioberti. Thirteen-year-old girls were usually more interested in movie actors than directors, yet she found herself attracted to the handsome, if comical Italian. But earlier in the afternoon, while posing for his still camera, she had felt confused and even a little threatened by his questions. Was she a virgin? Did she play with herself? Would she like him to show her how to give good head? Such questions intimidated Natasha, but the promise of more pictures, this time with Sagan, made her warm to Gioberti.

When they got to the house they discovered from a neighbour that Sagan had gone out. The girl, however, agreed to pose for more pictures before the light was lost. Though disappointed that the movie star was not there, Natasha was nevertheless impressed by the house itself and by Gioberti's familiarity with it. The photographs were for a commission he had been given by the French men's magazine Vogue Homme to produce a pictorial feature on the beautiful young girls on the West Coast. Gioberti found out about Natasha the year before during a brief affair with the girl's mother, a hard-living, hard-drinking divorcee and failed actress he met at a Bel Air orgy.

Before getting out his cameras again, Gioberti opened a bottle of Dom Perignon. The girl had one glass, and then a second, though she knew that champagne and her asthmatic condition did not mix. As she sipped on a third, Natasha began to feel a familiar discomfort creep up on her.

"I feel sick, Mr Gioberti."

He was all sympathy. There was a combination hot-tub and jacuzzi at the other end of the house. He suggested it would make her better. "And I can take some shots of you."

"But my bathing suit," said the girl. "I need my suit."

"No, you don't."

Before she could speak, he took her in his arms, kissing her hard and urgently on the mouth.

"Rudy, please, I..."

"Shut up," he growled. "Don't say a word." He kissed her again until her lips parted, and her small hands reached up and tentatively touched his face.

"I'm gonna throw up."

"Jesus, not over me you don't, bitch." He pushed her towards the nearest bathroom.

Feeling even worse after vomiting, Natasha lay down on a bed in one of the guest rooms. It was then that Sagan returned.

The girl had no idea how long she had been out. As she came awake and looked down at her naked body, she could see that her knees were arched and her legs were spread, and that the head of Rudy Gioberti, who was also naked, was somehow buried in her crotch. The sensations were unfamiliar but not really unpleasant: the unaccustomed feel of hair tickling the insides of her plump thighs, then of heat and dampness filling her up and an object, moist and rather rough in texture, stroking her clitoris.

Fascination was at first her only reaction. It was as though what she was seeing was happening to someone else, but then, as her mind cleared, her body stiffened.

"Stop it, please," she cried, her speech slurred by the drugged Dom Perignon, ineffectually attempting to kick out at Gioberti. Her head began to swim. She closed her eyes.

Moments later she was awaken by something being thrust into her open mouth. Gioberti was astride her, kneeling on her shoulders and arms, forcing his full erection in, frantically rubbing the swollen glans against the roof of her mouth. Suddenly he groaned and shuddered and her mouth was filled with warm, sticky liquid. She gagged. He let go of her and she ran to the bathroom and spat it out. Natasha had never tasted come before, though she knew what it looked like; her boyfriend had taught her how to give a good hand job.

"You all right, honey?" asked Gioberti, following her into the bathroom.

"Can I go home now?"

"Sure, honey. You ain't gonna say nothing 'bout this scene?"

"No."

"And your mother?"

"Ha. My mom's too busy humping every stiff dong she can get her hands on." Natasha grinned. "You should give her a try, Rudy. She's more your scene than I am."

Natasha and Susie Watkins talking.

"I mean," said Susie, "I didn't lose my virginity until I was fifteen, and there were only two other girls among my friends who hadn't been to bed with a guy, and they still haven't, so I suppose you could say I was the last. I really did like the boy, but there definitely was a feeling of getting it over with."

"Most of my friends lost their virginity when they were fourteen or fifteen," said Natasha. "My sister lost hers when she was twelve. I know girls are always more advanced about sex. Guys don't lose their cherry till they're sixteen or seventeen."

Susie nodded. "Guys are so much more uptight. They're scared of the responsibilities of sex, the attachments. They worry about whether you're gonna have an orgasm or not. I waited a whole year to have one. When it happened I was so pleased I sent a telegram to my best friend."

"At High School we talked about sex all the time. It was a real status thing. We'd say who we'd done it with, how many boys, you know, and how many different positions we'd tried, oral sex, things like that. We'd read the 'Joy of Sex' and try out things it said. Some of the boys were a lot less experienced than us girls, and we'd have these great conversations, you know. I can remember two of us on the subway comparing how many times we'd made our guys come the night before."

"Where did you do it?" asked Susie.

"Oh, mostly at my parents' house."

"Did they know?"

"Yes, most times." Natasha smiled. "When I look back now, my parents were really supportive. My mother paid for my contraception."

Susie smiled in agreement. "My dad used to tell me: 'You'll ruin your enjoyment of sex in later years by screwing around so young.' But I know better now. Sex is still fun. In fact, I don't know whether it's because I've got more experienced or whether I'm choosing better lovers, but sex is better now. Much better."

"At High School," said Natasha, "it was all pretty straightforward stuff but when my parents divorced and Mom and me moved to the Coast, 'cause she wanted to be an actress, some of my new friends were, are, into violence, SM, leather, things like that. I've never made it with another girl although I've got one friend who's a lesbian and several who are really bisexual. I've never done any group sex either."

"Same here."

"You know what, Susie? I had my fourth anniversary last week, since I got popped, and I've balled eleven guys. Some girls I know have had hundreds."

The sleek black studio limousine took the last bend, and there in the valley below, in the shadow of the sheltering hills, lay Sparta Studios. From the start Susie Watkins would think of SS in capital letters; it was a place she had to help Rudy escape from every night. The Sparta lot was the very image of Hollywood imprinted on the minds of a large percentage of the world's filmgoers. That famous aerial photograph of the vast spread of the studio's hangarlike sound stages was as familiar a symbol of tinsel-town as Paramount's De Mille gate. Not by chance, either. Rex Gideon managed to insert that shot into the promotional material of every film his studio released.

The chauffeur steered the limo slowly through the gate marked 'Artists' Entrance' and stopped at the guard's checkpoint. Rudy wound down the window.

"I'm Rudy Gioberti."

The guard consulted his clipboard. "You got a pass?"

"It's okay. I'm Rudy Gioberti."

"I don't care if you're Jessica Lange. You can't get in without a pass."

"My company just bought this studio, man. I'm the new president and you, man, are fired."

As the chauffeur drove through the entrance and onto the lot, Susie turned to glance backward out of the rear window and saw the guard talking on the phone.

It was only 4.30 on a Friday afternoon but already the lot had the look of a ghost town about it. Up in the hills and in the canyons beyond, the partying had already begun. Susie knew all about that life, those little gold or silver spoons, the straws, the lines of white powder. Afterwards, when everyone was high, out would come the video cameras to record the action, to be viewed at the start of the next party. She looked at Rudy. Meeting him was the best thing ever to happen to her.

It took them less than a minute to find a security man with keys to the office of Robert Gideon, which had been sealed like a tomb since the day of his arrest. Leaving the chauffeur in the limo, Susie and Rudy followed the man in uniform down a corridor of the executive office building.

"Here we are, Mr Gioberti," said the guard, opening the door to reveal an outer office and reception room of modest size. "Mr Gideon's private office is straight ahead, through those double doors.

Here's the key."

"Thanks."

The guard left them alone. They looked at each other.

"The keys of the kingdom, darling," murmured Susie.

He grinned. "Yeah." He turned the key in the lock, pushed open the tall, elegantly carved double doors, reached inside for the light switch, then stepped aside to let Susie enter first.

It was a huge room. Susie crinkled her nose. "Not bad, I suppose. All very functional, except for that."

"What?"

"That couch."

The wide, backless black couch was all by itself against the wall. The material in which it was covered, the softest of glove leathers, was worn shiny in several places.

"Do you think he balled his starlets on that?" she asked.

Rudy inspected the worn areas and smiled.

"I think so, honey, and often."

A spark of sexual electricity jumped between them. Susie's breathing quickened and her cheeks flushed. He laughed, pulling her down on the couch beside him. She arched her back, ran her hand along his thigh. He kissed her.

"Not here," she gasped. "The guard, anyone might walk in."

"Don't you find it exciting?"

She didn't answer. They kissed some more. He unzipped his fly to let her see his need.

"Rudy, this is crazy."

"I know."

He slipped his hands under her skirt, rolled her panties down, and thrust his erection between her pale thighs. She cried out, wrapping her long, sleek legs around his waist.

"Oh, Rudy, yes, oh."

He brought her to orgasm, her body jerking, her face sweaty, surprised.

A convoy of trucks trundled towards a rented resort home near the Mexican playground of the rich, Acapulco. In the trucks were twenty thousand red roses, fifty cases of champagne, one hundred bushels of white orchids, crates and crates of crab and baby lobster, and countless tureens of beluga caviar. The girl born Joanna Van Dross, on 17 February 1933, in London of Dutch and English descent, and known to the world as Joanna Jerome, was getting married for the fourth time in her tempestuous career. The groom-to-be was Lloyd King, showman extraordinaire, who had courted Joanna in a way that few women had ever been wooed.

Lloyd spent ninety-five thousand dollars on the engagement ring, thirty vulgar carats of diamond as big as an ice cube. Since first meeting the girl frequently described as the world's most beautiful, he had treated every Friday afterwards as an anniversary and showered her with gifts of ruby necklaces and diamond earrings, emeralds, sapphires, mink coats and dozens of hats, as well as designer dresses and evening gowns.

He paid thirty thousand dollars a year to rent a luxury private plane he called the 'Lady Joanna' and then spent another fifty thousand on the interior fittings and furnishings chosen by Joanna. He bought a yacht and a Rolls-Royce Silver Cloud, in which he installed two telephones and a bar with separate Lloyd and Joanna trays. The yacht was christened the 'Lady J'.

In an extravaganza of wheeler-dealing, Lloyd King bought two movie houses in Boston and called them His and Hers; he took out a lease on a mansion in Beverly Hills; rented a house in Palm Springs; spent thirty-five thousand dollars on an eighteen acre estate in Westport, Connecticut, which boasted swimming pools and tennis courts as special features.

It was an altogether special time for young Joanna Jerome. She had been a beautiful child, and her flawless porcelain complexion, eyes of deepest azure, and head of coal-black hair would have been enough to ensure the adult Joanna of much admiration by themselves. However, before her sixteenth birthday, the child had blossomed into a woman of almost indecent sensuality; the voluptuous curves of her slim and rather short body caused as many gasps for the teenager as the perfection of her face had for the child.

Joanna was seven years old when she arrived in Los Angeles in 1940 with her ambitious and domineering mother, Ruth, who had been an actress herself when young and was completely captivated by the glamour of Hollywood; so much so that she decided to push her shy daughter in front of the cameras and make her a star. Joanna's father, Erich, had stayed behind in London to hand over his art gallery business to his uncle, but joined them a few weeks later to open a gallery in LA. He was not pleased about Ruth's plans for their little girl. He worried over the effect the pressure of preparing for auditions might have on Joanna, but the seven-year-old assured him that she really did want to be a movie star.

Little Joanna auditioned for two studios, Metro-Goldwyn Mayer and the much smaller Sparta, and both made offers. Joanna begged her mother to sign with MGM, but the smaller company had offered more money and Ruth told her daughter she would be better looked after there. The founder and boss of the studio, Rex Gideon, was more interested in looking after Ruth, who obliged him only when Joanna began to get bigger and better roles. The affair was short-lived, however, and if Erich knew about it he never said.

So Joanna's career prospered. She co-starred with a cute Alsatian in My Pal, a sentimental animal picture; had a featured role in the big-budget production: The Valorous Hills, and was loaned out to Twentieth-Century-Fox for a small but telling part in that studio's version of Rose Fayre, the classic novel by Georgette Porte, with Aaron Lyles starring as Mr Lanchester and Jean Fountain in the title role. But it was the part of 'Silky' Blue, a twelve-year-old girl who rides the winner in the Kentucky Derby in the movie version of Derby Pride, that turned Joanna Jerome into an international star.

Ruth was enraptured by her daughter's success, and from that moment on her little girl's career became the ruling passion of her life. But Joanna was not so little anymore, she had turned fifteen, and during the making of Derby Pride her ever-enlarging breasts had had to be strapped down. Following Rex Gideon's statement about her, the joke went round the Hollywood cocktail circuit that was to mark the turning point in Joanna's public and private life and transform the cute kid into a sex goddess:

"Have you heard about Joanna Jerome? Gideon says she is now two of the studio's most outstanding assets. And her asset's not bad either."

None of those party jokers were speaking from experience, however, and Joanna went to the altar an eager but virginal bride. Ruth could not believe her eyes when she walked into Ricky Milton's sixty-room mansion in Bel Air. There were sixteen bedrooms, twenty-six bathrooms, and five kitchens, and an army of uniformed servants to polish the gold-plated fixtures in each room, as well as look after the five bars and ten marble fireplaces.

Werner Richardson Milton, the twenty-four-year-old son of the chairman of the Milton Hotel corporation, had invited his bride-to-be and her parents to his house for dinner. It was too dark to see the three hundred rose bushes in the rose garden, but he could point out the badminton and tennis courts and the swimming pool because they were lit up for night use. As heir to the Milton Hotel fortune, Ricky was everything Ruth Van Dross wanted in a son-in-law, and she refused to take any notice of his reputation as a playboy.

So the wedding date was set for April 6 1950. As their gift to the young and nubile starlet, Sparta Studios presented Joanna with a stunning white organdie and chiffon bridal gown in which to float down the aisle on the arm of her handsome father. More than a thousand fans were waiting on Santa Monica Boulevard to catch a glimpse of the beautiful bride the morning of the wedding. When she appeared in the spring sunshine, and beside her proud father, the flashbulbs popped and the crown applauded and cheered as the couple made their way towards the waiting limousine.

The church ceremony lasted twenty minutes, then Monsignor Franklin D Kilpatrick pronounced the groom and his seventeen-year-old bride to be man and wife. Joanna threw her arms around her husband's neck and kissed him so long and with such passion that laughter rippled among the congregation. At last, Monsignor Kilpatrick leaned toward the happy couple and suggested that they stop. It was only a temporary respite, for in the back of the limousine, and during the ten-minute drive to the reception, the groom introduced the bride to the special joys of the quickie, while the driver pretended he was deaf and blind.

The Crown Prince and Princess of Lithuania, sadly deposed fourteen years before, were on board of the 'Queen Christina' when it sailed from New York on April 24 1950, bound for Southampton, England. The glamorous royal couple insisted on meeting the even more glamorous honeymooners, and sent them a note inviting Mr & Mrs Werner Richardson Milton II to dinner.

All was well between Joanna and Ricky for the first two months. Their desire for each other's bodies verged on the animal; their lovemaking was very passionate, vigorous, and direct; two spoiled, self-centred people taking what they needed and to hell with kindness, gentleness, compassion. But the public adulation of his wife caused problems for Ricky. He was not used to playing second fiddle to anyone, not even his father. He wanted a wife who would stay at home and do as she was told; Joanna wanted an attentive but not a possessive lover who would allow her to lead her own life. They began to quarrel, bitterly.

On the night of November 6 1950, exactly seven months to the day since she married him, Joanna stormed out of their Pacific Palisades home. The fairy-tale-romance was over.

The stress of the break-up sent her to hospital for a week. A few days after she came out, Joanna, pale and trembling, walked into a Los Angeles courtroom and asked the judge for an interlocutory divorce on the grounds of extreme mental cruelty. She did not want alimony, but she did want her maiden name back. The judge agreed, with the stipulation that she could not remarry for a year.

Now that she was free, the no longer innocent Miss Joanna Jerome decided to have a ball; in fact she balled every young, handsome, available man she met, and she met quite a few. Ricky Milton was rather bemused by it all. He commented to a friend: "Every man should have the opportunity of sleeping with Joanna Jerome, and at the rate she's going every man will."

The studio, meanwhile, quietly bought up the lease on the Pacific Palisades house from Ricky and wondered what was to be done about his ex-wife. A scandal was brewing.

The Press were sniffing around Joanna like blow flies at a carcass. Rex Gideon had the brain wave of packing her off to England to star in The Talisman, from the novel by Sir Walter Scott. It was to be shot at Sparta's British studio at Pinewood and on location in Spain for the desert scenes. It was hoped that the pressure of acting in her first really grown-up role in the company of respected, professional co-stars might slow her down. Six weeks after her arrival in England, Joanna declared to the world's newspapers that she was madly in love.

The lucky man was David Gilding, the forty-year-old British matinee idol who had been squiring her around London's swish night spots. He was separated from his wife and Joanna begged him to get a divorce and marry her. David was unsure of his feelings, however, because of his continuing involvement with the legendary German-born star, Hanna Thane, but Joanna kept making the point that at eighteen she could give him the children he had always wanted, which the fifty-year-old Hanna could not.

When the movie finished shooting in September of 1951, Joanna flew to New York wearing an engagement ring of sapphires and diamonds. David arrived shortly after to promote his latest film and told the Press he was not engaged to anyone. In Hollywood he and Joanna stayed at the home of fellow Britons Ewart Ranger and his beautiful wife, Joan Ribbons. They were doing well in America. Joanna continued to pester him to marry her but David realised that to afford the kind of lifestyle she was used to in California, he would have to be making a lot more money that Gaumont-British were currently paying him. And he told her so.

Joanna went to see Kurt Lubitsch at Sparta Studios. He was Rex Gideon's right-hand-man, but when Gideon fell ill the following year Lubitsch took the opportunity to oust the old man from power. Joanna told Lubitsch that she was going to marry Gilding, and unless the studio offered him a lucrative movie contract she would give up her career and live abroad with her husband. Kurt offered her a deal. He would draw up the contract if she would lick his lollipop. Joanna agreed.

She and David were married at Caxton Hall, Westminster, London, on the morning of February 17 1952. It was the bride's nineteenth birthday. Her first child, David Leslie Gilding, was born on February 6 1953 at three in the morning. The birth was difficult. A month later Joanna was still too fat to begin work on her new picture.

Kurt Lubitsch, now in charge of the studio, demanded she'd go on a strict diet, and put her on reduced-pay-suspension at two thousand dollars a week until she lost the excess weight.

Meanwhile, the marriage was going sour. Money, or the lack of it on her husband's part, was the trouble. Gilding had a lackadaisical attitude to work and much preferred to stay at home, painting a still-life or relaxing by the pool. He was often suspended by the studio, thus losing his weekly paycheque of three thousand dollars. More and more of the bills were paid by Joanna, and the thought of another divorce horrified her.

One of the handsome young men she dated after leaving Ricky was her co-star in the movie An American Tragedy, Macdonald Hilt. In her usual bossy way Joanna had steered the shy, sensitive boy relentlessly towards the bedroom, where she did a strip-tease. The total non-effect of her naked nobility on him convinced Joanna that the rumours she had heard about Mac were true: he was a homosexual, but the dignified and gracious way he handled the whole situation endeared him to her and they became firm friends. On the night of May 5 1956, the Gildings held a dinner party for a few good friends. Rex Gideon's widow, Ellen Raintree, was there with her latest companion, a young man called Curtis Brown. They could hardly keep their hands off each other all evening. Also at the party were pretty singer and actress, Vicky Sothern, and her husband, the popular crooner, Freddie Lisher. On the surface theirs was a marriage made in heaven, like the Gildings, but they too were having problems. At first Mac refused to come, pleading that he was too tired. Joanna kept phoning until he gave in.

Mac brought a friend, a handsome young actor called Kelvin Harty, who was the brother of the radical writer, Sarah Harty. When Kelvin left the party at midnight, Mac got in his car and followed him on a zigzag course down the steep canyon road. The amount of drink Mac had consumed, plus the pills he had taken earlier in the evening, slowed his reflexes and he began to weave his sporty coupe from one side of the road to the other. Suddenly, Kelvin heard a tremendous bang, and looking back in his mirror he saw a cloud of dust. He pulled up and ran back to find Mac's car crumpled up by a telegraph pole. Gasoline was spilling from the coupe's engine which was still running. Without checking on whether his lover was alive or dead, Kelvin returned to his car, jumped in, and in a state of increasing panic, drove furiously up the canyon to the house and rapped on the door.

"Mac's had just an awful crash," he yelled, as he stumbled into the living room.

"Is he alive?" asked a distraught Joanna.

"I don't know."

David phoned for an ambulance. Joanna squeezed his arm.

"I must go to Mac," she gasped to her husband. He touched her hand.

When Joanna reached the wrecked car she heard moans coming from inside. She scrambled in through the back window, crawled over the seat, and got down beside the injured actor to cradle his bleeding head in her lap. The windscreen was shattered and the dashboard smashed in, pinning Mac beneath the steering wheel which had broken some of his front teeth. The pieces were stuck in his throat, choking him. Joanna thrust her hand into his mouth and pulled them out.

It was a week later when she asked Macdonald Hilt to marry her. Joanna was wracked by guilt, for she knew the accident would never have happened had she not insisted that he had to come to her house party. Mac needed a special denture and extensive plastic surgery before he could step in front of a camera again. It was to take six months, and in that time a lot was to happen.

Thinking her proposal a get-well-soon joke, Mac laughingly agreed to the marriage, but when, on June 18 1956, Sparta Studios announced that Joanna and David were separating, he was furious and made it clear to the nursing staff that Mrs David Gilding was not a welcome visitor. Joanna countered by having him moved to a private and very exclusive clinic where she could mother him to her heart's content, and keep his homosexual friends at bay.

"I'll never love another woman like I love you, Joey," he told her one day in September, and Joanna announced their engagement the next morning. She bought a thirty thousand dollar pearl ring and gave it to herself. By this time Mac was well enough to fly to Nassau with Joanna for a short vacation. They took connecting hotel suites and Joanna slept in Mac's bed. This was for the benefit of the hotel staff, who were being bribed by journalists eager for any titbits of information about the famous couple. Mac's homosexuality was an open secret; everyone knew except the public. News of the engagement had shocked the Hollywood cocktail circuit. How had she done it? What, in fact, did they do together? The permutations exercised many a mind in Beverly Hills and Bel Air and occupied their after dinner conversation for some weeks.

Sex was on the mind of Joanna Jerome too. Climbing into bed beside Mac one night, she burrowed down under the sheets and performed fellatio on his surprised but delighted person. At his climax he cried aloud and thrust his fingers into her hair.

"My God," he sighed when he had recovered his breath. "I didn't think girls did that."

Joanna laughed. "Some girls do. Some girls will do anything for the man they love. Anything."

He was silent.

"We must talk about this, Mac."

"I know, I know."

She touched his arm. "You have a beautiful body. I can

understand other guys admiring you. I've seen women giving me admiring looks too. Beauty is sexual, after all, and there's no separating the two."

"Did you enjoy," he hesitated, "what you just did?"

She smiled. "I enjoyed giving you pleasure, that's the important thing, don't you think? Would it be such a hardship to return the compliment?"

"I'll try, Joey."

She sucked him to full erection and he quickly mounted her from behind, but he was unable to maintain his erection long enough for Joanna to reach a climax.

"Am I not tight enough there for you?"

"I'm sorry."

"Don't be."

He began to cry.

"No, baby, shush, shush." She rocked him back and forth in her arms. "It'll be all right, you'll see."

Though David was not contesting it, the Californian divorce was taking too long for Joanna. She wanted to marry Mac before the year was out, so once back in LA she went to see Kurt Lubitsch again. The price was higher this time but she was willing to do anything, and, as a result of the satisfaction Kurt found between Joanna's buttocks, the studio hired a flock of lawyers to rush through the divorce papers Joanna had filed in Nassau. In October she and Mac returned to Nassau to wait for her petition to be granted. They did not have long to wait.

On the morning of October 25 1956, at a small civil ceremony in Nassau, Joanna Jerome married Macdonald Hilt. The wedding night was, surprisingly, a great success, and Joanna had Kurt Lubitsch to thank for that. He had so ably sodomised her that day in his office that her discomfort was minor and her pleasure great. Indeed she had achieved an orgasm. Mac needed a little coaxing at first, but once full anal penetration was accomplished he was as delighted as Joanna, and the results for both were spectacular.

In late November they were called back from their honeymoon by the studio to begin work on a five-million dollar Civil War picture. Thundertree Acre was one of the most ambitious movies ever to come out of Sparta Studios, and took ten weeks to shoot, with the second unit filming exterior, crowd, and battle scenes for another three weeks. Kurt Lubitsch had high hopes for the movie when it was released in the spring of 1957, but its failure at the box office, at a difficult time for Hollywood generally, brought about his dethronement from the presidency of Sparta Studios.

The huge flop of Thundertree Acre did nothing to dampen the personal popularity of Joanna and Mac, who continued to be mobbed wherever they went. However, disturbing rumours were beginning to circulate concerning Mac's drug taking and the nature of his sexual relationship with his wife. Of course there had been rumours before, but these were appearing in print in the gossip columns of some of the seedier LA and New York magazines. No names were given, yet there could be few reading the accounts who would be unable to put names to the couple described, so famous were they. One report mentioned the co-star who accidentally came upon the pair in 'flagrante delicto' and they were too engrossed to notice. Sodomy was rather tastelessly hinted at in the column as well for those who could read the code words. Few Hollywood insiders could not.

Lloyd King was now in charge at Sparta Studios. Not only that, he owned the place. He had bought out the Gideon family's controlling interest in a take-over battle that was bitter and prolonged. He was very concerned about the image of the studio's top female star. One morning he called Mac into his office. As he was later to tell Joanna, he and Mac talked over the need to keep the public affection Joanna had built up over the years. It would be a crime if anything should damage her career at this stage.

Mac drove out the studio gates only minutes after the meeting ended. He normally exchanged a few words with the gateman, but those who saw him that morning said he looked preoccupied. Perhaps he was considering King's suggestion of a divorce, or maybe he had rejected that idea in favour of another. Whatever the reason, he made a wrong turn on the corner of Sunset and Vine and a Greyhound bus cut him in two.

The funeral was held on June 1 1957. It was only natural that in the weeks that followed, Joanna should turn to Lloyd King for comfort. He was as grief-stricken as she and his guilt feelings touched a sympathetic chord in Joanna. When she returned to work in August she was in love. Every weekend a chartered plane arrived on location to carry her to New York and Lloyd's Park Avenue penthouse. During the working week he sent flowers and phoned her each day.

Lloyd was then fifty years old. Born to poor but pious Irish Catholic parents in Chicago, his real name was Raffeety. By the age of seven he was running the streets of his neighbourhood: shining shoes for a nickel and selling stolen cigars for three cents. Then he graduated to peddling dud watches in a carnival side-show. He grew up in a travelling show and made his fortune with a string of sleazy peep shows he produced. He was a brash, cigar-chomping, larger-than-life character; his sense of humour was as coarse as his face. Now he was about to sink his fortune into a picture designed to make movie history and recoup that fortune many-fold. There would be fifty stars and seventy thousand extras in 'Across the Globe in Sixty Days', which was to be filmed in fourteen countries. His engagement to Joanna Jerome was announced on the night of November 16 1957 to coincide with the New York opening of the movie. The one piece of news he did not give out to newsmen was the fact that Joanna was pregnant.

They married on January 2 1958, in Acapulco. Joanna was an hour late and a little the worse for wear after spending the morning sunbathing and drinking champagne. This was with Vicky Sothern and Freddie Lisher. Vicky was her matron of honour and Freddie was Lloyd's best man. The ceremony was conducted in the main room of the villa, and Joanna made her entrance wearing a blue chiffon gown with plunging décolletage, thus offering up her magnificent breasts to the pop-eyed gaze of every man in the room. As if that were not enough, she was also flashing an eighty thousand dollar diamond bracelet, her wedding gift from Lloyd.

"That was some entrance, baby," he approvingly murmured to her later, over the cracked crab and the pink champagne. For the next five months Joanna honeymooned with her husband as they travelled the world to promote his film, and in May they returned to Beverly Hills. Their daughter, Frances Joanna, was born by caesarean section on June 6. The doctors told Lloyd that Joanna should not have any more children or her life would be put at risk. She took the news badly, but not as bad as he, so proud was Lloyd of his new daughter.

It was little Frances Joanna, who they called Frankie, who helped the couple overcome their depression. "This kid is so gorgeous she makes her Mom look like the Bride of Frankenstein," Lloyd told reporters. The sensuality of Joanna was never more apparent than in the months following the birth. Both she and Lloyd publicly revelled in their need for each other, and were not afraid to flaunt it.

At a Manhattan dinner party hosted by Ellen Raintree, King was asked what it was like to be married to such a nubile young lady.

"Listen here," he replied. "Any time this chick spends out of bed is a total waste." Ellen Raintree obviously thought the same about her young boyfriend, Curtis Brown. Three times during the course of the evening she and Curtis disappeared for up to twenty minutes. Upon returning, it was silently noted by their guests that their faces were flushed, their eyes sparkled and their clothes had acquired some extra creases. Lloyd was highly amused by it all. Winking at Joanna, he waved a chicken leg in the air and said to her in a loud voice: "I'm gonna eat this and then I'm gonna eat you."

Joanna gave him a sultry look, slowly running her tongue over her full lips. On the short drive home to their suite at the Waldorf-Astoria they began to quarrel. There was nothing new in this, even the limousine driver smiled, for the feuding of the Kings was world-famous. They had more fun, they said, than most people had making love. In the elevator the argument continued, but when Lloyd grabbed her shoulders she wondered if things had gone too far. When his hands moved down to cup her breasts she knew they had, but by the time she noticed her skirt being hoisted above her waist and her panties lowered Joanna no longer cared. Arguing was almost always arousing and led to sex. This, however, was the first time they had done it in the elevator of the Waldorf-Astoria. The threat of discovery was an extra thrill that spurred them on to a furious bout of humping and grunting, and at her climax Joanna felt the tingles of pleasure spread from her vagina like ripples from the centre of a deep, dark pool, and run up her backbone and down the back of her thighs, even to the ends of her fingers which were dug into his shoulders.

Seconds later Lloyd, yelling a string of obscenities, ejaculated four long spurts of come into her, and she was off and running with a second and even better orgasm. They slid to the floor of the elevator, which had been motionless for some time. Thankfully the doors were closed. She felt him tremble in her arms ...

The heart attack proved fatal.

Los Angeles was once famous for being crude, flashy, and vulgar. Once upon a time Los Angeles had fresh air and uncontaminated oranges growing in every backyard. LA used to have big red tramcars that could take you from the inland valleys to the Pacific Ocean for the price of an ice cream cone. For years the City of the Angels was nothing more than a sprawling cow town with enough sunshine to keep the burgeoning movie studios happy, and enough moneyed people living in fine houses to fascinate and inspire the likes of Raymond Chandler and F. Scott Fitzgerald.

Then LA got respectable. High-rise buildings began to clutter the city skyline as scores of major US corporations moved to the Coast, forcing up rents and property values. Suddenly, with the smog and the endless freeways, Los Angeles became a place to escape from, not to. Hence Venice West.

At first glance Susie Watkins didn't find the place very impressive at all; just half a mile of man-made beach and a motley collection of low-rise bungalows, hotels, and shops among the palm trees. At dawn she awoke on the beach to be confronted by the sight of a bohemian Cannery Row as painted by David Hockney; all awash in pale blues and beiges. But with the warmth of the rising sun, Venice came to life for her.

She heard the first drowsy notes of a creaky clarinet, floating in the crisp morning air, as she packed up her sleeping bag. In the distance a disco beat began to pound as a few early roller skaters set up their sound systems. A professional beggar in a white turban rolled along the boardwalk, strumming his electric guitar powered by a portable battery. He winked at Susie as he went by, while in a vacant lot nearby the local Hell's Angels chapter were revving up their engines.

Susie had arrived in LA from New York with very little left of the money she had brought from London, a year before. The Big Apple had been tough for a single girl but LA was worse. She had been unable to find work as an actress and instead did some nude modelling for glamour mags to pay the rent. 'Acting' offers did come in, for hard-core porn flicks, and then there were the invites to "get down and party". Cocaine and quaaludes were the usual cocktail mixers at these parties and the jacuzzi the place where all the guests waited to be serviced. Prostitution was but one step away.

And then a friend mentioned Venice. "Venice, Italy?"

"No, silly, Venice beach."

As the street vendors opened up, the air became tangy with the smell of pizza, falafel, and soul food. Susie ordered a pizza and watched as the early morning joggers sprinted blithely around the still-slumbering forms of the winos. On the tiny pier the Khalsa Sikhs were doing hypnotically slow martial arts exercises, while a couple of bikini-clad girls practised roller skating slalom runs before going to the office.

By mid-morning Venice was a medieval fair. Nearly nude bathers and body builders, grandmothers on skate boards, paranoid millionaires and dope-smoking bag ladies, escapologists, tarot card gurus, sun worshippers, sacred and profane, easy riders, hustlers, whores, and Vietnam veterans; all mixed together with those permanent pillars of Hollywood's poverty establishment, out-of-work actors and would-be screenwriters.

Susie ran into an old friend, Ron Casey, an impressively handsome black actor, six foot tall and 210 pounds of rippling muscle. He was one of the body builders being gawped at by the tourists.

"Susie? Hey, babe, you're looking good."

She smiled. "So are you," she said, stroking a gleaming pectoral.

"Got a place to stay?"

"No."

"Wanna take a walk with me, babe?"

"Okay."

"I'd like to be home before the cops come out. They keep arresting me."

"But why, Ron?"

"They think they recognise me, and they're right. I've played every kind of criminal on the tube and in the movies."

Susie nodded. "You were in that Patty Hearst flick."

"Yeah. Man, I'm sure tired of raping white women."

"Could you manage one more?"

They went to a bar and got drunk. Once in his apartment Ron kicked off his shoes and announced he was going to take a shower.

The water was only tepid, but Ron was grateful for the uneven, lukewarm tattoo, and he closed his eyes; the noise of the water on the old-fashioned tin siding blotting out the sound of her approach, but he felt her presence as she stepped in beside him. He opened his eyes.

"Hi." She reached passed him to turn the water pressure to full, then handed the soap to him and turned her back. "Come on."

Ron hummed softly as he began to work up a lather on her

flawless skin, pale in comparison to her tanned neck and legs. Her shoulders slumped and she swayed gratefully under the pressure of his powerful hands as they kneaded and soaped her shoulders and back.

"Now you," she said, turning round.

"Wait." He could see her neck start to mottle as his fingers stroked her large, full, slightly pendulous breasts, the long nipples stiff, erect. Her breathing quickened. She took the soap from him and began to lather her thick bush of pubic hair, spreading her legs wide, one hand caressing her sleek and trembling thighs. Then she reached out to massage Ron's jutting erection in the foaming suds.

"You know, Ron, this is my first time with..."

"With a nigger?"

"Yes."

Clutching at each other, they staggered into the bedroom. She was glowing when he had finished towelling her.

"You smell good, babe."

He kissed her toes, her knees, the inside of her thighs, her arched hip. He gently positioned her face down on the bed and began to kiss her back and waist and buttocks, cupping each firm, out-thrusting cheek, and sliding his tongue into the cleft.

"Oh, darling, yes," she gasped. "Now."

He guided her up on all fours and entered her with a single thrust of his hips.

"Oh, God, Ron." Her back arched, Susie reached back to grasp his bottom, forcing the entire length of him into her.

"Baby, baby, baby." Brutally, rhythmically, he ploughed her with his huge hardness, driving it all in again and again. The size of his organ, the sensation of it inside her, was a surprise to Susie; painfully, wonderfully surprising.

"Ohhhhhhhhhhh, oh, darling, darling ... Ah, ahhh, ah-ah, oh."

"Baby, urrhhhhrr, you're so tight. So good."

"Ah, ahhh, I'm coming, ahhhhh-oh-oh-ohhh, Ron, ahhhhhhh, ahhhhhhhhhhh."

In her orgasm, Susie was twisting and bucking so violently Ron had a difficult time remaining in her as his own climax overtook him.

Later, they lay on their sides staring at each other. She touched the thick tufts of black hair on his chest, running her fingers over the swelling pectorals.

"You're so black."

He laughed.

"Mmmm," she purred, "I just love making love."

"I'd kinda noticed that."

She rolled on top of him, giggling. Her fingers, lips, and tongue got to work on his limp manhood, stimulating him anew. With thighs spread wide Susie mounted him, kneeling astride his prone form and squealing in delight as she impaled herself on his rampant organ.

"Darling, oh, oh, darling."

"Baby, baby."

Susie bucked herself to another satisfying orgasm, and leaving Ron in bed asleep, took a shower, dressed, and went out to grab a late lunch. Walking down the sunlit street towards the beach, she suddenly realised she felt very happy. It was an odd emotion. At a sidewalk cafe she ordered a piece of pie and sipped cappuccino while watching the sandpipers scurry away from the ocean breakers.

It was now late afternoon but down on Ocean Front Walk the parade of fluorescent leotards, skin-tight jump suits, transparent body stockings, and bum-hugging shorts was as constant as ever. Susie enjoyed the free show, but a well-known artist, whose starkly modernistic beach-front studio flaunted 'No Peddlers' signs, and her Bel Air friends, martinis in hand, gazed rather patronisingly at the scene. Their chilly respectability turned Susie off.

She stayed with Ron for three weeks. Then the bikers started snatching girls off the boardwalk and gang-banging them on the beach. She went back to LA.

It was Ron who saw her off at the bus depot, as she waited to board the Los Angeles-bound Greyhound.

"What you gonna do, girl?"

"Become rich and famous," she said, grinning. "What else is there to do in this bloody world?"

"How?" he asked.

"Easy, darling. Marry a rich and famous man."

He laughed.

"No wonder I'm still poor. I'm the wrong sex."

It was Susie's turn to laugh now.

"Not for me you're not. Oh, no, you're just the right sex. Bloody perfect."

She stood up on tiptoe to kiss him gently on the cheek as the bus pulled in.

"Take care of yourself, Ron," she murmured huskily, a twinkle in her eye. "Don't let your sword get rusty while I'm away, will you?"

"I'll keep it well-greased, just for you."

Another hug and she was gone...

Susie Watkins was an artist, and her greatest creation was herself. If she had lived in the 18th century she would have been a great courtesan, the king's favourite bed partner; a woman admired, envied; a woman of influence and power. In 1982 she did the 20th century alternative: she had an affair with Jean-Claude Duparier, the richest man in the world.

Bequia was a small but beautiful Caribbean island, part of the chain of islands called the Grenadines, and Susie's favourite port of call on the cruise through the indolent blue waters from St. Vincent to Grenada. The first time she saw Jean-Claude Duparier she was sunning herself on the deck of a big yacht in Bequia's picture-postcard harbour when the noise of a passing powerboat made her sit up. She waved at the two men in the sleek Riva as the two-masted schooner rocked gently in the speedboat's wake.

Susie was wearing only the bottom half of a black bikini, little more than a G-string. Her ripe, nubile body was deeply tanned; her long, dark hair wet from a recent swim. Almost naked, without make-up, she was, thought Jean-Claude, a dazzling vision. The two men inclined their heads toward each other as they spoke in order to make themselves heard over the noise. Susie knew they were talking about her. She recognised one of them as the polo-player Simon Barnes. He had been on Bequia all winter, and Susie had seen him every time the yacht had anchored there. The other, she realised, with a tingle of pleasurable anticipation, must be Jean-Claude Duparier, the shipping and property tycoon.

Beautiful women are drawn to the international rich as moths to a flame. Such girls are the satellites of rich men: their travelling companions, confidantes, mistresses and, sometimes, their wives and ex-wives. Of all the trinkets a gold American Express card can purchase, a pretty girl is the most prized by those men who have everything. On the day Jean-Claude first saw and desired Susie Watkins, she was travelling with two lovers: one the owner of the yacht; the other a banker, once accused, and later acquitted, of stabbing to death his wife and her lesbian lover. When Simon told him this, Jean-Claude was disappointed. She was too easy, too available; just another instant lay. And yet...

When Susie walked into the Frangipani, Bequia's main watering hole, with her two lovers, one on each arm, the billionaire quickly forgot his sense of disappointment of that afternoon. He wanted her, but he knew how to play the waiting game. Just before midnight he got up and left the party, walking out of the circle of light to disappear into the black, warm West Indies night. Susie was shocked by his sudden departure. All evening she had been conscious of Jean-Claude, conscious of being watched. She had laughed, smiled, spoken only a little, never quite closing her mouth entirely. She knew she was being admired and lusted over, and had abandoned herself to the delicious sensation.

Then, suddenly, Jean-Claude Duparier was standing just behind her chair. He was so close to her that she could feel the warmth of his body and smell the scent of his skin. He smelled clean and very healthy. She turned and looked up at him, and found herself gazing into deep blue eyes that shone with gentleness, not lust, and was lost, instantly. He poured a handful of shiny pebbles into her hand.

"Next time they'll be diamonds," he murmured into her ear. It was the first time he had spoken to her; the first time she had heard his voice. She closed her fingers around the pebbles. They were still warm from his touch, and she felt his warmth throughout her body. It was as if he were touching her.

"I have to go," she whispered back, conscious of the cold stares of her two partners. She got up. "The diamonds are lovely. Can I keep them?"

"Of course."

She left quickly, before he could say anymore. Susie Watkins joined the two men waiting a little distance away where the floor of the bar area met the white sand of the beach. The small wooden dock was only a few steps from the bar, and their three voices carried clearly over the water as they rowed back to the yacht. Jean-Claude stood and listened until their voices subsided into the darkness.

The Frangipani was deserted now, and Jean-Claude crossed through it and out the opposite side. He walked up the steep hill to the large suite of rooms he had reserved for his use in Bequia. Built in typical Caribbean mode, they had thatched double-height cathedral ceilings, windows with wooden shutters but no glass, and a wide veranda running across the front of the structure. The rooms were furnished with rattan chairs and tables and lacy khuskhus rugs dotted the terracotta tile floor.

He undressed. Clean, white mosquito netting was suspended like a flower from the ceiling above the bed. Naked, he went out onto the veranda and looked out over the harbour. The brilliant constellations of the southern skies glittered down, casting a cool light upon the black, shiny water of the harbour. The lights of the yacht were off. He imagined Susie crouched on all-fours in her dark cabin, accepting the rampant erections of her two lovers, and wished he was there to fill her third orifice, whether mouth, vagina or anus. The thought made his own organ grow stiff. Standing there, in the open air, he quickly masturbated to a climax, his right fist pumping hard, until, with a grunt and a jerk of his hips, his jism spurted out in one long, white stream.

"Where's the schooner?" asked Jean-Claude, trying not to sound panicky. It was seven in the morning and Susie's yacht was gone.

"St. Vincent," said Simon Barnes. It was the next port of call upwind. Simon wondered but did not ask what had happened the previous night. The last thing he had seen was Jean-Claude pouring pebbles into Susie's hand. Although they had not touched, the erotic aura was so apparent that Simon, the second son of a British aristocrat, turned away, somewhat embarrassed.

"Please excuse me," said Jean-Claude. He went to the small office of the Frangipani and phoned Barbados Air Charter to order up a seaplane for noon. Simon was there to wave him off from the small wooden dock.

"Give her one for me, Jean," he yelled.

The Frenchman grinned.

"No offence, Simon, but when I'm fucking her the last thing I'll be thinking about is you."

The Cobblestone, on the quayside in Kingstown, the capital of St. Vincent, was a two-hundred-year-old stone building which, in earlier times, was a sugar warehouse. Foot-thick stone walls, graceful brick archways and narrow, shaded paths wound through the complex which had been divided into shops, a bar, a restaurant and a small hotel overlooking the harbour. The yacht rested at anchor with only its crew aboard. Jean-Claude looked into the bar and saw the two lovers of Susie sitting there, talking to other boat skippers. There was no sign of the girl so he walked on, through the inner garden and back toward the shop selling Swiss watches, English china, Japanese cameras and French crystal. He found Susie sitting alone on a bench. She looked up at his approach.

"I didn't want to lose you," said Jean-Claude, by way of explanation. He could not see the expression in her eyes, hidden as they were behind tinted shades, but her full, sensuous lips were smiling.

"I know," she said.

EBONY AND IVORY

The girl was in her early twenties, tall and strikingly beautiful. Her cheekbones were high and the skin pulled taut across them was olive, the eyes flashing milky-white around the black pupils. Her coal-black hair was long and flowing loose around her slim shoulders, almost waist length. She wore a plain, pleated skirt, her pretty calves were bare, her painted toe-nails visible in sandals. Even sitting down it was obvious to Rudy Gioberti that her figure was sensational; trim waist and ripe, low-hung breasts pushing at the blouse, the hard edges of her long nipples indenting the cloth.

Cherie Halvinne was from Hawaii, of Japanese-Philippino origins. She was a model. He saw her one evening in the Marina del Rey Hotel and knew he had to have her, but he was already with a girl that night. Rudy spent the next three nights searching every club and bar in Marina del Rey and gasped with relief on the fourth when he saw her at a window table in El Torito, calmly enjoying a plate of enchiladas Suizas.

She treated him with arrogant disdain, but, eventually, agreed to go to his hotel suite with him. Once there, Cherie undressed slowly in front of him, very slowly. He took in the sleek, olive-skinned body, the full, firm breasts, the raven hair, and the dark triangle at her engorged pubis.

They sipped Dom Perignon and she took him by the hand and led him into the bedroom. The ease of the gesture made him wonder how many other men had brought her to this hotel, perhaps this very suite. The idea excited Rudy.

They lay down on the bed. His fingertips, frosty and tinged with white from the champagne glass, traced a slow line around her nipple and felt it stiffen. His hand opened like the petals of a flower in sunlight, and cupped the breast. She purred like a cat.

He felt her hand move to the buttons of his shirt, undoing them, and then she was moving across his body in a seesaw motion so that her breasts hung above his chest, the swollen nipples touching and rasping his flesh. He closed his eyes, felt the breast, warm and fragrant, on his face and took the nipple in his mouth, nibbling and sucking gently. She grasped his hand and guided it into the mystery of her sex, wet and pulsing, then took his fingers, one by one, into her mouth.

She unzipped the fly on his jeans. His erection sprang free.

"My God," she gasped, "You're huge."

He laughed.

She lowered her head and pulled the moist phallus through her long, thick hair. He sensed the warm forest brushing and tugging at him and the desire to open his eyes was overwhelming. But he resisted. Then she kissed the glistening crown. Her tongue began to stroke it. He opened his eyes.

Cherie was looking at him fully in the face, unsmiling but unashamed, then she took him in her mouth. Rudy watched, fascinated, as she made a few circular movements before plunging upon him, sucking furiously. When he came, his ejaculation copious, she jumped off the bed and headed for the bathroom to spit it out, while he slept.

She awoke him by bringing him to the brink of orgasm again, and his eyes opened on the sight of her kneeling astride him, the ripe breasts pointing the long nipples at him like gun barrels. She tightened her vaginal muscles and he groaned in delight.

"You will take me to Hollywood with you?" She squeezed his prick again and laughed. "Darling?"

"Oh, yes, yes, anything ... Ahhhhhh."

The edge of the sword sparked dangerously in the light, and a flicker of emotion passed across the face of Fraser Karl. The vast room was as still as the grave. It was a moment he had dreamt about for more years than he cared to remember. A moment he had longed for and also dreaded at the same time, like losing his cherry. And now, time seemed suspended.

He sensed rather than heard the faint swish as the blade came down.

"Arise, Sir Fraser Karl."

He rose from his knees to bow stiffly from the waist. The adrenaline was flowing through him as his eyes took in the details of the room anew; the priceless portraits, the glittering chandeliers, the smooth, assured courtiers, their coolness in marked contrast to the nervousness of the assembled guests in their hired morning suits, the women under exotic hats.

Karl had rented a black limousine for the day, rather than use the Rolls. Too ostentatious. They had made the trip from Hampstead through the morning traffic, he stiff and anxious in his morning suit, his wife as tiresomely horny as a randy goat on speed. He had to finger-frig her twice during the journey to calm her down. At the Palace gates groups of onlookers stared into the arriving cars as they stopped to be vetted by the two duty policemen. As their limo slowed, the chauffeur gave the invitations to the bored coppers. Karl smiled at the faces pressed against the glass. The invitations were handed back and one of the policemen pointed out to the chauffeur the entrance to a courtyard. Karl could see the red-uniformed soldiers quick-marching to their gold edged blue sentry boxes. He looked behind him at the iron gates and the people on the outside of them.

Fraser Karl was inside.

After the ceremony they drank tea from delicate china cups and the Prince of Wales moved amongst them. He spoke to Karl for several minutes, as did the Princess. Her quiet, earnest, interested questions and her polite conversation soothed many a jagged nerve that day. Later, Sir Fraser and Lady Karl posed for the photographers and uttered the ritual noises about what a proud day it was for both of them, etc. Inside, Karl was laughing. Inside, he was still the same East End lad, son of a Polish flier killed in the Battle of Britain. His mother was a whore who abandoned him at the age of three to a series of foster parents and children's homes.

Now he had received a knighthood for services to the British film industry.

And then it was all over. They found their chauffeur, Steven, leaning on the bonnet of the limo, away from the other drivers who talked, smoked, and moaned about their employers. But Steven stood alone. He was paid well, and as a bonus he screwed Karl's wife and nympho daughter every chance he got, which was often.

"Congratulations, Sir Fraser, Lady Elizabeth."

"Thank you, Steven."

Employer and employee shook hands while Lady Karl smiled. She intended to thank Steven in her own way later, when Fraser was with his mistress. The chauffeur saw the look in her eyes and knew what it meant. Elizabeth was a good lay but daughter Gemma was the real ball-breaker of the family. He opened the car door. As she climbed in, Lady Karl stroked his groin with her hand.

The car purred down the Mall and under Admiralty Arch. In the Charing Cross Road, Karl asked Steven to pull over. He got out.

"Steven will look after you, darling. I have some business in town. Take care, love. Bye."

"Bye, Sir Fraser." She smiled broadly.

Karl waved at the disappearing limo then crossed the street. At the Savoy, the reception clerk gave him his key and informed Sir Fraser his guest had arrived.

She came bounding out of the bedroom to greet him, deliciously nude but for high heels and a crimson garter, worn high on her left thigh. He looked, and that ripe ebony body seemed to suck him in. His hands were on her firm melon breasts, slim waist, and full buttocks, while hers were unzipping his pants and releasing his swelling penis from the prison of his undershorts.

"I'm glad to see a knighthood hasn't dulled your appetite."

"Monique..."

He lifted her from the waist, up, and then down, impaling her on the rampant pole of muscle jutting from between his legs.

"Oh, darling."

She felt herself being opened, stretched, filled, leaving her gasping, open-mouthed, like a fish out of water and wriggling on the skewer. She clung to him in desperation, her senses disordered, as he carried her to the bed and laid her down. She watched him strip, then he was upon her, mounting her, in her. He rode her with sweet force, and she rode him, as they moved back and forth across the bed, the springs protesting their innocence ever louder. And then the release, the dizzy, flowing descent, the slow decline.

The sun was a gold ball in the azure blue of the cloudless sky. Down in the valley the dirty brown smog hung like an evil haze over the city, but up in the low hills the air was fresh, clear, and the sun hot on your skin.

Scott Brinkley fingered the radio dial, looking for a music station he liked amongst the welter of LA voices giving the latest updates on the weather and the freeway traffic. Then the voice of Chrissie Hynde, lead singer with the Pretenders, cut through. She was singing 'Back on the Chain Gang', an oldie from 1983. Brinkley smiled, squinting his eyes against the harsh blue glare of the swimming pool. That was the year he left Spurs and the dour image of English football behind him for the showbiz dazzle of American soccer. Six months into his lucrative contract with the New York Cosmos the injury occurred that was to end his sporting career.

Still in all he looked magnificent, only seven pounds heavier than in his playing days. The extra weight was evenly distributed on his powerful and muscular frame. He worked out every day, starting with a run before breakfast, then on to a series of punishing exercises, followed by twenty lengths of the pool. Most afternoons he played tennis or hardball, and still managed to get in some weight training at a Beverly Hills health club twice a week.

The body that had been so obviously in its lack of colour the body of an Englishman, had now the rich, amber patina of a Californian surfer. The crinkly blond hair which had been shoulder-length was now cut fashionably short and sun-bleached, while the handsome face looked every one of his thirty four years. There were lines around the blue eyes and the sensuous mouth above the firm jaw, and those eyes showed the world a more cautious, less open, and altogether darker expression.

He heard footsteps approach, and the quiet clink of ice cubes against glass as she set the tray down beside him. He opened his eyes and smiled at Cherie as she made them a Buck's Fizz each.

"That looks nice."

"Me, or the champagne and orange juice?" she asked.

"All three."

The first time he saw Cherie Halvinne was at a television producer's party at a house in Coldwater Canyon. Brinkley's date that night was a well-known model and starlet with silicone-enhanced breasts of enormous size, and bizarre sexual appetites. Among orgy goers Annie was popular with men because she enjoyed sodomy, and with women because she enjoyed lesbian sex, but as she confided to Brinkley as they danced, her real favourite was horse balling. Not anything special, you understand, just Shetland ponies.

She was over the moon to be with him she said, and kept asking him to take her upstairs. Finally he did.

"Jesus, baby."

"Oh, yeah, oh, yeah, yeah, harder ... Darling, harder ... Yes, ohhhhh."

"Honey, you're great ... Ah, ah, so tight."

"Ohhhhhhhhh, ohhh."

"Ahhh … Ahhhhh, ahh, baby."

"Oh, that's beautiful … Yes, yes … Ohhhhhhhhhhhh."

"Baby, I'm coming."

"Scott, I love you, ooooooooooo, ohhhhhh, ahhhhrrr, ooohh, ohhh, oh."

He returned to the party alone and it was then he saw Cherie. He spotted her in a crowd of people grouped around the huge half-moon-shaped cocktail bar, which ended at vast sliding glass doors opening onto a mock-mosaic patio. She was now a big star, thanks to Rudy Gioberti, and after him there had been other men. It was she who had asked the producer to invite Scott Brinkley. Now she took in the body as he approached; the firm, flat stomach, the powerful thighs and strong shoulders. She must have him.

"Hello, Miss Halvinne."

"Hi."

Three hours later, at her home in Bel Air, she lay nude on her bed with her legs over his shoulders yelling:

"Bang me, you son of a bitch, bang me."

Three days later she realised she was in love with him.

Like Stavros Niarchos, Jean-Claude Duparier thought that the man who could count his money was not really rich. And Duparier was really a very rich man indeed.

His empire was run by five separate companies. Duparier Resorts owned resort hotels in Marbella, Cannes, Palm Beach, Montego Bay and Maui. Duparier Hotels owned skyscraper hotels in Milan, Rome, Geneva, Madrid, Paris, Berlin, London and New York. Duparier Shipping owned a world-wide fleet of oil tankers and other types of merchant marine which it leased to the highest bidders. Duparier Properties owned select real estate in all the major capitals of the free world. Last, but by no means least, was Duparier Entertainments, based in Los Angeles.

The rich are different, as F. Scott Fitzgerald observed. It is not the things money buys that makes the difference, but the freedom from and the freedom to. Freedom from the suffocating prisons of a boring job and an unhappy private life. For money buys freedom of choice and a sense of infinite possibilities. The freedom to indulge or deny; to work or not to work; to play or not to play; to hurl yourself into life or to withdraw from it; the freedom to build or to destroy; the freedom to give and the freedom to take. At different times in his life Jean-Claude had made all the choices.

BALLING THE JACK

The black girl pirouetted on the catwalk and Lord Randolph Deveer leered hungrily up at the dark, curved legs. Up to this moment the fat man had been wondering why he had bothered to come. He added more Mumm Cordon Rouge to the tulip champagne glass while the next model strode into view.

Deveer was one of the richest men in Britain, a millionaire many times over. Because of his enormous wealth, he was one of the few members of the landed gentry who felt no need to open his country home, Ramshead Manor, to the public. He was Randy to all his friends and resembled nothing so much as a character from some Henry Fielding novel; a bawdy, belching, wenching, drinking, farting aristo, all bottom slapping, breast feeling, and rolling in the hay. Sex was a passion to be pursued with the same energy his father had chased foxes. Indeed, the only difference was that the foxes Randy hunted ran on two legs and had to be stripped before their brush was visible.

With his thinning hair and ever-thickening waistline, Deveer was no Warren Beatty, but his charm, allied to his money and power, almost always proved a potent aphrodisiac and his beds and guest rooms at Ramshead Manor and his Mayfair town house were rarely empty. Gossip about his sexual exploits was legion. His parties, the impromptu Mayfair ones and the organised affairs in the country, were very popular, and an invitation to the Manor was a highly-prized possession among London's jet set.

The drink had been flowing since early evening, it was a charity fashion show, so when Monique jiggled into the limelight to be greeted by a chorus of lecherous calls and whistles, Deveer took notice. The girl had the body of a centrefold. Her breasts were far too large for a fashion model, as were her buttocks. Jerry Hall would look anorexic beside her, but Deveer thought Jerry Hall anorexic anyway, and his organ stiffened as he imagined himself between those shapely black legs.

At the reception which followed, he met the fashion editor of the magazine for Sloane Rangers, The Tatler. Her name was Edwina Lawrence, a tall, attractive woman in her middle forties who had been the star performer at Deveer's last country thrash. Unknown to her, he had videotaped the entire proceedings in the orgy room, and soon many more people would know about her blue-veined, pendulous breasts and her penchant for oral sex than the eleven men and four women she made it with.

"Hello, Edwina."

"Randy, darling. How are you? When are you going to throw another bash? I did so enjoy the last one."

"Soon, Edwina, soon. But first, darling, you must introduce me to that stunning black girl we saw."

"Monique Starr? She's Sir Fraser Karl's mistress."

Cherie Halvinne's voice went husky: "Bang me." Her mouth caressed his neck. Scott cupped his hands under the full, bare breasts and eased her body down beside him on the lilo. Cherie slipped a hand down the front of his shorts. "You horny bastard."

She blew into his ear and squeezed his erection hard as he kneaded her breasts, then, at her urging, he pulled at the silk cord holding her bikini briefs in place and felt the material fall away as her legs opened. He struggled out of his shorts and mounted her. She gasped. He felt her long legs lock about his waist. He came quickly, copiously. She cried out, telling him she could feel his semen flowing into her.

Karl threw down the red-covered screenplay and let it lie with the other scripts on the leather couch. He walked over to the large picture window and stared down at the Thames, glittering in the reflected glow of the spotlights shining on the Houses of Parliament. It was a view to inspire anyone, and he had bought this huge penthouse apartment in a South Bank tower block because of the view, but this evening Karl was in a furious temper.

He was looking for a vehicle for Monique, not a starring role, not yet. A good featured part would be ideal, but none of the projects he had examined were any good. Angela Cummin smiled. The fact that the powerful Sir Fraser Karl was angry didn't faze her in the slightest. She knew she was one of the best writers currently working in films, and she had a Best Original Screenplay Oscar on her mantlepiece to prove it. Warner Brothers had offered her a million dollars to do a rewrite and polish job on their new Meryl Streep film. Angela, though, had turned it down to work for Karl.

"Any suggestions?" he finally asked her.

"Yes, Fraser. Perfect 40 by Joy Joy de Ferrare. It was serialised in the Sun before publication. Now it's a big best-seller on both sides of the pond. I think there's a super part in it for Monique and, if we could interest Cherie Halvinne in the title role, the finance would follow, no problem."

"Can we get Halvinne?"

"Yes and no. She's part of a package."

"And what's the other part?"

"Her latest boyfriend, Scott Brinkley."

"The footballer?" Karl thought for a moment. "Well, what the hell. He might turn out to be a great actor. Talk to Judith about it. Is the meeting set up?"

"Tomorrow. I'll give her a ring to confirm."

Judith was at the very edge of orgasm when the phone rang. The answering machine took the call but Judith's concentration had been disturbed. It took an extra half-minute of tight-lipped effort on behalf of her partner before she climaxed satisfactorily.

Judith De Paul was one of the most experienced and accomplished film producers to come out of Britain. Taking a jacuzzi at The Sanctuary, she climbed gracefully out of the swirling waters of the hot tub, her sleek, svelte body voluptuously nude, to welcome Angela Cummin.

"Good morning, Angela."

"Judith."

"Just a moment while I put something on."

She slipped into a robe. They sat down. Angela gave her a copy of Perfect 40 by Joy Joy de Ferrare and went over what had been discussed with Karl the previous evening.

"What do you think, Judith?"

"Sounds interesting. I think I could get really involved in such a project, and you're right about Cherie Halvinne."

"Even with Scott Brinkley in tow?"

"Oh, yes, and I should be able to persuade Marilyn Chambers to play herself in the orgy sequence."

Angela smiled. She knew that American-born Judith, a former singer with the Metropolitan Opera, was a highly organised, efficient,

and demanding producer, who demanded the same energy and
commitment from those she worked with.

Joanne Layde thought Bequia an enchanted isle in the blue
Caribbean. It was certainly a vast improvement on the South London
slum where she had been born some twenty years before. Raped by
her favourite uncle at thirteen, sodomised by her headmaster at
fourteen, and forcibly introduced to fellatio by her brother-in-law at
fifteen, Joanne left school at sixteen a pretty, big-breasted brunette
with the only qualifications that mattered: an inexhaustible desire for
sex, an immense need to be the centre of attention, and an utter
contempt for men.

Her breasts very quickly became her fortune as posing topless for
the tabloids led to full nude spreads in the better soft-porn glossies.
There were glamour spots on TV and bit parts in a couple of movies.
There was talk of becoming a "serious" actress and of opening a dance
studio but nothing came of that. The hard-core video merchants
offered a kind of work. The money was very tempting. She did one
and was so disgusted with herself afterwards that she tried to commit
suicide. Some years later Badyr Al Hussein bought up all the
available copies of the video, plus the master, and had them
destroyed.

So she became a star baller. Power was her turn-on. She went to
bed with a randy prince and an Australian newspaper baron paid her a
small fortune for an exclusive on her saucy revelations. A West
German magazine later paid her almost as much for the same story.
Then there was the ex-husband of a Monaco princess, followed by an
Italian count, a Californian cosmetic surgeon, and the son of the
President of the United States.

Located in the eastern Caribbean, in waters considered the finest
for yachting in the world, Bequia, part of the chain of islands called
the Grenadines, was the sort of sun-soaked paradise tropical isles are
meant to be. Its harbour was a superb natural anchorage, and boats of
all kinds, classic Alden yawls, nine and twelve metre yachts, Morgans
and Hinckleys, the racers of ocean sailing, and the turbine-driven
floating palaces of Greek and Arab shipping tycoons, all paused at
Bequia on the indolent cruise from St. Vincent to Grenada.

The island itself was green and unspoilt: there was no runway for
jets, so the sun shone and the breeze blew on deserted beaches, and in

the raffish, devil-may-care atmosphere the fact that the electricity worked only now and then was of little consequence to anyone.

On the southern shore of Bequia was a two-mile-stretch of white beach which could only be reached by boat. No roads led to Grand Anse. Fine, clean sands sloped into crystal clear waters, while palms and sea grape provided a form of natural shade and the hills of Bequia rose behind, a living, constantly changing landscape. Badyr Al Hussein owned it. He and his associates were planning to construct a resort there.

Badyr was a very rich man indeed, but he moved in a society where such wealth was taken for granted. He was handsome, powerful, sexually magnetic, the owner of a world-wide empire of hotels, resorts, and a Hollywood movie studio. One of the studio's stars, soap opera veteran Veronica Capital, was with Badyr.

The history of resort development is marked by the merging of the ideal location, plus lots of imagination and lots of money. Miami Beach was more or less Florida swamp till it was filled in to allow the construction of hotels in the early years of this century when America was booming. Acapulco was a small fishing village until, during the roaring Twenties, the jaded rich discovered the morning beach, the afternoon beach, the cliff divers of El Mirador, and the orchids and royal palms of that sun-soaked dream. Sardinia was a windy granite island full of sheep and bandits before the Aga Khan built the yacht basin at Porto Cervo, and developed the Costa Smeralda to take advantage of a twisting coast of sea swept coves and beaches of powdery sand. Bequia had the potential, thought Badyr, to become a new destination for rich tourists bored with Puerto Rico, Nassau, and the rest.

The first time Badyr saw Joanne Layde he was returning by speedboat from Grand Anse. As the craft cleaved an arc of power across Bequia's harbour, a goddess rose from the sea, a goddess wearing black bikini briefs and a tight white T-shirt made transparent by the water. Striding up the beach, she turned round at the sound of the approaching boat. Her beauty stunned Badyr who asked his companion who she was. The man did not know. Badyr thought her breasts were magnificent, the way she pointed her perky button nipples straight at him, and her thighs sleek and superb. Her face he considered perfect, while her mouth was the most beautiful he had ever seen. Her lips curved in a teasing half-smile as she stared right back at him. He could imagine those lips on his penis. And when finally the goddess turned to walk away, Badyr was treated to a view of her spectacular behind, the buttocks full, ripe, and firm, the cleft deep and inviting. The general Arab predilection for sodomy had not previously tempted Badyr, but he literally came in his pants at that.

The vision of the beach goddess stayed in his mind all day, and all the night, even to the extent of losing his hard-on while Veronica Capital humped and heaved and thrashed around above him. Panic fluttered instantly in his chest, but the voluptuous actress kneeling astride his prone bulk, and whose once-raven hair was dyed a chestnut flame, quickly reached behind her, arching backwards until she found his maleness. Her nimble fingers probed and teased and his huge erection was restored to full stand. Then she increased the force and rate of her thrusts as she swayed forward, changing from a grinding motion to a straight back and forth pump. As she quickened the tempo her body began to shake, arms flailing, head moving from side to side. Her orgasm was near.

He reached up to grasp the wildly swinging breasts. Her vaginal muscles tightened around his shaft as she cried: "I'm so close, so oooooooohhhhhhrrr. Oh, dear God. You are a honey, ahhhh, ohhhhhh, oooooo, I'm coming." She rammed herself down on him so hard she felt the very core of her being had been impaled, and then his come was spurting into her and she screamed.

They clung together, their sweat-sheened limbs entwined, waiting for their breathing and pulse rates to slow. And once again, though he was stroking Veronica's hair, it was the beach goddess that Badyr was thinking of, and how to meet her. The Frangipani.

The dockside bars of the Caribbean, like the Frangipani in Bequia, the Nutmeg in St. George, Grenada, the Mermaid in Carriacou, and the Cobblestone in St. Vincent, were, like their cousins in the white hunters' Africa, pickup places and social headquarters for the region. The Frangipani had seen everything, even Paul Newman, who waded ashore one night. Princess Margaret often stopped off in Bequia on the way to her holiday home on nearby Mustique, and Prince Andrew used the same house after the Falklands war. To elude the posse of pressmen on Mustique, Andrew and Koo Stark took the short boat ride to the Frangipani where they enjoyed a candle-lit dinner. But nothing could compare to the night Badyr Al Hussein walked into the Frangipani with Veronica Capital and walked out with Joanne Layde.

Ten hours after he had found her again at the Cobblestone, Susie Watkins and Jean-Claude Duparier were boarding his Learjet Intercontinental 36 at Seawell Airport in Barbados, enroute for Miami. The one-and-a-half-million-dollar-plane was Jean-Claude's office, and the nearest thing to a real home that he possessed. It was fuelled up and waiting for clearance from the tower. They buckled into the black leather seats of the master stateroom and the plane took off, banking west to east, flying away from the sun into the night.

SISTER GOLDEN HAIR

Among former inhabitants of the secret world, the early 1980's were, or so it seemed to Jackson LeMay, an open season for indiscretions. "There are people going public now," he said at the time, "who would never have dreamt of it before." As someone in whom the capacity to conceal goes deep, he was disinclined to follow the trend for self-revelation, but having written two or three books that grossed between two and three million dollars before publication, the right to conceal your past was bound to come under attack. In the case of Jackson LeMay, author, and the private self called Richard Cromwell, the gates were ready to be climbed from the moment Newsweek decided to make him the subject of a cover story.

It was back in October 1977 that the other major international news magazine, Time, put him on the cover, but even with eight years to blur any sense of duplication, it had to be assumed that Katie Graham, the formidable owner of Newsweek, would never have approved of giving LeMay the kind of double very rarely granted to authors unless she thought there was something more to be said about him.

LeMay, however, suspected that whatever literary insights the Newsweek piece might contain, the main effect would be to blow the whistle on his past. Jackson LeMay the novelist was being forced to step aside and make room in the limelight for Richard Cromwell the former spy.

In his comfortable, unpretentious chalet in Wengen, a ski resort four thousand feet up in the Bernese Oberland, LeMay brooded on this with his half-sister, the highly regarded actress Lyssette Cromwell. Wengen won his heart soon after he went to the University of Berne as a sixteen-year-old refugee from the traumas of public school experience. His apprenticeship in intelligence work dated from around the same time.

"You have hollow legs," murmured Lyssette at one point. Indeed, their long night of talking was helped on its way by the grape and the grain, and a few Normandy apples too, by way of the Calvados. For his sister it was all the confirmation she needed that the ability to handle alcohol was one trait Richard had inherited from a father with whom he had had a blighted relationship.

Reggie Cromwell, who fathered Richard, and then, eighteen years later, Lyssette, by the first and second of his three wives, was a man who could not look after his own money, or anyone else's for that matter. Reggie saw the inside of prisons in England and on the Continent, and died owing well over a million pounds.

"You know, when Dad went, I heard that four bank managers and half a dozen head waiters lost their jobs," said Lyssette, in a voice infected with wonder.

"Yeah," said LeMay, "giving Dad credit was a   hazardous business."

Being his son was no easy option either, and to cope with the implications of his father's behaviour while keeping face among his companions, the sensitive schoolboy developed a talent to deceive. The brilliance as a linguist that emerged during the young Richard Cromwell's teenage years in Switzerland was no handicap in the Intelligence Corps during National Service. But it was when he joined the Foreign Office, after taking a first in modern languages at Cambridge and teaching for a time at Eton, that he became heavily involved in espionage.

The Le Parc hotel was Los Angeles. It was as fashionable as the city itself. At 733 North West Knoll, West Hollywood, the luxury hotel was conveniently located between Hollywood and Beverly Hills, and close to the studios and major film outlets.

Le Parc offered the business traveller a home-like setting. Each of the spacious suites featured a sunken living room with fireplace, wet bar, kitchenette, and private balcony. The guest could play a set of tennis on the lighted court, work out in the gym, and, just next door, take an invigorating sauna.

There was the roof garden to relax in, the heated pool to swim in, or the whirlpool spa to unwind in.

It was at Le Parc that LeMay and his half-sister stayed while talking with Sparta Studios chief Rudy Gioberti about a big budget movie of LeMay's latest novel. The heroine of 'Riders On The Storm' was a strikingly good-looking young woman called Catriona. Her looks, lustrous cornsilk hair, and bright and captivating liveliness were patently the contribution, by way of her half-brother's typewriter, of

Lyssette Cromwell. To friends in London she didn't deny that she was quietly thrilled by LeMay's efforts to persuade Rudy to cast her as Catriona. Not so many years earlier his advocacy would have been a painful embarrassment to her, but that was no longer the case. She was now thirty seven and her career in theatre and television had been surging in its own right for some time. In England. She was an unknown quantity in the States so it all hinged on how receptive the boss of Sparta Studios was going to be towards her. Was the casting couch philosophy of "fuck it or forget it" still going strong in Hollywood? Viviane Ventura had told her that it was, but Jane Seymour and Rachel Ward pointed out that economic considerations were so important an eager starlet could screw fifty guys and not get in the movie. So when, during dinner on their second night at Le Parc, Lyssette casually laid her hand on Rudy Gioberti's upper thigh as he talked to her brother, she was mildly surprised when he responded.

Perhaps he was responding more to her reputation than to the reality of her. It had always been thus. In her short life and long career, Lyssette Cromwell had been both blessed and cursed with some powerful gifts. She had an unusual acting talent, a troublesome honesty, a vulnerability she often masked by truculence, and a ripe sensuality in face and form. Some years before, she advised a struggling interviewer: "I find it difficult to talk about my work. Why don't you just write about my big tits?" He did.

Over the years Lyssette had helped out other such scribes with quotes describing her liking for sex and lusting after truck drivers and fairground roustabouts, and the traces of her forays into alternative lifestyles and love affairs. One alternative she had explored was lesbianism. Lydia Goodride was a women's body building champion from LA. They met in the basement bar of Blake's Hotel in Chelsea when Lydia came down to breakfast at half-past noon. She was five foot two, small-boned, curly near-black hair, leonine nostrils, freckly chest and well-shaped breasts visible down the open V of her black shirt. The only hints to her profession were the fully-rounded thighs straining her tight black jeans, and the unnaturally-veinous, toughened wrists.

She ordered black coffee and smoked Gauloises throughout an almost uninterrupted monologue delivered in drawling Los Angeles. How she had moved from a career in dancing to weight training with

Arnold Schwarzenegger, how she ran the gauntlet at Gold's Gym, the Mecca of LA's male body building elite, of her performances of body sculpture in the US and Europe, and the letters from thousands of women fans who had been inspired to pump iron because of her example. Lyssette was so impressed that when Lydia asked: "How about a slow comfortable screw?" the young English actress could only say: "Yes."

That particular experiment in alternative living was six years in the past, but on her way to join her brother in Hollywood, Lyssette stopped off in Paris to see Lydia. They greeted each other as old friends, with a hug and a kiss on the cheek, rather than old lovers. The affair had ended because Lydia developed a taste for sodomy, both in the giving and receiving, accomplished with the aid of Lydia's varied collection of dildos. As always the American did most of the talking. She talked of her marriage to French poet and rock singer Sergei David, their life together in Paris; he was homosexual so they were ideally suited, and her partnership with American photographer and movie studio boss Rudy Gioberti, who before becoming the big chief at Sparta was already famous for his sinister photos of New York's SM scene.

The latest product of their partnership was a large and expensive coffee table book called 'Lady Lydia Goodride'. It was a collection of black and white photographs of Lydia in many moods: from femme fatale to fetishist, Goya-like smouldering portraits to sculptural details of her tensed, graphite-coated limbs. She gave Lyssette a copy and autographed it, adding the words: "Desire takes, Need hurts, Love endures."

It was over a decade since a sub-editor had summed up the popular image of Lyssette Cromwell with the triumphant headline: "Stratford's very own Sex Goddess." It was a label that would stick and to some observers there even seemed to be a reluctance on her part to get rid of it. In a recent BBC radio interview, when asked about luxuries she desired, she requested the QE2 "even without the sailors" and then some lavish silk underwear. An appealing 1960's tartiness lingered in her style of clothes and make-up, as displayed for Rudy Gioberti's benefit that night. For the occasion she wore her long blonde hair partly pinned up, partly wisping round her neck, black boots, black tights, a black skirt well above her knees, and a white sweater worn back to front, its deep V caught at the back with a sparkly brooch.

From her ears dangled an unmatching pair of delicate, iridescent earrings.

She lightly stroked his erection through the cloth while Rudy attempted to keep the conversation going. Which did she prefer, the stage or film work?

"Whichever I'm not doing at the time. As a consumer I prefer movies to the theatre. As an actress I hate the brutality of film. You see, the best thing to be in a film is the director. Everything and everyone else is a commodity to be used."

"But you want to do more films?''

"Oh, yes. All the reasons why actors want to do films are bad, and I have them all: greed for the money, vanity, because it's an ego-trip, laziness, cos it's easier than theatre. I even enjoy the dreadful perks."

"Such as?" prompted her brother.

"Well, people treat you like cut glass, laugh at all your jokes, cream their jeans to please you." She knew as she said it that Rudy Gioberti had just performed that particular service for her.

Lyssette Cromwell's first film was 'That Certain Age' in 1969. In it, as in most of the others, she appeared at some point, without any clothes. But her career actually began with the Nile temptress, in a National Youth Theatre production of 'Antony and Cleopatra' at the Old Vic in 1965. She was seventeen and training to be a teacher, but she moved the theatre critic of the London Times to note her "very creditable shot at a part from the heights of which her years debar her."

Lyssette and Richard had the benefit of a Russian grandfather. He was a colonel in the Czarist army and in England negotiating an arms deal when the Bolsheviks took power. He stayed, never returning to Russia, and married an English girl. Anglicising his name and habits he became a London cabbie.

"Your brother has written an explicit sex scene in 'Riders On The Storm'. Have you any worries about doing such a scene?"

She smiled. She was surprised at how quickly Rudy had regained his composure. This was developing into an interesting game.

"Darling Rudy, I'll take my knickers down for you anytime."

The two men laughed, the American a little uneasily.

"Don't worry," said Richard, "my sister likes to shock."

With dinner over, the three went for a soak in the whirlpool spa.

After half an hour Richard excused himself, leaving Lyssette and Rudy alone.

"Are you married, Mr. Movie Mogul?"

"Yes. To an English girl as a matter of fact, called Fiona."

"And are you happy?"

"Yes, I am. I like English girls."

"Good." She climbed out of the water, nude, shimmeringly erotic.

"Then I'll see you tomorrow."

"No." He held out his hand. "Like I said, I like English girls."

In her middle to late twenties, Lyssette found herself out of work for a considerable time, and in a state of desperation she entered into a relationship, first business, later pleasure, with soft porn magazine publisher and theatre owner, Peter Lagonda. They met at one of Lord Randolph Deveer's celebrated parties. Like most people, Lyssette had the media view of Lagonda in her head, for his amours with well-stacked young women were regularly documented by the gossip columnists and the News of the World, but in person she discovered that the Rampant Sex Beast was a shy, neat, middle-aged man with a little moustache and a slight stammer. He wore a well-cut suit but no jewellery save a chunky gold ingot studded with diamonds, which hung around his neck on a stout chain and appeared to serve the purpose of keeping his tie flat. He offered her twenty thousand pounds to pose nude for a magazine centrefold. She agreed.

Peter Lagonda was a convent-educated Liverpool lad from a broken home. He was called Ralph Herbert then. Now he was a millionaire with three theatres, two Rolls-Royces, and four girlie magazines which were big sellers on both sides of the pond. His father, a haulage contractor, left the family when Ralph was six. He and his two brothers were brought up by his mother, whose own father was an inspector in the Merseyside police. Ralph left school on his fifteenth birthday. His first professional break into show business was as a drummer in a band in an end of the pier show at Blackpool. He got a pound a week. While in the RAF he ran hops at the local dance hall, and his National Service over, he continued to run dances as well as staging bathing beauty contests and putting on variety shows. Clawing ever upwards Lagonda, having re-named himself after the famous luxury automobile had, by the early 1950s, his own agency, booking acts for little theatres all over the country. It was all good clean family fun until one day in Manchester, the theatre manager told the budding tycoon that there must be nudes in the show. Lagonda asked two of the girls if they would bare their breasts for an extra pound a week. They said "yes" and the takings trebled.

But by 1957 the local theatre network was fighting a losing battle with television, so Lagonda bought some premises in Soho and opened the Lagonda Nitespot. The police raided the place within ten days and repeated the visit twice more before six weeks were out. But it rapidly became a huge success.

Lagonda invited Lyssette back to his penthouse in Belgravia for a night-cap. She accepted, warily, and when she saw the gaudy interior of the place she knew why she had been hesitant. There were white fur rugs and polished marble everywhere, while in the bedroom there were mirrors on the ceiling above the huge circular waterbed.

"It's not as bad as it looks," he said cheerfully as he handed her the small vodka and lime she had asked for.

"You mean, you're not as bad as this looks," she countered, equally cheerfully.

"Quite."

"And who looks after all this for you?"

"I have a maid who lives in. She's from Glasgow and a real character, an absolute dear."

"Why don't you marry her? She sounds ideal."

He laughed loudly. "She's almost as old as me."

"You like your girlfriends young?"

"I would much prefer an affair with a glamorous thirty-five-year-old, but I seem to meet the teenage ravers only. The girls around town, ambitious, tough, cold-blooded, you know the sort. Once they know who I am they suddenly turn into Miss Charming. They'll screw on a first date, and if you make the mistake of letting them into your life you have a hell of a job to get rid of them again. They start talking about how you can help them in their careers, you know. Maybe star in one of my shows, or make a record, or become a hostess on a TV game show."

"Very boring."

"Yeah. But they're good in bed, so one endures the chatter. Sex is the only thing these girls are good at and when they find out I don't have the connections they thought I did, they pack their bags, making sure they take all the furs, trinkets and stuff I've bought them."

"You don't sound too upset."

"I'm not."

"Well, perhaps I should come back when I'm thirty five," said Lyssette with a smile.

"Good gracious no. Let's get the contract signed, then I can give you the cheque."

"And then?"

"And then I'll drive you home."

"Oh."

They did not become lovers for two months.

On her thirty-fifth birthday, Lyssette phoned up Peter Lagonda, who she had not seen for years. It was just a stab in the dark, a joke call really, but the young American girl who answered the telephone at Lagonda's penthouse was not amused. She introduced herself as Natasha Landi, told Lyssette not to ring again, and hung up. Lyssette mentioned the incident to Rudy Gioberti one day during the month she stayed with him in California. In the intervening two years Natasha Landi had become Mrs. Peter Lagonda and Rudy had some comforting words to offer.

"That kid has humped more tools than it takes to launch the Space Shuttle into orbit. She must have started at about six, judging by all the guys who say they've made it with her."

"Have you?"

"Yes."

"How was she?"

"Nothing special. There was the thrill of having some under-age pussy but that was it. And she has an absolute bitch of a mother, a real lush who could not make it in the movies herself, so she pushed her monstrous brat at every horny yes-man in town. Now the kid's a big star with the image that butter wouldn't melt in her mouth. If the fans only knew just what sweet-little-girl Natasha had to put in her mouth to get into movies."

Lyssette tousled his newly blow-dried hair and laughed at his expression when he scowled at her.

"So what am I?" she asked, "Over-age pussy?"

"You are just incredibly special."

"Glad to hear it. Now tell me all about Natasha Landi."

To hear Natasha tell it, her romance and subsequent marriage to

Peter Lagonda was a match made in heaven. Few others shared that opinion. Her mother was pleased that her daughter had married a rich man but not so pleased that her new son-in-law was old enough to be Natasha's grandfather. Indeed Lagonda was fifteen years older than Norma Landi.

Natasha was nineteen; Lagonda was fifty five. For some time she had been looking for a way to break her mother's stranglehold on her. All Lagonda was looking for was a good time with no complications. He was in New York on company business. She had a featured role in an off-Broadway musical. After seeing the show and introducing himself to her backstage, he envisaged that her role in his life would rate no higher than 'featured', but having once sampled the delights to be had between her slim, muscular thighs and tight, round buttocks, Lagonda became the victim of a hopeless infatuation.

Back in England, Lyssette began rehearsals with her colleagues in the National Theatre for the new season of plays, still uncertain whether she had got the film role or not. She was happy to be working though, and as the weeks passed without any word from Hollywood, or from her brother, she resigned herself to the thought of another opportunity lost.

It was October, and Lyssette was happily at home on the South Bank as Strindberg's heroine, Miss Julie, when, at a party to celebrate the publication of a new history of the National, she met Edwina Lawrence, who told her that Natasha Landi had got the part.

"The cow. That bloody little cow."

Lyssette read a magazine article by Edwina Lawrence called 'The Year of The Sex Olympics':

After the sexual high-jinks that went on in the Olympic Village at the Los Angeles Games in '84, the big question must be: "Does sex before the main event spoil the chance of success?" We asked top athletes for their views and they were amazingly candid.

Former swimming star turned television personality, Maureen Willis, and her latest boyfriend, Lance Crosby, think lovemaking before a major contest is just what the judge ordered.

"Screwing is a good way of taking your mind off a competition the next day," said twenty-three-year-old Maureen, who has now retired from serious competitive swimming.

American pro-footballer Lance, twenty four, a millionaire quarterback for the Dallas Cowboys, said, "Playing in a big game next day makes no kinda difference to me. I still roll in the hay the night before. Mo says it's good for me."

But Superstars champion Helenne Landau rules out love. She likes to be alone to think out her gymnastic routines.

Helenne, twenty four, former British gymnastics champion who scooped the International Women's TV Superstars title last year, said, "I don't think I'd ever want to get my leg over the night before a big show." Her current lover is English soccer player Eric Evans but Helenne added, "Even if I was married, I still think I'd want to be alone. Of course, when the competition is over I go out and have a ball, especially if I've won."

Chris Hicks is the fastest woman in the world ... on water skis. But in the passion stakes she's a non-starter. "If you are going to be No. 1 in your sport then you can't afford to expend much time or energy on a social life of any sort," said Chris, twenty two, who set her blistering 81.62mph world speed record, on one ski, in September.

"Unless you're very lucky you don't have much of a sex life either," she added.

Chris, whose boyfriend is Britain's Formula 2 water ski champion Charlie Horn, spent five weeks alone in her hotel room when competing for the world title in Italy.

"All I had for company was my vibrator."

The great sporting stars of the past did not believe in denying themselves any joys that came their way. The legendary American baseball player Babe Ruth is said to have had sex with at least one woman almost every day of his playing life.

Gorgeous athlete Rhiannon Gray tried long distance running for the first time when she took part in the London Marathon earlier this year. Though it was a fun run, Rhiannon kept to her usual competition rule ... no sex the night before.

"With twenty six miles in front of me, I didn't want any distractions at all," said Rhiannon, twenty five, a former modern pentathlon world class performer.

Rhiannon, in training for the next world championship, also said, "When we are competing in international events abroad, we are kept away from the male athletes. The team manager who travels with us is my mum, so I get a lot of little talks about keeping fit for competitions. Sex before an event is something I would not contemplate. Your mind is totally concentrated on coming first."

Rhiannon said that her boyfriend never goes with her when she competes abroad.

"The day after the competition is different. Everyone goes mad then. You know there's a rumour that modern pentathlon is really six events not five, and number six takes place when the main contest is over. That's when we all try to score."

Long distance runner Cindy Ball believes in training hard ... and enjoying all the good things in life.

"I would not abstain from screwing before a race," said Cindy, who is thirty two and has competed in eighty six marathons all over the world. "I try to avoid a really late night and too much wine, but otherwise I don't think having sex makes any difference. Anyway, you want to avoid spending too much time on your feet the night before."

Physiotherapist Cindy, who likes to go out to clubs and restaurants, added, "Maybe some people think they will be more aggressive if they don't get laid, but I'd say it was psychological."

When, some days later, Lyssette found herself sharing the jacuzzi with Edwina Lawrence at the Sanctuary, she asked the journalist how the candid quotes were elicited.

"Darling, really. In bed of course. Before I started therapy I used to worry an awful lot about being a nymphomaniac, but there's no denying that people are more inclined to talk freely after a good lay, and that's the only sort of screwing I do."

Lyssette felt conventionally shocked. She allowed herself a brief moment to enjoy the emotion.

"Good God, Edwina. You must be a friend of Judith Chisholm."

"I am."

In 1982 reporter Judith Chisholm kept a tape recorder running when Welsh superstar Richard Burton took her to bed during the European location filming of the nine-hour television series 'Wagner'. After days and nights of pillow talk, Ms. Chisholm told Burton she had to return to London. When he demanded to know why, she could not bring herself to tell her famous lover that she had more than enough words for the story an American scandal sheet had sent her to write.

Lyssette smiled in response to Edwina squeezing her thigh.

"Do you want to ... er ... interview me?"

Edwina nodded silently, one hand in intimate exploration beneath the bubbling water.

"No thanks."

"Lydia Goodride told me you were an ace lay."

"I am. Now take your hand away."

"Please Lyssette."

"No."

"Please."

"Piss off, Easy Eddie. If you're that horny, go hump a doorknob."

"Bitch." She clambered out, in a furious temper, and flounced off.

Lyssette turned, smiled her most dazzling smile at the other women in the jacuzzi, and settled back.

More than she would ever admit, even to herself, Lyssette was hurt by the knowledge that Lydia had actually spoken about their relationship to another person, and a bitch like Edwina Lawrence at that. Suddenly her modest South Kensington flat, where Koo Stark had once been a neighbour before her marriage, seemed drab and empty. So did her life, with only her work to satisfy her. Her friends rallied round in an attempt to cheer her up, but all the invitations to parties were turned down by the increasingly despondent Lyssette. It was Linzi Baker who gave her Michael Cord's telephone number.

The South London gigolo was every bit as good as Linzi said he would be, so good that Lyssette took him to France for the weekend. They stayed in a secluded country hotel and, hardly needing the excuse of foul weather, they did nothing but screw for three days.

Almost three years before, Judith and Steve Krantz were standing in the sunny courtyard of the same French hotel, holding hands and gazing devotedly at each other. The happy couple were revisiting their hideaway honeymoon hotel thirty years on. But this time they were back on business, very big business.

With the Krantzes, it is difficult to separate work from romance. She is a sweet and demure Nancy Reagan/Jane Wyman look-alike, whose steamy novels of sex and money have made her one of the world's richest women authors. He is a slim, tanned film producer who turns them into television blockbusters. And together they are worth a fortune. Judith's third novel, 'Mistral's Daughter' tells the story of a French artist and the three generations of women who love him. Her first two, 'Scruples' ... about rich people who don't have any, and 'Princess Daisy' earned her £1.8 million, and in 1983 the latest offering had shot to the top of the American best-seller lists and had sold ninety five thousand copies in Britain two weeks before publication.

This time Judith had toned her purple prose down a shade.

"Apparently, I shocked a lot of people with my first book," she told Edwina Lawrence. "They were so worried by the sex that they couldn't pay full attention to the story, so I've included the same amount of sensuality without using quite the same words. I still think sex is very important. If a story's about romance, it isn't going to end at the dining room table. But it's all a fantasy. I love fantasy. My readers want to hear about worlds that they don't live in. The first book was a romp, a glimpse of incredible luxury that people don't have to pay a nickel for."

Judith believes in watching the nickels. Her neat, mauve and white two piece was serviceable rather than elegant, her blonde hair greying a little. Ignore the heavy gold bangle, the pearl and diamond eardrops, and she looked like any wife whose life had revolved around her husband and sons. But four years before, Judith's world went haywire when she fluffed her flying lessons and turned to the typewriter for consolation. The result was 'Scruples'.

"The instant stardom jolted the family, especially our two teenage sons," said Steve. "They were worried by the erotic nature of Judy's success and the notion of having a sexual mother. They read her book in secret. But then their friends stood in line, asking to have copies signed, and the boys realised it was something they could be proud of. I thought I might become another Dennis Thatcher. The phones rang, and they were never for me. People ignored me at parties and clustered around Judy."

But Steve had made a fortune of his own, producing films like 'Fritz the Cat' so he was not worried about being upstaged.

"It brought us even closer. She's still the most delightful woman I've ever met."

"He helps me enormously," said Judith in response. "He's the best editor anyone could have. I was no Marcel Proust when I started out. I spent all of half an hour researching my first novel"

The third book absorbed six months advance work in Provence and Paris ... an investment that turned out profitably.

"The money's made no difference," said Steve. "Judy bought herself some diamond earrings and a photocopier after the other two novels. This time, she got a sable, although I'd already given her one. That's all. We've still just got one house in Beverly Hills."

Judith's only other luxury is her Hollywood exercise teacher, who keeps the White House staff in trim.

"The first time you go to him, he makes you stand in a bikini and walks round you for about an hour," said the slender Judith, toying with her lunch steak. "If Steve can find a born-again Picasso, three statuesque redheads, and a country mansion near Avignon for the movie of 'Mistral's Daughter' then everything will be perfect."

For Lyssette and her stud, everything on their weekend in France had been perfect, but once back in London real life took over. She said good-bye to the South London gigolo. Linzi Baker rang and they agreed to meet for lunch the next day at the Cafe Royal.

"Sorry, I'm not very good company today."

Lyssette reached across the table to squeeze her friend's hand. "I know. I understand ... Julie?"

Soft-porn-star Julie Moxon died after five days on a life-support machine following a motor way crash three years before in 1983. Her £20,000 Mercedes hit a fence and burst into flames. She suffered appalling burns.

Former Sheffield model Julie worked as a shop assistant before her slim, raven-haired, dark-eyed beauty won her recognition on the beauty queen circuit and in films. She romped from bed to bed in the blue movies 'Emmanuelle in Soho' and 'The World Striptease Extravaganza', and also had bit parts in the Joan Collins films 'The Bitch' and 'The Stud'. Her success earned her a £65,000 home in Acton, West London and an expensive wardrobe of furs.

Linzi Baker looked up, her face strained. "Yes. It's been three years. I still miss her."

The two friends got quietly drunk, Linzi more so, and when it was time to go she was in no fit state to drive home. Lyssette put her in a taxi.

"Come home with me, Lissy."

"I've got to get back."

"Please, Lissy ... Please."

"Okay, love. Move over."

"Would you, could you, make love to me, Lissy?"

"I... I'm sorry. You're a dear friend, but..."

"You must. I helped you."

"And what about Jon? Don't you love him?"

"Of course I do. What's that got to do with anything?"

They were sitting on the couch in Linzi's favourite room of the house she shared with her husband, the photographic genius Jon Revere.

"I loved Bailey too," said Linzi.

Before he married lovely model Marie Helvin, David Bailey had had the pick of the world's most beautiful women, and his photographer's patter had frequently landed him in bed with his subjects. It was reputed he got his best results, on film, by telling each model to think of their last good screw.

"Very slowly, very carefully, David looked me over, and somehow I felt that he had touched every part of my body," top model Viv Neaves once recalled. "As I lay posing naked on his studio floor, he talked to me in the language of the bedroom. David knew he would get what he wanted, and in the end I gave it to him. By God, he can be a rotten so-and-so in bed, but I liked it. And the more beastly he was the better it became."

But Bailey's rough and ready approach did not impress nude model Nina Carter at their first photo session: "He didn't address me by name, or even as 'you there', but by the most blunt of four-letter words."

Like Nina, Linzi found Bailey coarse, but like Viv she succumbed, and when Jon Revere came along she succumbed again.

"Love me, love me," screamed Linzi, tearing open her blouse and thrusting her bare breasts into Lyssette's face.

Lyssette slapped her once, hard across the face. And stood up.

"I've got to get back to work, Linzi. Unlike you, I don't have a rich, successful husband who loves me, nor a beautiful home. Don't throw it all away. Forget Julie, forget Michael Cord, forget me."

She turned her back on Linzi and walked out, shutting her ears to her friend's pleas. But all afternoon the guilt gnawed at her. Rehearsals were a pain. That night she ate a late supper in front of the TV, not caring what she was eating or what she watched. Finally, before going to bed, she rang Linzi. There was no answer.

In the morning she rang again. Scott Brinkley answered.

"This is Lyssette. Can I speak to Linzi?"

"No, you can't."

There was a pause. Lyssette thought she could hear sobbing.

"Scot... What is it?"

Another long pause. And then ...

"Darling, there's been a slaughter."

"What did you say?"

"Cherie is dead. I found her. She died in my arms. She said Michael Cord did it... Linzi, Jon, Sheena, Mickey, Maureen Willis and Lance Crosby, they're all dead. Dear God, it's an awful mess here. I've had to give the police your address. They want to talk to all the friends of the dead."

He hung up.

Jean-Claude and Susie made love for the first time in the curtained-off section of his jet. Afterwards, he held her, gently. He held her until she fell asleep in his arms. It was a lovely feeling, thought Susie. Better than sex, because it lasted longer.

FOUR WOMEN

Sabrina Howard was the beautiful young widow of the late, and much lamented, Roger Howard, the charismatic New York lawyer, whose defence of the Mormon minister's daughter in that 'Murder in the Orgy-Room' trial had made Roger famous around the world. So much for history, thought Robert Gideon, but why does she want to see me?

He pressed the intercom.

"Ask Mrs. Howard to come in, Meg."

"Yes, Mr. Gideon."

Meg Cunningham was as voluptuous as Sabrina Howard was model-girl slim, as fair as Sabrina was dark. Meg watched her open the door to Robert's office and walk in, smiling. The door closed. Mrs. Howard certainly knows how to look good, thought Meg: matching shoes and bag by Gucci, matching skirt and jacket from Ralph Lauren. She felt a twinge of envy which was quite uncalled for. With her high, full breasts and proud, out-thrusting buttocks, Meg always looked her best without clothes.

Robert Gideon had been a man of few weaknesses until he met Meg, newly divorced, and a swinger, in a singles bar in New York. Recently divorced himself, they found that they had much in common, and after he had got to know her better Robert discovered that she was not only willing but happy to cater to all his sexual desires and needs. She introduced him to the orgy scene in New York, and even managed to teach him a few things he had never heard of. He once wondered out loud why she had not turned her talents to where they were best suited, and become a courtesan, but she told him, laughing, that she preferred the mask of respectability.

Robert had brought Meg back to California with him. Neither felt ready for marriage yet, so Meg had been given a job in Robert's office at Sparta Studios which gave her an excuse to be a part of his life. Gideon was tall, with silver-grey hair, and piercing blue eyes in a tanned, ruggedly handsome face. Meg knew how attractive Robert was to women.

Sabrina Howard certainly found him so. The first thing she noticed about Gideon, after taking in the details of face and form as she strode towards him on long, slender legs, was that his suit matched his hair colour. The second thing she noticed was more important: he didn't seem to remember her.

"Should I?" he asked, when she mentioned it.

"Maybe not." She smiled. "It was all rather hectic."

Intrigued and irritated, Gideon could feel his tool stiffening, becoming uncomfortably erect. He hoped he wouldn't have to stand up for a while.

"Where exactly was this, Mrs. Howard?"

"Oh, no. Please call me Sabrina."

"Very well ... Sabrina."

"Good." She laughed, a bright, musical sound, like tinkling glass.

"We, who have been so intimately connected, if only for a brief time, should use first names with each other. Would you like a blow job, Robert?"

"What?"

"Your secretary, Meg, is that right? She gives good head. I saw her at Plato's Retreat that night, the night you were there. She was having a ball."

"Was I?"

Sabrina laughed again and stood up. "So what about that blow job now?"

"My goodness, what a beautiful lady you are. You know, you'd be a great model. Let me call up someone who can really help you get started."

She stepped around his desk and knelt down as he began to dial. She crawled slowly towards him on her hands and knees, her eyes bright, fierce.

"Frank? About the party tonight. Right, I know, but there's a new lady I'll be bringing ... Sabrina Howard. Really beautiful ..."

His voice went on, without a pause in it, or a hesitation, as she unzipped and freed him, then used her tongue and fingers to bring him to a full erection. Still talking, he grabbed her by the hair and pushed her mouth onto his shaft. He filled her mouth, hurting the soft part at the back of her throat, making her gag. She clutched at his thighs with both hands. She enjoyed the sensation of servicing him, obeying him, belonging to him, but God, he was big, so big that her throat ached and her jaw hurt from holding her mouth open to take all of his shaft.

Now that he was off the phone, Gideon came quickly, his semen flowing into her throat. Sabrina had not swallowed a man's come since she was sixteen and in high school in Fort Worth. Thinking about it, and herself at that time, she could not help but grimace. She had been plump and so damned innocent in those days, but those five boys thought she was just a pricktease in her tight, tight clothes. They cornered her one afternoon when she was alone in the changing rooms and took her repeatedly.

Sabrina told Gideon about it later, while they were taking a shower together. They had made love for hours and she was feeling very, very good. Head back, letting the water stream down on her closed eyelids, her hair, her nose, she told him exactly what the boys had done, what they had said, and how she had reacted.

"At first, I was extremely frightened, so much so that I wet my lace knickers. They joked about that when they pulled them off me. I was so damned afraid I kept struggling and trying to scream until they slapped me a few times to shut me up. Then they each took their turn. After the first one had done with me," she giggled, "it didn't feel quite so bad."

"Go on," he said, "your story's got me fascinated."

Grinning, she continued, doing a kind of sensuous dance step, raising her arms above her head and swaying her body. Gideon wondered idly if the hash she had persuaded him to let her use earlier was beginning to act.

"While one was doing it, the others held me down, but they told me I wouldn't be hit again if I let them do what they wanted. So I gave in. From then on it was one really wild party. They taught me how to go down on a guy, and that was something I'd never even dreamt of."

"Bet you were a quick learner?"

"Sure was." She paused, her body still gyrating slowly under the hot, steaming water. The bathroom was murky and clouded, and Gideon felt, with a kind of surprise, his penis become rock-hard again. Sabrina giggled, and he jabbed it up against her, between the firm cheeks of her buttocks.

"How did you survive such a seeing to? It's a wonder they didn't screw you to death."

"They weren't as big as you are, not any of them. Nor was my late husband, for that matter. But you make me feel like this is the first time, when you do that to me."

Her delighted wriggles belied the complaining tone of her voice.

"Shall I keep going?" he asked.

She moaned softly. He filled her, making her fear she should be torn in two at any moment. Then he was humping her, hard, his hands slippery on her hips, and she loved it, even the pain. He did not say anything more, but his breath rasped against her neck as he bent over her. She closed her eyes.

"Hurt me, give it to me," Sabrina heard herself scream as his fingers dug deep in her flesh and she felt him swell inside her, start to throb and then to spasm. At that moment her own orgasm overtook her, but she was still able to realise that Gideon had not yet come.

"Darling, don't hold back, I'm coming, I'm coming."

Gideon grunted in reply and began thrusting viciously into her, moving very fast and hard, and came. He withdrew, hurting her again, but leaving her sore, throbbing, yet satisfied all the same.

Much, much later, after the party, Sabrina was alone in her apartment in the Wilshire House luxury tower apartment building. She was soaking in the jacuzzi and wondering how it had all happened. The party had, of course, turned into an orgy, and, as well as movie exec Gideon and photographer Frank Jay, one of the men she made it with was TV anchorman Martin Rich. My God, she thought, my mother watches him every morning. What would she think if she knew?

But there was worse. Sabrina was bisexual and quite open about it, with everyone but her mother. When Meg arrived at the party, partnered by Rodeo Drive boutique manager, Joe Panama, this to spite Gideon for not taking her, Sabrina was delighted. Later in the evening, after the action had begun, she arranged an all-girl scene among those of similar tastes, while the men watched or took pictures. Meg was so high by this time that it was easy for Sabrina to get her to join in, even though Gideon was looking on.

Yes, she thought, what would Mom say about that? Sabrina giggled. She had enjoyed it...

Frank Jay's San Francisco studio was located in an unexpectedly plush apartment house; a high-rise with a view of the bridge and the bay. Sabrina had assumed it would be a run-down, sleazy little place on Market Street or the Haight-Ashbury, maybe even the Fillmore district, over a shop that sold adult books. She stepped gracefully out of the cab into the spring sunshine, ignoring the cabbie's leer as she paid him and turned away. In the lobby, she picked up the phone and called his apartment. Frank Jay was a long time in answering. He sounded high.

"Come on up, baby."

When the buzzer sounded she opened the door, taking the elevator as instructed to the fourth floor, where he opened the door to his apartment after another long wait by Sabrina.

"Hello, Mr. Jay."

"You look sensational."

"Thanks."

She smiled and walked nonchalantly into the carpeted room, pausing to kick off her shoes. The gesture was calculated to focus his gaze on her slim, lithe calves, which it did. She dug her bare toes in the carpet's deep pile.

"Oh, bravo," said Jay. "That was charming, and so well done. I really like your style."

"Thanks again."

Frank Jay was a small man with a thin face and mousy-coloured hair, thinning from the temples, and a typical Southern California tan. His wiry, hard-muscled body was developed and kept in shape by frequent visits to a health spa.

He showed her to a bedroom where she changed out of her clothes and put on a short Japanese robe he had left on the bed for her. She tied the belt tightly around her slender waist to emphasise her small breasts and slim hips, and emerged from the room.

There was a kind of improvised platform, doubling as a couch, running the length of the big windows of the main room, and with brightly coloured pillows scattered along its padded expanse. Jay was already fiddling with his camera equipment, and there were wires strung out all over the floor. When he saw her, Jay motioned her onto the platform.

"Okay, baby, drop the robe now."

She unknotted the belt. Jay was squinting through the viewfinder at her and adjusting the lights, turning them up so they impaled her with their heat and brilliance, and Sabrina was surprised to feel herself trembling slightly as she obeyed his instruction. Was it fear or excitement? She was not sure, not sure at all ...

1974

At that time Madelaine Sale was only nineteen. Her long, straight hair was dyed blonde, and her breasts, though large and firm, were nothing like as huge as they would be after the surgeon had pumped them full of silicone. But that was some years in the future. Now she was on her first trip to California to be photographed for 'Libertine' magazine, and being met at the airport by Vaughn Townes, an executive in the 'Libertine Organisation' and soon to take over the British end of the set-up.

"Hi there, Madelaine. Welcome to California and welcome to LA."

"Thank you. Are you Mr. Townes?"

He certainly was and she found him enormously attractive, right from the start. He ushered her to a waiting limousine and told the black-uniformed chauffeur to take them "to the mansion".

"You'll be staying at Sly Gioberti's place," Townes informed her.

The 'place' was a huge estate with rolling lawns and imposing wrought iron gates, with the initials SG prominently displayed. The limo pulled up by the security guards' booth.

"We have Miss Madelaine Sale," said the chauffeur. One guard checked a list and nodded; the other pressed a button and the gates swung open. The limo swept up a long, long driveway where, atop a low hill, stood the Libertine Mansion West, as out of place in Southern California as an English castle.

"Goodness," gasped Madelaine.

"Goodness had nothing to do with it," said Townes, and they both laughed, Madelaine a little nervously. The mansion was as impressive inside as out. Huge floor to ceiling windows set in stone, monstrous fireplaces, leather couches, a wonderful library with backgammon tables and, everywhere, there were butlers scurrying around carrying trays. The indoor pool had its own waterfall. By swimming under the fall the swimmer arrived in a second pool in a cave-like room which also boasted a large jacuzzi. Other features of the Mansion included tennis courts and a bath house. During her stay, Madelaine was to get to know all the facilities.

Shooting the picture spread took four days. At the end of the second day's work, Townes informed her that there would be a party that night, and a movie. Sly Gioberti wanted her to attend.

"I'd love to."

She came down at the appointed hour to find that the huge living room had been converted into a small movie house for the night, with seating for fifty or sixty people. A screen had been set up over the front windows and a projector was concealed in the wall between the living room and the library. As it turned out there were more movie stars in the audience than up on the screen, and Madelaine later could not even remember what the film was called, much less what it was about, because she spent the entire time star-spotting.

When it was finished and the lights came on, everyone headed for the pool or the jacuzzi. Townes walked over and took her arm.

"Sly very much wants to meet you, Madelaine."

"I er ..." She paused. "Okay."

After that night, Madelaine became part of the family and was given a special gold card. Such a card allowed the owner to come and go as they wished. All other people, no matter how famous, needed an invitation. The freeloaders needed nothing, once they had a gold card. Every night they were at the mansion for the movies, the food and drink, the straight parties, and the regular orgy night action, which usually took place on a Thursday. On such a night the family saw a porno flick before getting together in the bath house, the pool, or the jacuzzi.

Madelaine had never seen the hard-core 'Deep Throat' before arriving in California, but during the weeks of her stay at the mansion she was to see it several times. On one occasion, Linda Lovelace herself, escorted by Chuck Traynor, were among the guests when it was shown, though they didn't take part in the orgy that followed. Madelaine attended on most Thursdays but without any enthusiasm, agreeing only to intercourse with Townes, always hoping that Sly would make an appearance.

Orgy-night was not always announced in advance. Sometimes the evening started off in a normal way: music, backgammon, socialising, and then the word would be passed down. At this point the true celebrities made their excuses and left, as did most of the young women, hostesses, centrefold models, and starlets, who wanted to maintain their amateur-status reputations. Of those girls who stayed to take part, many were hookers. Many of the male orgy-goers were members of the mansion's family.

One Thursday night, when the action in the jacuzzi was in full swing, Sly came down from his private suite, wearing a bathrobe and carrying a large-size bottle of baby oil. He watched what was going on for a few minutes before removing his robe and climbing into the whirling waters of the hot tub. There were four men, including Townes, in the jacuzzi, and eight women, including Madelaine and a porno movie actress called Andrea True, who co-starred with Linda Lovelace in 'Deep Throat Part 2', and would later have a hit single in the American and British charts.

Gioberti began rubbing baby oil on the breasts, belly, and buttocks of each of the women in turn. Madelaine watched as Andrea was simultaneously penetrated, front and back, by Gioberti and Townes. That was a great honour for a girl in this select company, so when they both withdrew from Andrea without coming, and the baby oil was now being rubbed on her own breasts and ass, Madelaine was thrilled.

Towards the end of her stay at the Libertine Mansion West, Madelaine was taken to a very special LA night-club by Townes. Despite her pleas, he would tell her nothing about the club before they got there, so when the chauffeur drew the limousine into a crowded parking lot, Madelaine began to feel a little uneasy. This was a particularly seedy area of Los Angeles.

"I'm not sure about this, Vaughn," she said, though allowing him to take her arm and guide her across the street to a rather imposing building with a door that was a slab of stainless steel. At his ring, it slid open.

"Good evening, Mr. Townes. Nice to see you again." The voice belonged to a young, large-breasted, Mexican woman sitting behind a desk. Her long, stiff nipples jutted seductively beneath the black tee-shirt she was wearing, on which, in gold script, was the legend: NYMPHS & SATYRS. She asked Townes to pay the admission charge and gave him a card to sign. He in turn offered her his credit card. When the formalities were complete, the girl smiled, pressing a button to allow Townes and Madelaine to pass through the turnstile.

"Have a ball now, won't you?" she said, winking at Townes.

They went passed black, padded vinyl walls edged in gilt, and down a carpeted staircase. They now stood at the entrance to a smoky cavern, the air heavy with the cloying odour of hash, and loud with the urgent pulse of the music, to which a crush of men and women danced. Most of them were naked or wore only shorts or towels; a few still had their street clothes on. At the edge of the dance floor, two young women moved sensuously together, each girl wrapping her arms around the other's neck, their bare breasts touching, their mouths open, joined in a hungrily devouring kiss. Nearby, another woman, older, with pendulous breasts and heavy thighs, thrust and rolled her hips at her equally naked partner, then ran her fingers down over his pot-belly and grasped his erect penis.

Other people, also in various stages of undress, lolled on sofas or leant against the mirrored walls of the room, watching the dancers. Townes led her passed bodies glistening with sweat; bodies on couches, bodies on mattresses, or on pillows banked against the walls, bodies kneeling or bending beside each other, moving gently or writhing wildly above or beneath other bodies.

None of this was new to Madelaine, of course, but that was at the house. Out in the real world, she did not expect people to behave in this way, and was surprised the police had not closed down the club. She also noted the several ways these orgy-goers differed from the freaks and jaded thrill seekers who attended at the mansion. Here, the men and women looked and were ordinary, affluent, middle class people; the majority of whom were also middle-aged.

The music throbbed after them as Townes led Madelaine down a long flight of stairs to a lower floor of the club.

"Why do people come here?" she asked.

"To escape," he said.

"And why do you come here?"

"To make love."

Townes gently pushed Madelaine forward, and they moved through narrow, darkened corridors opening onto saunas and steam rooms. They arrived at a large area full of pool tables and pinball machines. Madelaine slipped her shoes off and sat down on one of the floor cushions, pulling Townes down with her and cradling his head in her lap.

A few feet away, a man, dropping his towel, tumbled onto a floor mat, followed by a woman whose only garment was a single black lace garter on her upper thigh. The man, in his forties, was dark and swarthy; the woman younger, and blonde. She was slender yet very muscular, and Madelaine recognised her as a women's body building champion who had come close to winning the US title. As the woman began fellating the man, another man, pale and balding, joined them, penetrating the woman anally.

Madelaine put her shoes on and stood up. They went into the bar, where more people had their clothes on, but some of the glances of the male drinkers made her uneasy and she asked Townes to take her away. At the jacuzzi, the sexual activity was vigorous and noisy, and again Madelaine signalled her discomfort and they moved on, through an area of cubicles, some shut, some with their doors open. From beyond the thin walls she could hear whispers, laughter, the slap of flesh against other flesh, and against mattress or floor. Townes smiled, took her hand, and led her into a large room.

"Are we alone?" she asked, a little surprised by her own nervousness.

"Yes."

The room contained a large swimming pool, enclosed on all sides by a ledge of polished tile, and there was a sauna at the far end. While Townes sat on a bench and watched, Madelaine pulled off her sweater, removed her skirt and panties, and naked, dived into the pool with the ease of a trained swimmer. She got out after a few laps.

"What's the matter, Vaughn? Why don't you get undressed?"

He gazed at her for a long moment before speaking.

"I love you, lady. I love you."

Madelaine blushed.

"Then, sir," she murmured huskily, "you had better prove it."

They rose, and moved towards the sauna, Madelaine carrying her clothes. Opening the door for her, Townes switched on the light. A smell of wood shavings and dry bark met them as they stepped inside, and Madelaine placed her small pile of clothing on the top bench and sat down on the one beneath to watch him undress, which he accomplished without undue haste.

Naked, he sat down next to her, his shoulder grazing her back, the scent of her hair mingling with the pungent aroma of the wood, his mouth on her neck, his lips finding the soft mound behind her ear.

"Mmmm ... nice," she whispered.

His hands slid over her large, glistening breasts, stroking and squeezing the tanned flesh.

"Like melons," he grunted, his voice thick with emotion.

Madelaine giggled, making the flesh jiggle in his hands. She felt his erection against her thigh, ramrod stiff and trembling, and turned to him. They kissed while his fingers explored between her legs, gently probing, finding her moist and open.

They drew together. Lying back on the wooden bench, Madelaine arched her body, her legs around his hips as he lowered himself into her. He bore down, her nails scraping his back, impaling Madelaine on his jutting manhood. She gave a brief, low moan and Townes paused.

"Honey?"

He felt her hand caress his buttocks, then she thrust her body up at him, eager, gasping, wanting to force the pace. He took up the challenge, matching his rhythm, his desire, his need to hers, and on the hard saddle of the wooden sauna bench they rode each other's taut yet yielding flesh to the rough, quick climax they both wanted.

Next day, when Vaughn Townes asked Madelaine to go with him to England, she happily said yes ...

1980

A new and surprising emotion was troubling Meg Cunningham: Guilt. It was not that she had arrived at the party with Joe Panama, or made it with him afterwards, that was merely casual and a fitting rebuff to Robert Gideon for dumping her. No, it was what had happened at the party, the scene with Sabrina and the other women, which was worrying.

Meg had never considered herself a lesbian, nor yet a bisexual, though she had indulged in lesbian lovemaking during orgies before. What made it different this time was the aching, continuous desire she felt for Sabrina's body. The thought of having to watch her strolling in and out of Gideon's office on a daily basis was too much for Meg to bear. She resigned her job at the studio.

That evening in the Polo Lounge, Meg got a little drunk and let herself be picked up by four men, who took her to a house in Laurel Canyon where they all snorted coke and then undressed her. When she was naked, one of the men led Meg to another room. There was a thick carpet on the floor, the walls lined with cupboards, but no furniture in the room in which she was left alone for some minutes.

Three women came in, dressed in the manner of eighteenth century tavern wenches, with long, plain, heavy skirts that reached to the floor and tight bodices that made their breasts rise and swell. Each girl wore a thick leather collar around her neck and leather straps on her wrists.

Wordlessly, the three began to dress Meg in the clothing they had with them: seamed stockings, black garter belt, and black bra, and their voluptuous captive clearly enjoyed the attention of their cool fingers, which frequently strayed. Only when the prettiest of the three produced a length of thin, but strong-looking, cord did Meg become concerned, though she did allow her to bind her hands behind her back. Meg was then blindfolded and guided to yet another room where, she was told, the men were waiting for her.

Stumbling a little, Meg was made to advance into the room, and could feel the heat of a log fire on her thighs and calves. A hand, male, closed around one breast and squeezed, while the other breast was scooped from its low-cut bra cup and the nipple sucked and bitten. At the same time, her legs were forced apart. Hair grazed the inner surface of her thighs as the lips of her sex were gently worked open.

Someone suggested that she ought to be made to kneel, and the hands that had been caressing her breasts were now at her shoulders, pushing her down. Her own hands still bound behind her back, Meg was helpless to resist their urging, and they kept pushing till she was bent right over, her face buried in the pile of the hearth rug, her haunches higher than her torso. One of the men gripped her buttocks and sank his shaft fully into her vaginal passage. When he had finished, his place was taken by another, even bigger, and a lot less gentle. The third took advantage of her position to sodomise Meg. Panting loudly, he forced his way into the narrower passage with hard, violent little thrusts that wrung a wail of agony from her lips, but once in, he was quick to ejaculate.

Moaning, tears streaming down under her blindfold, Meg slipped sideways to the floor after he let go of her. The savage usage of her body, the effect of the cocaine, the tightness of her bonds; all these things conjoined to bring about the descent into unconsciousness into which she now fell.

She did not wake till the next morning and was not surprised to find herself in the room without furniture. She was lying on a mattress over which a sheet had been carelessly thrown, her head supported by a rather lumpy pillow. Her body felt surprisingly clean, relaxed, good. She sat up. Her stockings were badly torn, and she was about to remove them when the door opened and one of the women came in. The pretty one.

"How are you, Meg?" she asked, softly.

"Confused."

She smiled. "Don't be. My name is Joy Joy de Ferrare." Her voice, low and ardent, was exactly in keeping with the lean, slender look of her body, while her white skin contrasted absolutely with the coal-black sheen of her hair, which was close-cropped. The shape of her eyes, green-brown in colour, was almost oriental, and Meg enjoyed being the object of their gaze.

Joy Joy knelt down beside Meg. "Let me," she said ...

1973

The location was a chateau in the French countryside, sixty miles from Paris. Outside, it was an afternoon in early spring, while in the master bedroom, behind heavy drapes and under subdued lighting, the celebrated film director Franz Strasserman was about to shoot an intimate scene between the unnamed anti-hero and the frustrated wife of a rich businessman. Handsome, well-spoken English actor, Edmund Roc played the man; the seductively alluring French actress, Joy Joy de Ferrare, after several years starring in French and German films this was her first major English-speaking role, played the wife. Both were naked.

Strasserman had, as always, fully rehearsed his actors beforehand, but a nude scene, whether explicitly sexual or not, presented certain difficulties, not the least of which was persuading the actress to do it. However, Joy Joy was no giggly starlet, she had a self-confidence borne of maturity and a pride in her splendid body which transmitted itself into a willingness to strip once she had been convinced.

The film was 'The Night of The Fox' based on Randolph Savoy's best-selling novel about a plot to assassinate the West German Chancellor. The terrorists hire an English assassin, code-named 'The Fox', to do the deed. While on the run from the police he turns up unexpectedly at the woman's home after a one-night-stand with her in a country hotel some days earlier.

The director called for a take. The 1st assistant director called for silence. Lighting, camera, and sound set-ups were checked one more time, then Strasserman yelled: "Action."

Joy Joy rolled on top of Edmund and began humping and thrusting. The violent churning of her hips was meant to simulate the final stages of sexual intercourse and, judging by the arousing effect it was having on the camera crew, the performance was a huge success. Strasserman grinned. Poor Edmund, he thought, the fully-clothed rehearsals couldn't possibly have prepared the actor for this assault. The director, however, knew her reputation for dedication, and was not surprised.

What Joy Joy knew, after long service in the sex film industry of Hamburg and Nice, was how difficult men found it to fake orgasm. Truth being the most convincing act, the trick was to make your partner come without penetration while faking your own climax at the same time. So Joy Joy's frantic hip actions allowed her belly to stroke his flaccid organ to erection and ejaculation out of sight of the director, crew, and, most importantly, the camera lens, which had to make do with a picture of the ecstatic Edmund clutching Joy Joy's superb buttocks.

Strasserman nodded and the 1st assistant director called: "That's a print." Before the lights were turned up, the wardrobe mistress threw a sheet over Joy Joy and Edmund, and a hospital screen was wheeled in and placed round the bed. A break was called, the crew drifted away. Strasserman was about to congratulate his actors on a scene well done, but something in the attitude of the couple held him back. He told his assistant to make sure they were not disturbed for ten minutes.

Edmund Roc, meanwhile, was in a daze, finally opening his eyes when his co-star rolled off him.

"Wake up, Edmund. Come on now, it wasn't that good. I'm sure you've had better."

"I have, but never without having the lady as well."

Joy Joy laughed softly. "Oh, you poor thing. Let me make it better..."

January 1984

Twelve thousand feet below him the Nevada desert was a grey sea in the early morning light. Simon Barnes tightened the chin strap of his crash helmet, adjusted his goggles, and when the signal turned to green, moved to the open door. Larson and Dax were ahead of him. They moved up together, their boots in unison, stamping on the ringing metal floor of the Rockwell Commander troop transporter.

Larson turned, kicked into space. Dax was a second behind. At the threshold now and feeling the vicious pull of the prop blast on his face, Barnes confronted the horizon, his hands grasping the cold steel jambs, his knees bent, and vaulted into the sky.

The slipstream buffeted him but he was ready for its turbulent threat. He corrected the leftward tug of the propeller wash by pulling one arm into his side and closing his legs, then reverted to the star position: arms and legs wide, head back and belly out. The wind whipped against his jump-suit. From behind the goggles his eyes checked the readings of the altimeter and timer mounted on the reserve chute on his chest. Though the ground was rising to meet him at thirty-two feet per second it seemed, at first, that he had not fallen but that he was held suspended in the air, a plaything of the winds. But then, as his eyes adjusted to the fast approaching earth, he became aware of the changing contours and rapidly enlarging dimensions of the land, and the illusion was dispelled. The timer clicked into the red. He was now two thousand feet above the ground and hurtling towards the desert at two hundred miles per hour. Drawing in his arms, his left arm in front of his face, right arm over his chest, he reached for the ripcord and pulled. The wind grabbed at the pilot chute and the main canopy, sucking in the air he had just passed through, billowed out above him. Like a giant pendulum, the world swung gently back and forth beneath him.

The drop zone was marked by a white cross. Barnes located its position and tugged on the guide strings of the chute to bring him nearer. He spiralled down gracefully, turning in and out of the wind at will in order to adjust his forward speed. He landed lightly on his feet and gathered up the chute as it collapsed round him, then struck the quick-release button and removed his crash helmet and goggles along with his chute harness as Larson and Dax approached. Barnes, a tall, handsome man of about forty, with chestnut hair, grey, flint-hard eyes, and a sharply-moulded face which carried just a hint of cruelty around the thin-lipped but sensual mouth, continued to pack away the nylon parachute.

"Hey, Limey," said Dax, by way of greeting, his weak, bland face creasing into an ugly, unprepossessing grin. Larson did his best to imitate it. His real name was Tatagglia and, like Dax, he was from New York. Both men were tall and stocky; their blank faces and glass bead eyes devoid of all genuine emotion. It was a look Barnes had seen before.

"Used to work for Gus Bartelli, didn't you?" asked Barnes.

"Yeah," said Larson. "What's it to you?"

"Ever wondered who got him?"

Larson came on, drawing a .45 Colt automatic from inside his jump-suit. Barnes stood up and to one side, all in one fluid movement, and shot him in the wrist. The .45 went off and flew away, and Larson went straight up in the air in shock. When he came down Barnes' arm was round his neck and they danced towards Dax; Larson screaming and bleeding like a stuck pig.

All this had happened in less than ten seconds, and Dax was a little slow in reacting. Holding the struggling Larson in front of him as a shield, Barnes aimed the .357 Smith & Wesson and shot Dax in the head.

He died instantly. The bullet penetrated the skull through the right eye, bursting the eyeball and driving slivers of bone into the brain. A triangle of skull and hair the size of a fist was torn away at the exit wound, and Dax tumbled backward. At the moment of brain death the tendon in the finger curled round the trigger of the .38 pistol began to spasm, and the gun began to empty itself randomly at Barnes, who let go of Larson and dived to safety. The unfortunate Larson was not so lucky.

The first bullet struck him in the chest from a distance of nine feet, splintering bone and shredding lung tissue as it tore through the rib cage from right to left. The second hit him in the left shoulder. It passed clean through, severing artery and muscle, the impact spinning him round and down on his knees. The third bullet burst his skull, exposing his brain before slicing through it and out, taking off the nose and the right cheekbone. Larson flopped face down in the sand.

As Barnes got to his feet, the whine and chatter of engine and rotor blade caused him to stop. There it was: a black smudge hugging the early morning shadows, a 212 Bell copter by its outline, Barnes decided, and smiled. He quickly snapped a cartridge into the flare gun and fired it into the air.

William Darrow, founder and sole director of UNSIS, the United Nations Secret Intelligence Service, was the most respected, feared and hated law enforcement officer since J. Edgar Hoover. He stood at the living room window of his suite of rooms at the Waldorf Hotel, looking down on the steady flow of evening traffic in the Strand.

He was waiting for news from Germany that night in April, 1984, and he was not alone. As the phone rang, and the fat man moved wearily across the room to answer it, a pale, tense Lyssette Cromwell turned to UNSIS agent Dirk Chancellor, a close friend of Simon's.

"I just realised something, Dirk."

"What is it?" he asked, equally tense as he squeezed her hand.

"I've not thanked you for rescuing me. Those bastards would have killed me in the morning."

He gave her a tight little smile. "Finding you alive in that basement was the only reward I ever hoped for."

She put her head on his shoulder. "While it was happening, there was one thought I focused on to keep myself sane, that Simon was safe and would come for me."

"He is safe, Lyssette. I just know it. And he will come home."

SPRING IN BAVARIA

Simon Barnes awoke with an oily taste in his mouth and had no idea where he was. He swung his long legs down off the high double bed with its posts of oak almost as thick as telegraph poles. He was wobbly on his feet. He was dressed in a pair of old yellow cotton pyjamas he would not normally have been seen dead in. They had been washed so many times he could almost see through the material. The pyjama jacket hung unbuttoned on his lean, muscular torso. There was a tear under one arm that had been recently sewn up. He had the unnerving feeling he was wearing dead man's clothes.

He swallowed several times, finding his throat a little raw, and then a stomach cramp propelled him into the bathroom. He retched until he was worried he had ruptured something. Nothing much came up but bright yellow bile, the same shade as his revolting night attire. His head ached from his exertions. He looked around the bathroom through tear-filled eyes. Though he was over six feet tall, everything seemed to be on a vast scale. Obviously whatever drug or combination of drugs they had pumped into his veins was still having an effect. He felt like Alice after she had drunk from the little bottle. Half an acre of tiled floor led to a square basin big enough to bathe in, standing four feet off the floor. There looked to be many thousands of those little six-sided tiles covering the bathroom floor. Wherever he was, it was a shitty old place, older than the house in St. John's Wood.

Thinking of St. John's Wood and his wife Lyssette caused the tears to run and run until he washed his face in cold water. When he finished, his fingers still tingled but the stomach cramps had stopped. He looked in the mirror. His handsome face was now hollow-cheeked, and there were dark circles under the eyes. He stripped off the hideous pyjamas and strode naked back into the bedroom.

Simon had had a noiseless visitor. The curtains were now open, billowing in the morning breeze. The air, scented by a forest, felt and tasted good, melting on his tongue like a wafer. He suddenly felt very hungry, something that had obviously been anticipated. On a round table in the centre of the bedroom he saw a tray with an icily sweating carafe of fresh orange juice, together with a round of buttered toast and a jar of Oxford marmalade. He shrugged into a T-shirt and pair of boxer shorts that were laid out on the bed and settled down to a hearty breakfast. He had just finished when a sweet, clear female voice startled him by calling his name:

"Simon?"

He stood up and walked barefoot onto the balcony outside the tall windows and got his first look at his new surroundings.

Blue-green mountains and a far sparkling lake were the first things he took in and, nearer, fieldstone buildings with steep slate roofs in a naturally wooded setting. Nearer still he saw a garden with squared-off hemlock hedges, beds of marigold and gracefully curving footpaths walled with roses. Beside the house there was a private swimming lake studded with rock outcrops, and ringed by perfect rows of spruce. A wooden bridge arched above a spillway. A multi-level, flagged terrace in the wide angle formed by the wings of the house went down to the water's edge.

The girl swimming in the green water raised an arm when she saw him.

"Take the elevator down to the terrace, Simon. I'll meet you." She dived beneath the surface and he saw her stroking underwater, fluid as an otter, towards the terrace.

"Okay," he answered, though she could not hear him. He turned, going back into the bedroom and across to the door. Opening it, he stepped out into a hallway which was an interior gallery rich in wood, with a carpet like an abstract painting in tones of burnt orange, rust and brown. The gallery was lit by high opposing windows, three of them, each the size of a badminton court. The streaming hot light of the morning sun was regulated by stained glass louvres which appeared to have a religious motif.

He found the cabinet-sized elevator and descended to the first floor, walking through a chapel which had been turned into a dining room and out onto the terrace, passed a grotto with a trickling waterfall. Here religious statuary had been removed and replaced by a huge piece of stone that looked like a cross, except for the top part, which was in the form of a loop.

"It's called an ankh," she said. "It's the ancient Egyptian symbol of immortality."

He turned round. She was a voluptuous strawberry-blonde with incredible silver eyes.

"Welcome to Bavaria, Mr. Barnes. I'm Tanith. I hope you'll let me call you Simon?"

Before he could think of a suitably sarcastic reply, she continued to chatter on brightly.

"Those are the Harz Mountains. Isn't spring in southern Germany a wonderful season?"

"Spring? What month is this?"

"Why, April, of course."

"That's impossible," Barnes muttered. "It was January..."

His voice faded away. He walked to the edge of the lake. The half-submerged rocks at the water's edge were fringed with green-gold streamers, some sort of aquatic plant life. The water had a decided flow even this close to shore and it looked clean, so clean and clear he could see the round brown stones on the pebbled bottom out to a depth of seven or eight feet.

"I've lost two months."

He spun round to face the girl, who was vigorously towelling her hair. She was wearing a black one-piece cut high on the hip and low at the bosom. As she towelled her mane, her heavy breasts jiggled provocatively, the nipples making aggressive high-rise peaks in the material. The quantity of down on her arms and long legs glinted like hazy golden wire. She stood with feet apart, her pubic mound ripe and inviting, as she draped the towel over one sleek shoulder to fluff up her half-dry hair with her fingers until it settled back thick and lion-toned, shading to smoke, curling like woodshavings on her bare shoulders.

"What is this place?"

"Psi Facility. SPEAR Directorate have put me in charge of you, Simon. You must be ready when Mr. Caligari comes for you."

"Why Psi Facility?" asked Barnes. The Special Program for Extortion, Anarchy and Revenge had gone to a lot of trouble to ensnare him and Lyssette. When the time was right he would make them all pay, including this girl.

"Oh, come now, Simon. You know as well as I that Psi is the twenty-third letter of the Greek alphabet, and that the ideogram stands collectively for all paranormal experiences."

Barnes also knew, or guessed, that despite appearances, the campus at Psi Facility was as tightly guarded as any facility at Langley or Fort Meade, though he saw no helmeted security men with packs of vicious dogs or checkpoints overseen by machine guns in guard towers

and lit by floodlights. Before Barnes had been brought to it, part of the
SPEAR reservation had been used to experiment with new types of
protective sensors and hardware. The security system that monitored
several square miles of campus and woodland was based at the
meteorological weather station situated on a bald bluff overlooking the
far lake. It contained surveillance and tracking devices adapted from
all the latest cameras and telescopes which SPEAR crammed into its
spy satellites. The woods were gridded with sensors and honeycombed
with sector control bunkers. Each team of operators had at their
disposal arsenals which could soak the night sky with burning
magnesium, destroy bridges or create lethal pitfalls in the winding
approach roads. They could gas every living thing on a two-acre plot
around the main buildings in a matter of seconds. The surrounding
fields were sown with pop-up land mines that contained enough metal
fragments to shred an elephant. Heat-seeking missiles awaited low-
flying jets. It would need two battalions of crack paratroops supported
by helicopter gunships and tanks to take the facility. Unknown to
either Barnes or the girl, that was exactly what was on the way at that
very moment, courtesy of an out of synch CIA satellite that should
have been spying on East Germany. The NATO Bavarian command
centre in Munich had released a bland press statement concerning a
"snap" military exercise in south Germany as a plausible cover for the
rescue mission. However, it had been William Darrow who had
recognised the significance of the rogue data first, the seriousness of
which was confirmed after the successful SAS raid, led by Dirk
Chancellor, on an unfriendly embassy in London freed Lyssette
Cromwell alive and well.

"What did you mean, I have to be ready for Mr. Caligari? In what
way?"

"Psychically, of course, Simon. Your psychic energies are very
strong, but they lack concentration." She smiled. "It's my job to help
you concentrate."

She thought back to her conversation with Aubrey Caligari some
days before: "They say that fucking in the astral plane is nirvana,"
mused Tanith, dreamily. "For pure sensation it's supposed to eclipse
anything we can manage in the flesh, but we managed pretty good last
night."

The old man grinned.

"Yes we did. But, my dear, Barnes is somewhat adept in the

astral, you are not. And I'm a little worried about your proclivities toward the left-handed uses of sex."

"Now, Aubrey, don't fuss. Using drug and sex rites to implement paranormal experiences is standard occult practice. The release of sex energy through ritual copulation can be very creative, as I know to my cost," she said, hugging the ribs Caligari had belaboured in his loverage the previous night, and wincing.

He captured her firm jaw in the palm of his big, hairy-backed, virile hand, stroking her full lips with his thumb until she took it into her mouth and began to suck on it with a will.

"Oh, yes, yes. Sorry about my excesses last night, Tanith, but you do stimulate me so. Anyway, this morning you're vital as always, not badly used, as I might have expected after the many athletic hours we spent together."

She knelt down in front of him, unzipping his fly, her hand slipping inside to seek him out.

"You old bugger," she said cheerfully, "I forgive you, though I won't be able to sit down for a week. As for what I'm going to do with Simon Barnes, don't worry. It's white magic. I'm not fool enough to dabble in Black Magic."

"You will be focusing the libidinal forces of this man on yourself. He may prove to be quite extraordinary sexually."

"Oh, I do hope so," she said with a flippant shrug of the shoulders as she played with his erection. "Check out the videotapes afterwards. It could be a hot show."

"No joking matter, Tanith. I think Barnes could become far too much for you to handle."

"Ho, ho," she laughed. "After having you shove your nine-inch prick all the way up my backside, and making me like it, I doubt if there's anything I cannot handle." She began to pump his jutting organ with her left hand.

"Yes, Tanith. Oh, yes, yes. You must have a healthy respect for the kinetically destructive powers of the sexually aroused. It's very important to realise that you can satisfy, even exhaust, the physical body, as I well know. But what about the bioplasmic double on the ethereal plane? What happens when it is subjected to prolonged spasmic orgasms without the possibility of emission? Can you satisfy Barnes in the astral? What happens if you don't? You may find yourself confronting a tulpa, a living nightmare beyond your control."

At the mention of the unruly and often terrifying tulpas, part of the lore of Tibetan mysticism, Tanith took his cock out of her mouth.

"Tulpas are thought-forms, and I'm a hard-headed realist. And Simon Barnes is just a man, even if he did willingly share his wife with the High Priest of Mendes and others at a Black Mass." She shrugged. "At least, that's the story."

"Very well," Caligari murmured, as Tanith continued to fellate him. "I only wanted you to be aware of the possible dangers."

It was five-thirty in the morning. The stones of the house were sweating. Conifers in the gunmetal greenery of the garden stood limp with beads of moisture. Fathoms of curling fog, white as bone, wisped hotly from the surface of the black reflecting lake. Two noisy swans glided rose petal smooth to the far bank where the tall spruce, dark as midnight sentries, began to blur into the illusory distance. Birdsong was chilled, isolated. The wall-sized bay window behind them overlooked the swimming lake and the Japanese lanterns illuminating the perimeter of the terrace. The rain had all but stopped. Clouds like chimney smoke rolled away toward the mountains. In the first glimmers of dawn, the trees dripped diamonds. As Tanith deep-throated him, and his climax neared, Caligari looked to the higher ground where the fog was parting. Ahead of them the sun had risen; the blue and speckled day exploded...

There was a big shower in Tanith's bathroom, a modern instrument of torture like an iron maiden, needle spray coming at her from half a dozen different directions. The ribs which Caligari had bruised during their violent copulation ached horribly, but she stuck it out, using a loofah to get the blood rushing even more fiercely.

Tanith came out red as a beetroot, breathing hard and pleasantly exhausted, wrapped herself in a big white fluffy towel and lay down on the bed, tingling. Before she was completely dry she discarded the towel and reached for the little bottle of concentrated hash oil she kept close to hand. She measured a small drop of the liquid directly onto one fingertip. Sitting in the lotus position, she held the firm, viscous drop aloft to study it. Then she looked down at her ripe, round belly and the dark thatch of pubic hair covering her mound. Without uncrossing her long legs, she lay back, inserting the droplet-coated finger deep into her anus, then withdrawing it quickly to place it inside the vagina, letting the fingertip loll deliciously on the engorged clitoris.

Within seconds she was jumping up and down at the brink of what could be a night-long orgasm. Her skin flushed again and her head was a sensuously entwining ball of vipers. Tanith placed a drop of hash oil on each erect nipple, smearing some on her full lips too. She was desperate to put her hands on herself, to claw out and cling to the steamy, pulsating heart of her desire; to rub against walls and furniture and fall panting and grinding on the rough carpet, wearing the skin off her hips and backside while she wore out her need. But she forced herself to keep control.

She went quickly along to Simon's room, hearing him thrashing about in his sleep and crying out as she neared the door. He sat bolt upright when she came in.

"It's all right, Simon. It was only a bad dream. I'm here now."

He stared at her, becoming aware of her glistening, vibrant nakedness. Despite himself, his cock grew swiftly erect, forming a stiff little tent in the sheet over his loins.

"What are you doing here?" he groaned, holding his forehead.

"I was in the bath. I heard you cry out in your sleep, so I came...," she said, pausing meaningfully, "right along. Have you a headache? I know a good way to get rid of it."

There was a muffled detonation in the far distance as Tanith sat down on the bed beside him.

"What was that?"

"Electrical storm starting, by the sound of it," said Tanith. "We had a real doozey here just last week."

She hitched closer to him, making him fully aware of skin tone and stressed muscle, the pulse of her hot blood and the bawdy heaving of her breasts. There was another detonation, nearer this time.

"Let's see what you've got there," she murmured, pulling back the sheet.

"I want to fuck you," he said.

"I can see that."

His whole body vibrated with lust. She was astride him, a smile playing on her pert mouth as her slim fingers stroked his chest, going lower and lower. Bent over him, her lips were brushing his own, then her tongue was flicking at the lobe of an ear, while his hands went to her heavy, full breasts, teasing those nipples so that they stood out even harder and redder than they already were.

With breathtaking speed she mounted him, lifting herself up and impaling her body on his shaft as though she was mounting a horse, and instantly she was riding him in a headlong gallop to a finish that had her writhing, even after he flung her off so fiercely that she fell off the bed onto the floor.

He forced her voluptuous thighs as far apart as they would go and grunted his satisfaction as he plunged his cock into her warm, wet depths, the full weight of his body pressing down on hers, crushing her into the hard, bare floor with every jackhammer blow of his wildly thrusting hips. Her hands clawed at his strong shoulders, her legs locked about his middle, the ankles crossing above his pumping backside, clamping him to her as her rhythm matched his own.

Using her hips as handles, Barnes spent himself in her. They lay still. The booming detonations were very near now. He had known all along that it was no electrical storm. He rolled off her. The sounds of gunfire drew closer.

THE PRESIDENT'S WIFE

Sabrina Howard was thirty-two when she married Senator Alan Woodville. She was thirty-eight when they publicly separated and the mother of two small daughters, Lisa and Rachel. By this time it was July 1986, and Alan had been President of the United States for eighteen months.

She first set eyes on the up and coming Senator from California in 1967 in Hawaii, during the Christmas vacation. Sabrina had been sunbathing topless on a friend's secluded private beach all that afternoon, when the man whose skill at water skiing she had admired came over and struck up a conversation with her. They talked about student politics mostly, and the War. Only in the evening did Sabrina learn the identity of the handsome stranger she had so glibly chatted to.

The Woodvilles were the nearest thing in America to royalty. One brother had already been President. He was dead, and the next in line was preparing for the '68 election. Alan was the baby of the family and a bit of a black sheep as well. Though married, he was often seen and photographed in the company of pretty young women who were definitely not his wife. Sabrina's slim, dark, well-bred, model-girl looks certainly fitted the bill. She hoped there were no photographers around that afternoon. Yet she had to admit to herself that the youngest Woodville brother did intrigue her, despite the fact that he was twice her age and obviously spoilt and self-centred.

This she had discovered early on in the conversation when she mentioned to Alan that she intended to vote for his brother in the Californian primary. Sabrina thought the remark would please him.

"I'll tell Paul," he murmured, icily, making it clear that Paul Woodville was not a subject he wished to dwell on. He would much rather talk about himself. Sabrina got the distinct impression Alan was jealous of his older, more serious, successful, and celebrated brother.

It would be many months before they met again. During that time Sabrina dropped out of college and became a hippie. In Morocco she experimented with drugs, group sex, macrobiotic diets, and other aspects of commune life. But what seemed to worry her lawyer father most was her newly frizzed hair. Family pressure finally brought her back to Southern California and the family home in Imperial Valley, though not for long.

Less than a month after Paul Woodville's death, Alan phoned to ask her out on a date. Sabrina accepted. Their secret meetings were to last only a couple of weeks before her father discovered what was going on and put a stop to it by making Sabrina a virtual prisoner. It was a situation that could not go on.

"Will you stop treating me like a child," she yelled at her father one day.

"When you start showing signs of growing up, my girl."

"Oh, screw you."

She waited to be slapped with closed eyes, but it did not come. Instead she found her father looking at her with a pained expression on his face.

"Okay then, since you've brought up the subject, let's talk about your love life. If you want to go to bed with a rich, handsome guy old enough to be your father, that's fine with me, as long as I choose the guy."

The man he chose for Sabrina was successful New York lawyer, Roger Howard. They were married in April 1970. Ten years later, a national celebrity because of the sensational, usually sexual, nature of the trials he was involved in, Roger died of a heart attack while making love to Sabrina. As his wife, always in court to listen to her husband, Sabrina had a high media profile. As his beautiful young widow she was a celebrity in her own right. An affair with Hollywood producer, Robert Gideon, ended abruptly when he was arrested by the FBI because of his involvement with prostitution.

More headlines.

By this time Alan was divorced and making the rounds of Hollywood starlets and New York socialites alike. It was only a matter of time before they met.

There are a number of private sex clubs in New York. One of them, the most famous, is Plato's Retreat; another is the Boom Boom Room. It was during a celebrity orgy at the latter that Sabrina and Alan found each other. They were married three weeks later.

Life as a Senator's wife was fun, always interesting. In a Playboy interview she revealed that Alan had once made love to her in his office in Washington while a group of Congressmen and their wives waited outside. On another occasion, they did it on the steps of the Capitol building itself.

But life as the First Lady of the United States became, very quickly, anything but fun. After the highs and lows of the exhausting Presidential campaign, and the hectic, seemingly unending succession of celebration parties that followed Alan's victory, Sabrina expected that moving into the White House would prove an anti-climax. But it turned out to be much worse than that. From that cold January morning she first set foot in the White House, she found the trappings of power, the servants, and the austere official surroundings, so utterly stifling it was as if a great smothering blanket had come down over her.

She did her best to improve the decor of their private apartments at 1600 Pennsylvania Avenue, as well as those at the country retreat at Camp David. She considered herself successful at recruiting a team of people to help her run these establishments. These were the only tasks that the First Lady was allowed to perform. Anything else was frowned upon, and in time she came to see the servants and security men as jailers rather than as helpers and protectors.

Worst of all, surprisingly, was the idea of being a public figure. She had always enjoyed seeing her photo and reading about herself in the society columns when she was married to Roger, but she did not feel like public property then. Sabrina hated the way people felt they owned her and could criticise her appearance and behaviour with impunity. There was no way for her to answer back, and, increasingly, no one to turn to for support as she lost touch with her friends outside Washington. The pressures of the job made Alan remote, unwilling or unable to understand when she tried to talk out her pain one evening at dinner.

"My God, Sabrina, what is it? Do you want another baby? Okay then, we'll have one."

"How? You hardly ever sleep with me now, and on the rare occasions you do feel horny you're too tired to screw. I'm not likely to get pregnant that way, no matter how hard I suck."

"Keep your voice down for God's sake, Sabrina."

"I will not. I don't care who hears. I want out."

"Out?"

"Escape. Yes. From here. I must."

"What nonsense. This isn't the sixties, and you're no longer an adolescent, though you often act like one. You can't drop out anymore. You have responsibilities that you must face up to."

"Screw you, Alan. I'm drowning and all you can tell me to do is walk on water. Well I can't do it. I never could."

So began the First Lady's famous freedom trips, instituted by Alan as a means of holding the marriage together. Half a dozen times a year, for two or three weeks at a time, Sabrina would disappear from Washington with family or close friends, no Secret Servicemen, and unwind in some out of the way corner of the world. And for a little over a year the ploy worked. The marriage held. But the trips themselves became ammunition for Sabrina's detractors, and the more she tried to make her life work, both personally and publicly, the more her behaviour was condemned as outrageous. The pressure was unrelenting. Something had to give.

On a warm summer's evening in New York City, Sabrina, accompanied by two of the youngest and most handsome Secret Servicemen on the White House team, paid an extended visit to Plato's Retreat. There was no attempt to keep the outing secret, indeed there were photographers inside as well as out. Everyone, men and women alike, was eager to perform for the cameras with the First Lady of the United States.

The pictures were published in a special edition of Screw magazine, but the story made headlines all over the world, even in communist regimes such as Cuba. That was perhaps not so surprising since the President was visiting the island for talks with Fidel Castro when the scandal broke.

Alan returned to 1600 Pennsylvania Avenue to find Sabrina literally packing her bags.

"What am I to do with you," he asked. He spoke quietly, with great sadness.

"Let me go, Alan. What else is left for us now?"

"Oh, Sabrina. "

"Please don't. I've got to find myself, to search for my own truth. Your identity is here but I can't stay with you any longer. I'm so sorry."

To the rest of the world, the fresh departure of Sabrina Cary Howard Woodville from 1600 Pennsylvania Avenue was just another freedom trip. To the First Lady of the United States it was the first step on the road to a new life. The children were to stay with Alan. She knew they would be well looked after by reliable and caring nannies, and so she could concentrate entirely on herself, her well-being, and her future.

The first stopover was New York, where Sabrina bought an apartment in the famous Dakota Building on Central Park West. Security, which was already tight because of the celebrity tenants, became even tighter. And the guards were needed. Crowds of onlookers and sightseers gathered outside the iron gates at the entrance to the grey, brooding eminence of the Dakota when the news of the new occupant got out. For two weeks she was unable to venture beyond the secure environs of the building and had to content herself with answering the phone calls. Some were from friends, some from enemies, some were people looking for a connection, either business or pleasure, while others were merely obscene.

Sabrina had visitors too, a steady stream of friends and admirers, who came to congratulate or console her as each morning's crop of newspapers and magazines from around the world produced fresh approbation or opprobrium. One visitor in particular had the gossip columnists and feature writers in a real lather, a European toy boy called Prince Cesare Belmondo. The stunningly good looking twenty-year-old, one of Britt Ekland's cast-offs, was a member of a wealthy Italian landowning family, and was at the orgy club Plato's the night Sabrina paid her now-famous visit. Indeed, rumour had it that the woman from Screw magazine had taken several photographs of Belmondo in vigorous anal copulation with Sabrina. None were published, and it was said his family paid an enormous sum to prevent their appearance. Alternatively, the Belmondos had links with one of New York's five Mafia families, who put pressure on the publishers.

Whatever the truth, Sabrina was intrigued. She did not actually remember the young man at the orgy, but then it was such a wild night.

"Please come in, Your Highness."

"Thank you." The smile was dazzling. "The signora does not remember me." A statement, not a question. Sabrina blushed.

"Is it so obvious?"

"Only to a close friend, or someone who wants to be," he said, speaking very confidently in English, the accent soft, melodious.

"Ah, I see. Would you like a drink?"

"I'd like to take you to lunch."

"That might prove a little difficult," she said, indicating the window and the crowds on the sidewalk far below.

"No problem. The windows of my limousine are fitted with one-way glass. Shall we go?"

The limousine took them out to Kennedy Airport where they boarded the Prince's private plane, a Learjet Intercontinental 36. The in-flight lunch consisted of beluga caviar, lobster, cracked crab, all washed down with pink champagne. By the time they reached Paris, after a refuelling stop in London, it was time for dinner. He took her to the Coq Hardi in Bougival, eleven miles out of the capital, driving himself to the restaurant at the wheel of his gold Porsche 914. On the return trip he let Sabrina drive.

"Where to?" she asked, as they entered Paris.

"The Plaza Athenee." He informed her that his suite was the one in which the American automobile tycoon, Alexander Birmingham III, died of heart failure while making love.

Sabrina pretended surprise though she knew not only the girl involved, Roberta Gideon, and, of course, her father Robert, but also Alex III as well. Roger Howard once took on the might of the Birmingham Motor Corporation when defending a sacked car worker accused of inciting a riot at a Detroit plant. He lost the case, but by way of compensation Sabrina had a brief affair with Alex III.

In the hotel elevator, Belmondo took her hand. In the plush bedroom of his suite, he took her in his arms and kissed her.

"I didn't bring a thing with me," she gasped, when he finally let her go.

"Clothes, you mean?"

"Yes, and other things, female things."

"Ah. In the bathroom cabinet. I keep it well stocked. There is even a selection of vibrators and dildos."

"Really?" She looked at him round-eyed. "I don't think I'll be needing those tonight, but I would like to take a bath."

"Of course. I'll show you where everything is."

The bath was a large, round, sunken tub with gold taps.

"Fabulous. Big enough for a party."

"What does the signora have in mind?"

"The lady wants to screw."

She returned to New York alone the next day to find that the secret was out. On the tarmac at Kennedy she stepped off the Learjet and into a football pack of reporters, airport officials, and police. Questions were flung at her from all sides, in a whole variety of languages:

"What exactly is your relationship with the Prince?"

"Have you slept with him?''

"Do you want a divorce?"

"Do you think your actions have destroyed your husband's chances of being re-elected in '88?"

To all these her answer was an enigmatic smile and a firm: "No comment." She was hustled into a waiting limousine by Secret Servicemen and driven away from the airport terminal building at high speed.

"Are you taking me to the Dakota," she asked the chauffeur.

"No, Ma'am, the Waldorf-Astoria."

"The President?"

"Yes, Ma'am."

Sabrina smiled bleakly. "He'll be furious." Then the smile broadened and mellowed out as she remembered the night of passionate lovemaking with the Prince. How tall and athletic he was, how tanned his skin, all over. She remembered how his body felt to the touch of her exploring fingers, how broad his shoulders, how slim his waist, how firm his buttocks. They were together in the bath to begin with, and Sabrina was kneeling astride him. She remembered how the soapy water frothed and boiled around them as she worked her body up and down on his shaft. Cesare's organ was huge, a rigid pole of muscle fully eight inches long. It drove her wild that she couldn't get it all in.

The limousine rolled to a halt in front of the canopied entrance of the Waldorf. Sabrina was escorted quickly across the lobby and into the elevator. The presidential party had taken over the entire top floor of the famous New York hotel.

"All this just to welcome me back from Paris, Alan? You've absolutely no cause to be jealous of Cesare, you know. It was a fun screw. He's too young to marry."

Alan didn't lift his head to look at her till the aide who had ushered Sabrina into the room went out.

"You bitch. What possesses you to say such things when other people are around?"

"What other people?"
"Okay then, go on, act like royalty, but you're still my wife."
Sabrina grinned. "If I married Cesare I'd be royalty."
"Don't be so stupid." He stood up, his features set in so stern a
mould that they matched the steel-grey of his sleek hair, and the ice-
blue of his eyes.
Sabrina returned his gaze evenly, unafraid. She noticed a
movement almost below the edge of her vision. He had an erection.
"Would you like me to do something about that? You were always
more relaxed after a good blow job."
There was a long, tense silence before he replied.
"Sabrina, I love you, despite everything you say and do."
"I know."
She licked her lips and knelt down in front of him.
He stroked her hair. "I've missed you," he murmured, "very
much."
Afterwards, they talked, about their children, about themselves.
"I think," said Alan, "it would be best if you left New York for a
few months. London is a discreet town, if you want it to be. I can
arrange things. Your arrival will be unannounced. You'll have the
use of a small house in Hampstead and an equally small car, which
you will drive yourself. There is a cook but no live-in staff, and no
bodyguards."
"Sounds like heaven."
"When can you leave?"
"Tonight."
He walked her to the door. As she reached to open it, he took her
in his arms and kissed her. Sabrina responded. It was some moments
before they parted.
"Mister, you sure know how to say good-bye," she said, throatily.
"I wish I wasn't President."
"Don't say that. You can't flunk destiny."

The quiet life? After all that had happened to Sabrina, life in
London was quiet, even serene, but not for long. Getting her new
Hampstead home in order took a few weeks, then, suddenly, a great
empty void seemed to open up. How to fill it?
One way was to spend money. An average day would find Sabrina
shopping in South Moulton Row. An Ungaro coat or a Chloe suit,

then on to James Street and shoes from Charles Jourdan or Gucci, perhaps a silk dress from Laura Ashley or Yves St Laurent, maybe a Rolex watch. She thought nothing of spending anything up to five thousand pounds a time on these shopping trips. Then there were the lunches at the Savoy and dinners at the Connaught or the Inn On The Park. It was at the latter one night that she was picked up by an Arab businessman who thought she was a high-class hooker. He offered her two hundred pounds for a night's pleasure and specified what he wanted. Amused, and not a little flattered, Sabrina accepted.

His name was Badyr Al Hussein, a Saudi multi-millionaire arms dealer and international Mr Fixit who was close to the Saudi royal family. He, of course, knew who she really was, but saved the announcement till the morning. Sabrina laughed. They became good friends. Through him she met Robin Errol. Badyr was in the middle of a heavy relationship with the voluptuous American television actress, Veronica Capital, so Sabrina was soon won over by Robin's boyish good looks and roguish charm. He was an adventurer of the old school who owned a home in Bali and made his money as an art dealer. He became her guide and passport to everything that the jet set thought fun to do in London. Making love in the front passenger seat of his Range Rover illegally parked outside the Ritz at three in the morning, was one such. Sabrina noted that the Range Rover was almost always covered in peacock droppings from the birds on his estate in Buckinghamshire.

It was Robin who introduced Sabrina to Paul Ashley and his mistress, the exquisite Joy Joy de Ferrare. They were the deans of the international jet set in London that season and still in the 'honeymoon' period of their relationship. Sabrina admired and envied the way they treated each other so lovingly. Paul was the typical English aristocrat: articulate, slightly reserved, utterly charming. Joy Joy, on the other hand, was a complete extrovert in every way, determined to transform his sober life into an endless feast of partying and fun.

Born in Bangkok, Joy Joy spent the early years of her childhood in Thailand before the family returned to the States. Her mother was a French socialite and heiress who was not pleased when her American husband decided to retire from the diplomatic service to his farm in Iowa. The marriage failed, custody of Joy Joy went to her mother, who took her to live in Paris. As an adult Joy Joy renounced her American citizenship in favour of her adopted France.

She was twice-divorced by the time she met Paul Ashley. All she had to show from the first marriage was her surname; from the second she received enough money to travel extensively and maintain homes in New York, Rome and her native Paris. Sabrina found the former champion gymnast and accomplished swimmer, skier and ice skater to be surprisingly small and pretty, with green-brown lustrous eyes and waist-length coal-black hair, though her body had the lithe, hard-muscled tautness of a prima ballerina.

What Sabrina most liked about Paul and Joy Joy was their evident closeness. It was as if both had suffered at the hands of the same enemy. One morning, after a particularly splendid party, Joy Joy confided in Sabrina.

"I only knew him as Mr Brown. I was fifteen, on summer vacation in LA with my best pal Kelly, and her parents. Brown kidnapped me, raped and sodomised me, held me prisoner for five months. I was forced at gun point to appear in 8mm skin flicks. We were constantly on the move, but the FBI were closing-in all the time. I woke up one morning in our motel in Miami and Brown had gone."

It sounded like a well-rehearsed speech. Sabrina was almost willing to be convinced, and would have been, if one of the guests at the party had not already given her a different slant on Joy Joy's story.

The guest was Harry Reems, who partnered Linda Lovelace in the infamous 'Deep Throat'. He was also Joy Joy's partner in the porno movies she did for Brown. According to Reems there was never a more willing X-rated performer than Joy Joy de Ferrare.

"She was red hot. She loved sex, all kinds of sex, on camera and off. She was wonderful to work with. Nothing was too much trouble. She'd get it on with anybody or anything, you know. Boy, we had some scenes. Marilyn Chambers had the reputation for being insatiable but the title really should go to Joy. Joy Juice she was called in the movies. It was going to be Joy Bang till we found out there was an actress with that name, for real. That's one lady I'd like to get to know."

"I'm sure."

"Anyway, let me tell you about the pictures we made. You see, Joy Juice, maybe you can guess from the name, she had this thing about come."

"Oh, really?"

Looking back on that conversation, Sabrina decided that Reems' version of events sounded as false as Joy Joy's. She didn't know who to believe. There was once clue: Joy Joy personally organised every detail of her parties, and nothing was more important than the guest list. Reems certainly wasn't a friend of Paul Ashley.

It was shortly after this episode that Joy Joy and Sabrina became lovers. Paul and Joy Joy were moving into a new home. Four townhouses converted into one, built around an immense central drawing room draped with Chinese silks to form a vast Arabian tent, the inside decorated with priceless rugs and hanging tapestries, it would be a veritable pleasure palace for the international jet set. Joy Joy invited Sabrina to try the jacuzzi in the new house the night before the housewarming party.

"I'd love to."

But first there was the last, the very last party at Paul and Joy Joy's old apartment. The guest list was the usual mix of famous artists and writers, socialites and celebrities, and almost every movie actor, actress and starlet on location in London. The women who attended Joy Joy's parties had to be on the youngish side, pretty and/or sexy, and available. Joy Joy didn't, however, like them to be too young, for, in her skin-tight lycra cycling shorts and see-through lace top, she was meant to be the star of the show. And most nights she was, but not this night. Among the guests were Bliss Enlund, Sylvia Kristoff and her husband, sex queen Ginger Lynn, actress and socialite Viviane Ventura, and the pneumatic Annie Ample, an American starlet who was very popular at film festivals. She had stopped off in London on her way home from Deauville, and her entrance in wet tee-shirt, bikini briefs, and thigh length boots completely stole the show from Joy Joy.

Sabrina couldn't help laughing at the expression on her friend's face.

"What are you laughing at?" yelled Joy Joy.

"I'm sorry, Joy, but there's no way either of us can compete with that. Of course you could have your breasts done, but I'm sure Paul loves you just the way you are."

"Sounds like the cue for a song." They both laughed. "Darling," murmured Joy Joy, linking arms with Sabrina. "Would you like to be the first to try out the jacuzzi in our new home?"

The party was, as always, a huge success. Nobody got more than politely drunk, nobody was caught snorting cocaine in the bathroom, and nobody was discovered in 'flagrante delicto' with someone they shouldn't. This was not to say that such things were not going on. Sabrina walked in on a cosy threesome of record producer, his wife, and her best friend, nude-model-girl Linzi, who was busy fellating the record producer while the wife vigorously tongued the girl's anus. The husband invited Sabrina to join in but she politely refused and returned to the party, and an unsurprised Joy Joy.

"Oh, Sabrina, you should have accepted."

"What?"

"Then you could have told me what it was like doing it with The Man With The Most."

Sabrina grimaced.

"Maybe you didn't want your fanny licked by Sheena and Linzi?"

"You got it."

"Pity," murmured Joy Joy. "Here comes Robin to take you home. Don't forget our date tomorrow night, the jacuzzi, will you?"

On the drive back to Hampstead, Sabrina was quiet.

"Don't take what she says seriously," said Robin. "Joy is a fine lady but she has a wicked sense of fun, and she can be very naughty sometimes."

"I can imagine."

"What was that about Linzi?"

She told him.

"Well that's our Linzi all right. She was always a fun-loving girl."

"You know her?"

"Who doesn't? She's one of Vaughn Townes' girls. She was in his soft-core movie, 'Ecstasy'. I remember her in the orgy scene. She looked like she was really enjoying her work."

Sabrina smiled. "Is there a woman in London you haven't screwed?"

The Range Rover pulled up in front of her house. As Sabrina made to get out, Robin squeezed her arm.

"I can't make the house-warming."

"Oh, no."

"I'm so sorry. I've got to see a man about a Ming, in Turkey yet. Flying out in the morning."

"Then you can stay the night here."

He hesitated.

"Please, Robin, I need you. Don't let me sleep alone tonight."

"Oh, darling." He embraced her tightly. "Of course I won't."

They made love all that night; tender, patient, gentle lovemaking, the urgency of their flesh tempered by a willingness to respond to the other's needs before their own but all too soon it was morning and Robin was saying good-bye.

Sabrina caressed his cheek. "Hurry home, Mr Errol."

"After last night? You bet," he mockingly drawled.

"I'm sorry for being so selfish. You look very tired, and you've so very far to go."

"Don't worry, I'll sleep on the plane. You're worth a night's sleep. You're worth a whole lifetime."

She kissed him one last time. "Go on, go, before I change my mind about letting you go."

"Right then." At the bedroom door he turned. "Joy will look after you, and I'll be back before you know it. Good-bye. I love you."

"I love you."

She listened for the front door closing and then the Range Rover driving away. She tried to sleep but Robin's parting words kept coming back into her mind. She remembered the look of hunger in Joy Joy's eyes at the mention of the jacuzzi. Yes, Joy Joy de Ferrare would be only too happy to look after Sabrina. That was the problem.

WATCHERS AT THE FEAST

Miss June peered thoughtfully through her blonde fringe at the very sophisticated beauty in the glamour girl calendar.

"I don't think I look anything like the picture," she said. "It's really difficult to believe that that stunning creature, Miss June, is me. But it would be even more of a problem if you'd seen me hanging out my husband's shirts at the weekend."

Michael smiled indulgently. No way could he see a girl like Linzi doing the laundry. Linzi Baker was a glamour model. That meant tits, ass, and raunchy poses. At 25 she was at the top of the tree, earning as much as £11,000 for two weeks calendar work. There was no room for inhibitions and little time for any kind of conventional private life.

They were in the winter sitting room of the house in north London she shared with her husband, the photographer Jon Revere, five cats, twenty-five parrots, and a dog. The animals lived on the ground floor, where there was also a small studio, darkroom, and office. Revere bought the house twenty years ago. He and Linzi had been married for seven.

"When I first moved in," she told Michael, "I didn't like the house at all. Basically, I think it was because I was moving into another woman's home, and there were lots of things I had to move just to make myself feel that I existed in Jon's life and she didn't. Anymore."

"I understand," said Michael.

The house had a summer and winter sitting room and two bedrooms. The winter room was Linzi's favourite. The walls, floor, and ceiling were painted black, Jon's idea, while the vivid colours and contrasts of the furnishings were Linzi's contribution. One wall was full of mirrors which reflected the main feature of the room, a life-size painting of Linzi, nude.

"It was a Christmas gift from Jon. I like it, but I don't think it looks like me. Do you?"

"I'll tell you later."

She smiled back at him. She was very aware of her own face, with its high cheekbones and green, sparkling eyes. Her make-up had been carefully but rather thickly applied, but in contrast she was quite casually dressed in a man's white shirt, open at the neck, and with the sleeves rolled up, and a pair of skin-tight designer jeans. The Gucci high-heels on her feet were the same exquisite shade of egg-shell as her nail varnish.

"What about the audition. Was it a bit of a cattle market?"

She leaned back on the sofa, her shirt stretching over her large breasts. It was obvious to Michael that Linzi was not wearing a bra.

"I suppose so, but I wouldn't say it was undignified. I had to walk down a flight of stairs in a bikini bottom, just the bottom part mind you, and a pair of high-heels. The photographer and the art director had to see what I looked like. I mean, they couldn't be expected to judge me just from my old photos, could they? I could have got fat, with stretch marks and all kinds of things."

"That's true."

"The hundreds of girls at that first audition were a sort of insurance against any casting couch stuff. I was recalled for three more auditions before I knew I'd got the job."

"And no funny business on location?"

Linzi shook her head. "No. We were all treated like ladies. None of this 'Spread for me, honey,' garbage you get from some photographers."

Michael lit a joint. "How long have you been a model?" He passed it to her.

"Thanks." She took a good long drag. "I started over three years ago. It was Jon who encouraged me of course. He used to take a lot of photos of me, so one day I went along to an agent and it just seemed to take off from there."

"And you've been taking them off ever since?"

"Right," she giggled. "I've done some magazine centrefolds, and a lot of topless shots for newspapers, but mostly it's the bread and butter stuff of catalogue work. You know, corsets, bras, that sort of thing. They like using glamour models for underwear ads because we've got the best looking rear ends, and the best boobs."

"I'll say."

"You like them?" she said, running a hand across her ample chest.

"42in. they are. To be exact, I'm 42½-24-36. I'm really paranoid about my looks. When I'm not in front of the camera I'm in front of the mirror, checking out my body. The slightest blemish and I'm depressed, because in this business your face and your body are your fortune. Every morning I exercise with weights to keep my buttocks tight and my boobs firm upright."

"Some workout."

Linzi smiled. She slid her hand up the inside of his thigh to his crotch and squeezed the bulge.

"Okay then, Michael. Let's get our gear off."

It was a rough, vigorous copulation, the first time. Strangers to each other's flesh they grasped the moment. Eager for their own pleasure they forgot their partner's need. It turned into a race, a hurried, frantic, clutching encounter without gentleness or style. Michael was first passed the post. He found her so deep and warm and easy that it was impossible to hold back any longer.

"You going somewhere?" Linzi sneered, digging her nails into his back when he tried to withdraw.

"Sorry. Consider that a trial run. Next time will be better."

"I hope so. Cherie Halvinne told me you were very good."

"That was sweet of her."

"Wasn't it?" She cupped his buttocks in her hands and squeezed hard and long. "Lick my boobs."

"Is that an order?"

She gave his bottom a sharp, stinging smack.

"Ooo, nice. Do it again."

She felt him swell and stiffen inside her and could not repress a tremor of pleasurable anticipation when she caught the look of amused triumph in his face, the fierce desire in his eyes.

"Now then, madam. What was it you wanted me to do?"

Unaccountably, Linzi found herself blushing:

"Would you please lick my tits, suck my nipples, nibble my earlobes, run your hands up and down my thighs, give me a long, slow, comfortable screw, like I know you can."

"Isn't there a cocktail called that?"

Linzi grinned. "You supply the cock, I'll supply the tail."

They both laughed.

The second time was good, the third, even better. She gave him £200 and watched him dress. They shook hands, said good-bye, and Michael Cord, the South London gigolo, stepped out into a chill November night.

"Hey, aren't you the girl who humped off Jeff Bridges, the lucky son of a bitch, in 'Rancho Deluxe'?"

"Well, Mr Sagan, that depends. Do you want me to be that girl?"

"Oh, yeah, that was a really sweaty scene, horny."

"I know."

"You saw it?"

"It was on television the other night. Awful film."

"As a movie I've seen better sure, but do you remember the girl's..."

"Name?"

He grinned. "Right on."

"Patti D'arbanville. The film was made in '74. In '78 she starred in one of David Hamilton's soft porn films. Now what was it? 'Bilitis'. You see I'm a bit of a film buff, Mr Sagan."

"Call me Brett."

"Okay then, Brett," she said, smiling. "Did you know that a pop singer called Cat Stevens once wrote a song about Patti D'arbanville?"

"A bit of a music buff as well. What's your name?"

"Helenne Landau. Were they really doing it?"

"In 'Rancho Deluxe'? What do you think?"

Helenne blushed.

"Good enough answer," he murmured.

"You know, I thought that sort of thing only happened in hard-core porn like 'Deep Throat'."

"Honey, you'd be surprised." Brett Sagan, though turned fifty, was still devastatingly handsome, with his mop of sunstreaked, golden-brown hair a sharp contrast to his neatly trimmed grey beard and deep blue eyes. "It was 'Easy Rider' that did it."

"What?"

"Turned Hollywood upside-down. When Dennis Hopper, Peter Fonda, and Bill Hayward hit town they didn't just bring their home movie with them. They brought the whole youth culture, anti-establishment, drug scene, and it became fashionably daring to do the sex scenes for real after smoking a little grass, to get in the mood. Happens all the time on little movies like 'Rancho'."

"And big movies?"

"That would be telling."

"Oh, do tell."

He laughed. "You're a very pretty girl, Helenne. Should I know the name from somewhere?"

"Not unless you're into women's gymnastics."

"Only in the bedroom, or the jacuzzi."

She blushed again. "Brett, I'm not letting you off the hook till you tell me about the films."

"Okay. Well, there was Jane Fonda and Donald Sutherland in 'Klute', then Sutherland again with Julie Christie in 'Don't Look Now'."

"Another lucky son of a bitch, eh?"

"Right on. Who else? Jessica Lange and Jack Nicholson in 'The Postman Always Rings Twice'. The footage they did was so hot most of it was cut from the final release print and ended up in Jack's collection of porn flicks. Only Hugh Hefner has a bigger collection. Anyway, I understand Jack has been entertaining Warren, Diane, Roman, and other friends with the raunchy sight of him banging Ms. Lange like crazy."

She ran a hand through her blonde hair. "Mmmm, sounds like an interesting film. Anymore?''

"Bruce Dern and Maud Adams in 'Tattoo'. Bruce actually boasted he'd made it with his co-star, which is unusual. Maud denied it, of course, as did Maria Schneider after starring opposite Brando in 'Last Tango in Paris'."

"Oh, I saw that. I was under-age but my boyfriend got me into the cinema all right. The butter scene got him so horny he asked me to jerk him off. I said okay. Instead I surprised him by giving head. He yelled so hard when he came everyone looked at us, and there I was, on my knees with his log in my mouth."

Brett whistled. "Wow. How old were you then?"

"14. I was big for my age."

"Yeah. Look, I'm staying at the Savoy. We could have a late supper in my suite."

She appeared to ignore the remark. "Doesn't Joy Joy throw a good thrash," she said, eyeing the throng of famous faces around them.

"Yes." He touched her arm. "Well, what about it?"

Helenne pointed her pert nose at him and opened wide her green-flecked, grey eyes. "What about what?"

Brett grimaced. "The late supper," he said.

"Oh, I'd love to..."

"Ah, ah,ah,ah. Oooooo."
"Helenne, Helenne, baby. Oh, baby, baby, yeah."
"Darling, ooo, oo-ohhh."
"Gawd."
"Oh, darling, oh ahahaaaa, Brett. That's it, right, oh, just there."
"Baby, yeah."
Helenne shook her head vigorously, pouting, her face flushed,
sending beads of sweat in all directions. Her firm, muscular thighs
trembled as she eased her taut, sweat-slicked, glistening form up and
down his shaft, her full, round breasts jiggling.

Of her superb body, Helenne was most proud of her nipples.
During sex or masturbation they would swell and distend till they were
almost an inch long. Brett reached up and tweaked one.

"Ow, bastard ... Ah, ah. Make it last, darling ... Ah, oh, please,
it's so good."
"Yeah, yeah, screw me."
"Go on, ahahaaa, oooohhh ... Tell me, ah-ah, what you want."
"I want, Christ, to screw you, you ... oh baby."
"Tell me, oo, oo, oo, ooooohhhhaa."
"You're a tight-assed bitch."
"Oh, darling, ooooooo, darling, darling, darling, it's happening."

The following afternoon Helenne, leaving Brett still asleep in bed,
took the inter-city express north to Newcastle to tape another edition
of her dance and exercise show, and do some personal appearances in
the region. One of those was a three-hour stint at the opening of the
MUSCLE-IN exercise studio, where she demonstrated the fitness and
exercise machines, weight training, aerobics, the Californian Stretch,
et al. Her reward, apart from the fee negotiated by her agent, was a
three-some for dinner with the owner of the MUSCLE-IN and his
wife. Both were former body-building champions, and the three-some
continued in Helenne's hotel suite after dinner, where other appetites
were satisfied.

Monday morning arrived too soon so far as Helenne was
concerned, but she had to take an early train back to London to be on
time for her next job. She hoped to catch up on some sleep during the
journey, but her very short rah-rah skirt, and the wide expanse of
thigh on display, prompted a fellow passenger to pester her so much

Helenne was left with no choice. They went into the loo together and she gave him a blow-job.

Afterwards, she did get some sleep.

"Everything you can see in the penthouse is for sale," said Joy Joy with an expansive gesture that encompassed sculptures, paintings, furniture, and Japanese electronics. "Including, of course, the penthouse itself," she added.

A French maid wearing black stockings and suspenders wiggled by carrying a tray of sandwiches.

"What about the waitresses?" asked Brett. "Are they for sale too?"

This was the new way to sell a house, according to a bright young London property entrepreneur called Nigel. You show it off in its best colours by throwing a party to which you invite a crowd of potential buyers. Helenne was not in the market for a £150,000 penthouse overlooking Holland Park. She had gone to the party at No. 47, one of those massive Victorian wedding-cake houses divided into apartments, at the invitation of society hostess Joy Joy de Ferrare who was fronting the event for Nigel.

Most of the guests were called Rupert, and their sole occupation seemed to be looking at penthouses. A succession of Ruperts with disdainful young women, Sloane Rangers all, on their arms, inspected the amenities of No. 47.

"How are you all doing?" asked Nigel. "Have you seen the jacuzzi yet?"

Helenne was surprised. All this and a jacuzzi too. She had only enjoyed the delights of this erotic whirlpool bath once before, but the memory was as fresh as a new lover. It was at the Bucks mansion of Vaughn Townes. He and Madelaine Sale were playing host to a hundred friends for the weekend. The second evening she asked Madelaine where everyone was.

"In bed or in the jacuzzi. Come on, I'll show you."

Helenne followed her hostess, and in a vine-clad conservatory, with the strobe lights pulsating to the beat of disco music, she beheld a scene from Dante's Inferno, or possibly one of Ms. Marilyn Chamber's porno epics. In an enormous brick-enclosed pool full of foaming blue water, pink bodies thrashed.

"Come on, in you get," said Madelaine, wriggling out of her

clothes.

Helenne quickly stripped and jumped in. Surfacing among the copulating forms, she had only just found her feet when she was vigorously penetrated by not one but two handsome young men, each the mirror image of the other. The biggest surprise of all was that her vagina was accommodating the two phalli without the slightest discomfort.

"Are you twins?" she yelled above the noise.

Their answer was to ejaculate together and disappear back into the mass of heaving flesh all around Helenne, while, at the same time, an unseen protagonist assaulted her rectum. Impaled on his rampant maleness as she was, she was curious about her attacker. The buttocks, small, round, and firm, Helenne was squeezing seemed male, as did the broad shoulders she glimpsed behind her, but the narrow waist of her attacker, and the full breasts with their erect nipples rubbing against Helenne's back with each thrust, were obviously female. She wriggled free and turned.

"Mo," she cried. "Oh, Mo, you randy little hussy."

Helenne had not seen Maureen Willis since the Moscow Olympics. The former swimming star was now, like Helenne, making a career in television, films, and modelling. They kissed, open-mouthed, and Helenne happily allowed Maureen to mount her, but from the front this time.

Such were the memories in Helenne's mind as Nigel took her to see the jacuzzi in No. 47.

"But it's just a plastic bathtub with holes in the sides," she said. No room there for Mo and her extra-large dildo.

"Good for one's arthritis, though," said Nigel.

She left him there and rejoined the party in the main room.

"Not quite what you expected?" said Joy Joy, grinning.

"Let's go somewhere and screw."

"What about Brett?"

"What about Sabrina Howard?"

"Your place," said Joy Joy. "You have such a comfortable bed."

"Mmmm, that was nice," Joy Joy murmured, kissing the small of Helenne's back.

"Is this what you did with Sabrina?."

"We played tennis."

"Oh, really?"

Joy Joy giggled. "It's amazing what can be done with a tennis racquet and a jar of Vaseline."

"You gave her the shaft?"

"She loved it. She is the wildest, strongest, best piece of ass, man or woman, I've ever had."

"And what about me?"

"Oh, Helenne, you're a very special lay. You know you are."

"Prove it..."

"Ah, ah, Christ, ah, ah, ahhhhh."

"Oh, Helenne ... Oh, darling, yes, yes, yes."

"Ahhh ... Ahhohoooo, ooooooooo, ooo ... Oh, Joy.''

"Keep going... Oh, yes, oh, oh, I'm so near."

"Can't ... Ahhhhhhhh ... Ahhhhh, oo, oooo."

"Please, Helenne."

"Ooooooooo, oooohhhhh, I'm coming."

"Screw me, screw me, screw... me... love it, I love it, love it, love...ohhhhhhhhhh."

"Ahh, ahhhh, ahhhhhh, ahhhhhhhhhhhhhh, ahhrrrr, oh, ooo, oo, oo, oh."

Her soft blonde curls dark with sweat and clinging to her neck and shoulders, Helenne collapsed across Joy Joy's taut, glistening body, still straining to the rhythms of orgasm.

"Tell me about Sabrina. How did you manage it? She doesn't look the type, not really."

"Neither do you."

Helenne blushed.

"Sabrina came on like Princess Diana but she's no innocent. She ran with a fast crowd in Hollywood, and before that in New York. Private sex clubs, wild parties, group sex, pornos, she's done it all. The night before the housewarming party I invited her over to the new house to try out our pool. She took her clothes off, no problem, then she went all shy on me. We did some kissing, touching, a little mutual masturbation. No one came, but I didn't push it. The next afternoon we played tennis at the health club."

Helenne lay in bed alone, idly masturbating. The dildo she was using was the very same one so effectively employed by Maureen

Willis at the aquatic gang-bang at Vaughn Townes' mansion.

Though some ten inches long and topped by a truly awesome glans, the dildo was in every other respect a realistic model of an erect penis. Each ridge and vein correctly positioned and sculpted, it could have been moulded from life, as indeed Maureen claimed it was. Helenne closed her eyes as she worked the dildo back and forth in her vagina, and tried to imagine what a guy with a ten-inch dong might look like. She also thought about broad shouldered, square-jawed Maureen, who was her flat-mate when they were both poor sports people.

Helenne climaxed.

"Mo, screwing you is like diving into warm honey."

"Oh, Lance," giggled Maureen Willis, holding him tight between her strong thighs. "What a thing to say."

He slid into her and began to thrust. Maureen quickly picked up his need and tried to match it to her own.

"Mmm, mmmm, lovely man ... Mmmm, yes, oh, ooo... Easy, mmmm, slow down, we have all night, ooooo, yes ... Steady...Please love."

"I'm coming," he groaned.

"Well, good for you."

She felt his ejaculation pump into her.

"I love you," he murmured.

"I know." She brightened. "Oh, did I tell you? I'm having lunch at the Connaught tomorrow with Joy Joy de Ferrare. She's promised to introduce me to Joan Collins."

The morning after their return to Paris from LA, Susie Watkins went shopping. She bought three furs: a fisher coat, a sable pea jacket and a mink sweater lined, collared and cuffed with cashmere. Jean-Claude rewarded her with a pair of diamond studs for her ears.

"You're a darling," she cooed, as she clipped them to her lobes. "I'll never take them off."

Susie kept her promise, and Jean-Claude promptly forgot all about it. He did not remember until two months later, in June, when he saw her naked on a beach in Mexico, nude but for her diamond ear studs. She was married to Roman Duparier by then. They had eloped and were living in Acapulco, where Roman was making yet another attempt to become an heir worthy of his inheritance.

What stopped Roman from being richer and more powerful than his father was a secret sickness that Roman perceived as shame. Several times he had tried to take his own life, but he had carefully hidden the suicidal desperation from his father.

Susie would not learn Roman's secret until that summer of 1982. Right now, in April in Paris, less than three months since their meeting on Bequia, she knew that Jean-Claude had begun to tire of her.

HUSBANDS AND LOVERS

The burgundy red Mercedes glided to a halt amongst the noise and bustle of a busy London street at lunch time. The chauffeur got quickly out from behind the wheel, umbrella in hand to protect his boss from the English rain.

"Thank you, Charles," said a soft, feminine voice, as the richest woman in the world climbed out of the six-door limousine...

Roxanne Duparier felt the tranquilliser begin to work as the headwaiter showed her into the executive-dining room of the Adonisthenes London office in New Bond Street.

"So glad to see you here again, Miss Roxanne."

"Thank you, Henry."

"Will you be dining alone?"

"No. Mr Krug will be joining me soon."

"Very good, Miss Roxanne."

The day before, Felix Krug, head of the Adonisthenes European operations, had invited her to lunch. He had, he said, something to ask her.

They first met three months earlier, at a shareholders meeting in Paris, and though their talk was all business, Roxanne had been deliciously aware of his dark-blond, sun streaked hair and deep blue eyes. Only his mouth, almost too sensual, saved him from looking pretty.

As Roxanne took her place at the big mahogany table set with two Madeira linen place mats, she was depressed and uneasy. She and her husband had had another fight.

"Can I get you something while you're waiting?"

"Yes, Henry. A champagne cocktail, please."

It had been about Roman and Susie. This time, Roxanne, who usually avoided confrontations with her powerful husband, as she did with her glamorous and unpredictable father, had felt strong enough to oppose Nikos, and she had won.

Felix Krug arrived a few moments later, in the wake of her drink.

"I'm sorry I'm so late. Please forgive me."

"How are you, Felix?"

"The better for seeing you, Mrs Adonisthenes." He kissed her outstretched hand. She grimaced. "You're supposed to shake it."

Nikos had wanted to give them a wedding in the library of their ... her ... Belgravia house. Roxanne had refused, absolutely. She knew of Susie's affair with her father, Jean-Claude Duparier, and when she heard that Roman and Susie were to marry she felt a terrible premonition of disaster. Her father and her brother had always had a loving but competitive and tempestuous relationship, but it was Susie that Roxanne feared. Not that she thought the girl was consciously malicious, merely careless of other people. Susie exuded a vast carelessness that allowed her to smash things and people and then retreat into her own preoccupied narcissism, untouched.

Roxanne, on the other hand, was only too painfully aware. She had been a plain child in a world of glamorous men and beautiful women. Jansen of Paris had decorated her nursery. Dali, who had painted the murals for the dining room of a Paris hotel her father owned, had painted yellow elephants and rose lions for her. The film stars, celebrities, and business rivals who came to court her father, cooed over her first steps and words, praised the arabesques she learnt in ballet class, and hung the paintings she did in nursery school in their homes and offices. More than anything else she wanted to be loved for herself, not for her money.

Roxanne Duparier had an accent in every language she spoke. Her English sounded American to the British and British to the Americans. Her French had her grandmother's Russian 'r', her German the Austrian inflection of her tutor, while her Spanish had the Castillian accent of the Madrid school for the sons and daughters of the nobility she was enrolled in at ten.

Until Roxanne married Nikos Adonisthenes and bought her house in London, she had never thought of any one place as home. As is the custom in France, Roxanne was introduced to sex at fourteen, by her father. The ritual deflowering coloured her attitude to physical passion for years afterward, hence her marriage to Nikos, who was three years older than Jean-Claude. But it was the suicide of her brother, Roman, that touched her more deeply than any other single event of her young life. Even Nikos' suicide, two years later, did not affect her as much.

Roman was buried next to his grandfather in a family plot in the family estate at Southampton, New York. Susie Watkins made a beautiful widow. By her side throughout the ceremony was Sabrina Howard...

"Oh, God, Sabrina, yes," cried Roxanne, almost in disbelief, as the penetration, so forcefully begun, continued.

"Ohhhh, mmmmnnnhhr ... ahhhh, ahh," she moaned and grunted, wide-eyed, open-mouthed, the tongue protruding between the bared teeth in a grimace of undisguised animal lust. She was nude, as was the object of her adoring gaze, Sabrina, but for the harness of narrow leather thongs which hugged her hips and upper thighs, and from which were supported two replica phalli of very considerable length and thickness, joined base to base. So each woman copulated with her own dildo while rolling and thrashing together on the pink satin sheets of Sabrina's bed in her New York apartment.

It was to the Dakota building and Sabrina's apartment that Prince Cesare Belmondo, of the Sardinia Belmondos, came to renew an acquaintance. Implicit in that renewal was an offer of marriage. Sabrina declined, with great regret.

"Yeah, yeah, yeah ... Ohh, yes ... Oh, ohh, ohhhh, Jesus Christ, yes, yes."

Susie wrapped her legs even tighter around Sabrina's waist.

"Mmmmm, mmmnn... Do it harder, please, eh, Sabrina, Sabrina."

"Ahhhhhhh, ahhhhh, ohhhhhhhhhh... Ohhhrrrrrr, you darling child, ahhrr."

"Oh, am I, ohhhh... Am I really, ahhhhhr, your dar-ahhh-darling?"

"My darling...Ooooooo, ooohhhhhhh-ooooowwwowowow."

"Sabrina, I'm coming."

Badyr Al Hussein did not like coupling in planes, not even his own. He was lying in his king-size circular bed in a bedroom which took up enough space to accommodate sixty tourist class passengers on any other aircraft. The ravenhaired Princess beside him stirred, and in her half-wakefulness reached out for his body.

"Badyr?"

He kissed her lightly on the forehead.

"Sabrina."

She smiled. "What's for breakfast?"

He gave her a sour look.

"My darling, what is it? What's wrong? Are you ill?"

He shook his head.

"No, no, Sabrina, I am well, truly."

"Truly?"

"Yes," he said, hesitating. "It is just..."

"What?" asked the newly-married Princess Sabrina Al Hussein.

"I am superstitious."

"You don't like screwing on a plane because you don't see how you could ask Allah to give your partner a climax and keep the plane in mid-air at the same time," she said, smiling. "Right?"

He smiled back, then took her in his arms. They made love...

On Roxanne's eighth birthday, Jean-Claude gave her a doll's house. Only it was not a house but a miniature hotel, complete with furnished guest rooms and suites, a restaurant, a bar, and a reception desk. As a child Roxanne was always a good girl, ever anxious to please her busy and sought-after parents. Her first words were not "Mummy" and "Daddy", or any variation of same, but "bye-bye". Jean-Claude and Jacqueline did so much travelling that Roxanne's nanny was always prompting the small child to wave and say "bye-bye".

Roxanne grew up tormented by a feeling of inadequacy. She was sure that she would never be important enough for her father to pay attention to her, or pretty enough for her mother to be proud of her. So, to please the glamorous Jacqueline, Roxanne became immaculately well-groomed, and made a point of never leaving her bedroom unless she was dressed and freshly made-up. To please Jean-Claude, his dutiful daughter studied diligently at school and won herself a place at the Sorbonne. More than anything, as the plain child metamorphosed into a beautiful young woman, the shy, lonely, insecure teenager still clung to the daydream that she was not an only child, that somewhere she had, perhaps, a brother.

Marriage to the Golden Greek, Nikos Adonisthenes, brought her the first real happiness Roxanne had known in her life, though this did not mean that they never argued. One night in San Tropez, another couple invited Nikos and Roxanne to bed with them in a foursome. Nikos wanted to; Roxanne refused. On another occasion, in New York, at a party in a loft in Greenwich Village, the cabaret included a live sex show imported from Times Square. Roxanne left alone while

Nikos stayed until the party broke up at seven the next morning.

Despite such disagreements, the saying that everything changes after marriage held true for Nikos and Roxanne as it does for less materially-endowed couples. What happened in the early years of their marriage was that Nikos, who had seen Roxanne as a prize to be conquered and had carefully calculated his conquest, fell madly in love with her once she was his wife. He thought she was wonderful, and he became fascinated with everything about her. She was, to him, an exotic and rare species, and he became a scholar of her manners and habits.

She was, for example, a wonderful driver. Her shyness and awkwardness disappeared behind the wheel. She drove very expensive sports cars very well, with passionate concentration and a sense of abandon controlled by an edgy discipline. She and her powerful cars seemed to share the same nervous system. Her touch on the accelerator was the touch of a lover; she heeled and toed the brake-accelerator with Formula One precision, up-an-downshifting in perfect synchronisation with the rpms. On a hairpin curve on a mountain corniche or on the entrance to an expressway, she invariably entered corners on the inside and came out of them on the high point of the apex while maintaining road speed more steadily than any driver Nikos had ever ridden with.

At first, Roxanne's total inability to park bewildered Nikos. She, who could do anything with an automobile, could not punch it into a parking slot. And her inability did not bother her. She would leave sixty-thousand-dollars' worth of hand-tooled machinery every-which-way against the kerb. It was the rich-girl syndrome, and it infuriated the poor-born, self-made Greek. Roxanne had never learned to park because she had never needed to. There had always been someone to do it for her. And it never occurred to her to worry about the safety of her expensive, flashy cars. Whatever went wrong would be put right. All it took was money: "My money," he would remind her. His annoyance amused her greatly, for in this at least, she had the kind of confidence and carelessness only money, old money, could buy.

There were other manifestations of the rich-girl syndrome. Roxanne did not know how to buy a theatre ticket or an airplane ticket, because whenever she wanted one she would call her father's office and it was done for her. Going to the supermarket was an exotic treat and she had never ridden on a bus, not even when she studied at the Sorbonne for two years.

She was, Nikos learned, addicted to the telephone. She used long distance so casually that Nikos, who thought he could be impressed by nothing, was impressed. She ordered clothes from around the world. She called her new-found brother, Roman, at least once a week wherever he was. She called her father once a week wherever in the world he was. She had several close women friends, Sabrina Cary Howard Woodville, Joy Joy de Ferrare, Lyssette Cromwell, and Edwina Lawrence, to whom she gossiped for hours long distance. Her shyness disappeared over the phone. Roxanne became direct, intimate, intense, silly, frivolous, and often extremely salacious.

Behind the wheel of a car or over the telephone Roxanne became a different person: confident, strong, assured, and, little by little, with the encouragement of her husband, she began to take equal control of other areas of her life.

FAMILY TIES

The house they were living in in Acapulco was beautiful. Set high on a hill, it had a view of the resort city spread out below and the blue Pacific beyond, but to Susie Watkins Duparier it was a beautiful prison. She was starved of attention, of love, of sex. Her marriage to Roman was a fraud. Her husband was, for most of the time, impotent.

In the beginning he blamed his failure to achieve an erection on drink, tiredness, or business worries. Then he started to refuse to consider there was a problem at all. Finally he began blaming Susie. He told her she was too demanding; her sexual appetite was excessive and abnormal. He became angry with her for her desire and punished Susie by not touching her at all. Soon, Roman was not even talking to his wife.

In the first three months of their marriage they made love six times only, and each time it was Susie who made the first move. It was Susie's tenderness, passion, patience and skill that allowed Roman to acquire and keep a hard-on for long enough to give his wife a pleasant screwing, and Roman hated her for it.

Once, after she had made him come, he got off her and methodically broke every perfume bottle on her dressing table. The next time they did it he pulled roughly out of her before climaxing and spurted his jism in her face.

"I feel like pissing on you, you whoring-cunt-bitch," he screamed as he ejaculated. Then he stood up and struck her a glancing blow across the shoulder with the heel of his hand. It did not hurt so much as confuse and frighten her.

Roman was equally confused and frightened by his behaviour. He resolved never to hit or in any way to hurt Susie ever again, and phoned the Cartier store in Mexico City to order a jade and gold pendant suspended from a silk cord which Susie had once admired. He also decided that once the hotel project was up and running, he and Susie would take a holiday.

In Cairo, the relationship between Susie and Roman, which had begun in scandal, ended in violence.

Istanbul merges East and West and is therefore partially accessible to Europeans. Cairo, however, joins the Mediterranean and Nile cultures, and its polyglot impenetrability causes Western visitors to feel isolated and threatened, but also free of all civilised restrictions. Roman Duparier was attracted to Arab hospitality, and their cruelty, to the aura of fatalism and their tradition of funeral pomp.

The Duparier company apartments were located in a former royal palace between the British embassy and the El Tahrir bridge. Occupying the top three floors of the building, the apartments overlooked the Nile, where feluccas, the sailboats of Arab design with attenuated, triangular sails, plied the brown waters of the river in maritime traffic as dense as the human traffic that thronged the streets and alleys of Cairo itself. Across the river, the view extended to the lush, green Tahrir gardens.

"So you're pregnant," said Roman. "You could have told me sooner, Susie, or did you tell him first?" It was clear to both of them who Roman meant.

"Whose is it?" he continued.

Susie did not know what to say. Roman hit her twice, hard, across the face. They were in their bedroom, a large square room at the opposite side of the house from the servants' rooms. It overlooked the Nile on one side and, on the other, opened onto the inner courtyard. All the windows were open to catch any night breeze that might lessen the heaviness of the humid August air.

Suddenly, Roman produced a small handgun from a drawer and aimed it at her. Susie moved blindly, instinctively, out of the way of the path of the bullet, and reached for an unopened bottle of champagne to knock the pistol from his grasp. He caught her arm and twisted it up behind her back. The bottle crashed to the floor.

They were both soaked in sweat. Roman was behind her now, his hand slippery on her wrist, forcing it upward, hurting her. Susie felt his log stiff against her buttocks.

"Let's love," she gasped. "Kill me with your love, Roman. Love me till I scream for mercy. Love me till I split in two..."

Roman was Roxanne's illegitimate half-brother, conceived by a Warsaw hotel chambermaid during Jean-Claude's month-long stay in the Polish capital in the summer of 1958. Jean-Claude was a Sorbonne graduate, Maria was an uneducated peasant girl, but both were young and far from home. He left Warsaw without even knowing she was pregnant.

Roman arrived in Paris in March 1980, just twenty one, a little-known Polish film director, and was stunned by its beauty and luxurious ambience. He had read a great deal about it of course, and seen countless photographs, but he was still unprepared for the effect it had on him.

He arrived with little more than a change of clothing, a print of his movie, and several scripts he had been working on in Warsaw. During the summer of that year he was to get to know Paris a great deal better.

Roman had left a new wife behind in Poland, but although he made a brief attempt to remain faithful, the overpowering attractions of his surroundings were too much for him to resist. A friend in the Polish community introduced him to countless girls, most of them ambitious actresses. The Paris social scene was as bohemian and sybaritic as Roman had been led to believe from the books he had read, and the availability of women, plus the wide and wild variety of sexual goings-on, gave him a severe case of culture-shock. He was the kid in the candy store.

Very quickly, one of his favourite activities in this first taste of the forbidden Western fruit, was to participate in the shooting of hard-core pornos made almost nightly at various parties across Paris. At first he just went to watch. Then he was promoted to camera operator. Finally, he was allowed to join in as a performer.

It had taken Roman a long time to convince the authorities in Poland to allow him to travel to France to capitalise on his film's success at Cannes the previous year. His real reason, however, was to find his father. He found his stepmother first. At an orgy.

He knew her only as Jacqueline to begin with. She was a middle-aged lady, turned forty, but still very beautiful, lively, bright and exciting, with an enviably preserved, svelte, voluptuous body. According to the whispers, she was the wife of a prominent businessman...

"Eee, eee, eee, eee, eee, eee."

"Urrh, urrh, urrh, urrh."

She clawed at his back. "Goodness ... Eee, owww-ohh, I love your cock."

"You sex-mad bitch, ahhhh."

They were in his small, shabby flat, making love on a very

squeaky bed. It was 4.30 in the morning, dawn, the orgy had broken up an hour before.

"Yes, yes, yes, yes."

"Ahhhhhhhhhhhhh."

"My love." She held him tight in the vice of her thighs as he spasmed endlessly into her.

It was only by chance that Roman discovered the identity of Jacqueline's husband. She was very careful not to bring anything with her that might provide a clue to who she was, blackmail being the ever-present threat, but such was her passion for Roman that Jacqueline began to lose her fear. And to make mistakes. Mistakes which were to cost her everything.

English soccer player Eric Evans had just slid seven inches of erect penis into the receptive rectal passage of Helenne Landau, when the phone rang.

"Stay right where you are," commanded Helenne. "I'll get it."

She stretched out a trembling, sweaty hand and picked up the receiver.

"Hello?"

"Hello, Helenne, this is Lyssette Cromwell. Something terrible's just happened."

"What do you mean? Is it Mo?"

"Yes. I'm sorry."

As Lyssette continued her catalogue of horrors, Helenne's whole body tensed, including her buttock muscles. This was too much for Evans, but the former gymnast turned television personality was unaware of her boyfriend's semen ejaculating into her bowels. He spasmed three times then eased his still-rigid prick from her rectum and rolled off her.

"Jesus, that was good," he groaned.

Natasha Landi fell back onto her pillow, exhausted by the latest bout of lovemaking with her husband of one month, Peter Lagonda.

"Mmmmm, that was nice," she murmured, hooking one slim leg over his belly as she snuggled down against his shoulder.

"My pleasure," he answered. "Anytime your husband's out of town give me a call."

She giggled.

"I sure will, honey."

He looked at his watch.

"My God, it'll be daylight soon. I've just got to get some sleep. Do you mind, darling? Or I won't be fit for anything tomorrow."

"Ha," she snorted. "The way you talk you'd think I was a nymphomaniac or something."

"Perish the thought."

For a long time after Peter went to sleep, Natasha lay awake. She liked to re-live every detail of that night's copulation while masturbating to a climax before going to sleep, but on this occasion she was disturbed by memories of her raunchy past.

And by feelings of guilt. She smiled to herself. It must be love, after all.

She looked at the sleeping form of her husband. How much did he know about her life before she met him? Though only nineteen, Natasha had already collected a Karma Sutra of sexual experiences from Hollywood and around the world. One of the men, she did not count the women, was Rudy Gioberti.

Peter had worked hard to get her into movies. Did he know that by taking the lead role in Sparta Studios' new epic, Natasha had placed herself under the control of an old boyfriend?

Roxanne Duparier Adonisthenes, the world's most beautiful widow, looked at herself in the bedroom full-length mirror and smiled. She knew that underneath her gypsy skirt and skin-tight satin boob-tube was a body that no man could resist.

Naked, her breasts were not large but firm, rounded on the upper side, curving down to dark brown nipples which were naturally prominent, and swelled to an acute length during sex. Below her narrow waist her hips curved out high, giving her a tight, almost boyish, ass, and long slim legs. She had a wide mound of Venus covered by a large triangle of curly black pubic hair.

Through her friendship with billionaire arms dealer and international Mr Fix-it, Badyr Al Hussein, Roxanne met King Rashid at a very exclusive dinner party in Washington DC, and fell in love. And he with her, at first sight.

Badyr affected the introductions and, literally, bowed out. There was no mistaking the sexual electricity between his two friends.

"Your Majesty, you're making me blush," murmured Roxanne. "You have a very disconcerting gaze."

There was no chance of them being alone together that night but he did promise to send for her soon, in the next few days. Now, back in her hotel suite, looking at herself in the mirror, she hoped it would not be too long. She had a flash of herself being screwed by the King on the floor of his apartment, her Yves St Laurent dress hitched up around her thighs, her silk Dior knickers at her ankles as he pounded into her.

The invitation came the next morning. It was hand-delivered by a two-hundred-pound gorilla in a pin-stripe suit.

Natasha Landi sat in the aisle seat one row back in the near-empty compartment, first-class of course, of the Pan-Am jumbo to Miami. In front of her Rudy Gioberti had two seats to himself. She liked it when he took her on his business travels, and this trip promised to be something special. It was not the easiest thing, or the wisest, to transport a minor across state lines in violation of the Mann Act. Especially when she was to be used for immoral purposes. Natasha smiled. If there was any corrupting to be done, it was her that did it.

Rudy Gioberti had solved the problem by calling her his daughter, and he had paid the going market rate of five thousand dollars for the fake passport to prove it. So there were no problems with hotels, immigration officials, or anyone else. For the past seven months she had belonged to him, satisfying his unusual sexual needs as no other girl had ever done before, but Natasha had no complaints. She earned a very considerable income, though she worked hard for it, and actually enjoyed every moment. She twirled her fingers in her long black hair and stretched out her legs across the empty seats beside her.

"Hi, I'm Kelly. I'll be looking after you on this flight. Can I get you something?"

Natasha looked up and took in the stewardess. Kelly was tall, with cropped black hair and an open, engaging smile.

She was in her early twenties, the younger girl concluded, noting the way the white silk blouse stretched taut over Kelly's spectacular cleavage, and how the tight beige skirt emphasised her narrow waist and wide hips, clinging to Kelly's firm thighs and her absolute peach of an ass. The rest of the stewardess's uniform consisted of a bolero jacket matching the skirt and flesh-coloured stockings.

As for Natasha, Kelly found the younger girl equally interesting. And very beautiful in an incredibly sensuous way with her long black hair, brown eyes, pert nose, and pouting rosebud lips. Natasha was dressed like a schoolgirl but she was more woman than child. In a white shirt, blue blazer, long white socks, and flat sensible shoes she looked terribly sweet and innocent. However, her skirt was rather too short, and she was not wearing knickers. Rudy Gioberti liked her that way. It meant he could feel her up in public and semi-public places like cabs, elevators, and restaurants. His favourite was at the movies where, in the dark, he would sit her on his knee and hump her from behind, and sometimes, if she had been a naughty girl, in the behind.

"I'd love a Coke. You know this is my first time on a plane and I'm just dying for it."

The stewardess smiled. She was a little unsure what the girl was talking about. She dismissed the obvious. Not from a sixteen-year-old. Still she was a Hollywood child and they grow up quick there. Kelly went back to get the drink, rather pleased at the admiration in the young girl's eyes. It was quite normal to be looked at in that way by the male passengers. It was part of the job, the best part thought Kelly. She had lost count of the candlelight dinners, one-night-stands and, occasionally, lingering affairs that had come about from such openings as she served the drinks.

The basic fact was that Kelly liked to screw almost every night, and if she went without for just a couple of days she became irritable. Sometimes she became worried by her promiscuous behaviour and talked with the other girls about it, but they reassured her that casual sex was okay and they all did it.

She returned with the drink.

"Oh, thank you," cooed Natasha. "I've always dreamt of being an airline hostess like you."

"Well, it isn't exciting and glamorous all the time."

Natasha reached out and touched Kelly's arm. "Would you tell me all about it?"

"I think I can spare a few minutes."

"Oh, good." Natasha knew exactly what she was doing, and so did Rudy Gioberti, who was shifting uneasily in the seat in front, pretending not to hear, and Roxanne Duparier Adonisthenes, who was in the seat behind, was also intrigued. She knew that Natasha was not

124

Gioberti's daughter.

The conversation that was a seduction continued, and the two listeners continued to listen, excited. When the two girls went to the john together, Roxanne could no longer keep her hands off herself. She masturbated furiously, noisily, eyes closed and both hands inside her panties. She climaxed with a yelp of surprise. It was only then that she remembered where she was and opened her eyes.

Rudy Gioberti was standing over her. They did not speak. She saw his hard-on and reached up to unzip him. She lifted her bottom as he peeled the sodden briefs off her. The seat went back as far as it would go, and the copulation began.

"Oh, God, oh, God...Oh, God, yes, ohhhhhhh, ohhhhh, yes."

He thrust deep and hard and strong. He called her a foxy bitch, several times, and came. King Rashid couldn't screw any better than this guy, thought Roxanne, but she was to be proved wrong.

Kelly stood in the tiny aircraft john like a condemned convict in front of a firing squad. She could hardly believe what was about to happen. An under-age piece of jail bait was going to make love to her at thirty thousand feet above the North American continent. It was insane. Kelly did not think, had never thought, of herself as a lesbian, yet here she was. She should get out while there was still time but the spell was far too strong to resist. Then she heard Natasha's light tapping on the door and let her in.

The two girls stood facing each other, their breasts touching, their breathing, especially Kelly's, already fast. Without taking her eyes off the older girl's face, Natasha slid Kelly's tight skirt up around the stewardess's waist. Only then did she look down. Kelly wore red knickers, sheer nylons, and a red suspender belt. The knickers were soaked through.

"Oh, darling," moaned Natasha, as she eased the wet garment down to her knees. The sensual, musky smell of Kelly's exposed pubis filled the enclosed space. "Christ, ain't you horny," whispered the young girl triumphantly, her fingers exploring the glistening bush of pubic hair then slipping deep into Kelly's wetness. The older girl opened up to the probing gratefully, her fine, firm buttocks braced against the washstand, and pressing down as hard as she was able on the insatiable fingers. She yelped as Natasha teased her clitoris from a little button of flesh into an erect, swollen knob, red as a cherry.

Natasha bent forward suddenly and thrust her whole hand inside

Kelly, whose vaginal muscles had relaxed under the young girl's expert tuition. She looked up at the stewardess's face bathed in sweat, eyes half-closed, tongue protruding slightly from her open mouth. With her free hand Natasha reached inside the tight blouse to caress the full breast, taking the stiff nipple between her fingers and squeezing gently. She moved her right hand rhythmically back and forth in the other's pubis, the strokes long, slow and deliberate, and Kelly pushed against it, gripping the hand in the vice of her pelvic muscles, striving to increase the pressure, the delicious friction.

Kelly's juices poured down her thighs, soaking her stocking tops. She had never been so wet.

''How does it feel. Kelly? Don't you just love it?"

"Oh, yes, yes. I do. Ohhhh, please don't stop, ohhhh. I'm so near."

"Are you?"

She increased the piston action of her right hand and the stewardess threw her head back and screamed. It seemed as if a tap had been turned on in her vulva as the liquid spilled forth.

''Yeah, go with it, darling," murmured Natasha. "You're coming beautifully Kelly. Ain't it great?"

Kelly could hardly stand, her legs shook so violently as a result of the magnificent orgasm she had just experienced. She fell back against the washbasin. Her stockings looked as if she had taken a shower, her make-up was badly smudged, and her hair was a total mess.

"I've never made it with a girl before," she gasped. "Does it show?"

"Don't worry," said Natasha. "I prefer virgins."

Kelly laughed. "Me, a virgin."

Natasha smiled and, leaning forward, took Kelly's face in her hands, kissing the stewardess softly on the lips and running her tongue wickedly over Kelly's teeth. Then, reaching up, she began to lick gently at the beads of sweat glistening above her upper lip. Kelly moaned, returning the kiss.

Natasha sank to her knees before the older girl and began to lap up the love juice still coursing down the inside of her quivering thighs. Slowly she moved her lips and exploring tongue upward to the source.

"Please," begged Kelly.

The younger girl laughed and buried her face in the eager, open sex of the other, drinking it all in. She kissed the lips of Kelly's vagina as before she had kissed her mouth; nibbling, nuzzling, coaxing, tasting. Now with her tongue she explored the musky interior; revelling in the warm, wet, silky texture of it. To Kelly that tongue seemed to swell and grow as it licked with long, hard, conquering strokes that began and ended on the most sensitive spot in her vulva. She placed her hands on Natasha's head and pushed it against the open vagina, rubbing the young girl's nose and mouth in the juices, forcing her to drink it down. Natasha loved being made to do things. Kelly's fingers were in her hair, crushing her face between the stewardess's powerful thighs.

"You little bitch, ahhhhh, ahhhhh...Go on, go on. Such a good little twat-licker you are. Oh, yes, put your tongue in deeper, ohhhhh ... Deeper, deeper. Ohhhhhhhhh ... Suck me off ahhh. So near."

The "little bitch" knew Kelly was about to climax and positioned her mouth so that it covered the entire opening of the stewardess's pubis.

"I'm coming, I'm coming, I'm coming, ahhhhhhh, ahhhhhhhhhh."

Kelly's knees shook violently and her mind was wiped clean as she gave herself up to orgasm. All barriers were down and the floodgates were well and truly open, as Natasha was finding out. She was almost drowning in the liquid ejaculations of her conquest, and it was some minutes before either girl was in a fit state to leave the john. Natasha went out first and the first thing she saw was Rudy Gioberti's naked ass bobbing up and down. He was screwing the ravishingly beautiful woman the young girl had noticed was the only other passenger in the first class section.

"Hey, Kelly, look at this."

She looked, open-mouthed, while Natasha giggled. The woman's long legs had been hoisted over Gioberti's shoulders, and her heels were drumming an erotic tattoo on his back. She was screaming her head off.

"My God," said Kelly. "And to think I was worried by the noise we were making."

The two girls looked at each other. "C'mon," said Natasha. They went back into the toilet. "Now you can do me, this time."

The next time they came out everything was back to normal. Natasha sat down beside an angry Rudy Gioberti.

"Where the hell have you been? What the hell have you been doing?"

"Oh, please don't be annoyed with me, Daddy."

"What have you done?"

"Well, I've just balled that stewardess."

"Jesus H Christ. You did what?"

"I didn't think you'd mind because it was a girl. She's so pretty and sexy and she really needed to come."

She watched in secret amusement as his face turned red with anger, and his penis stiffened in his pants.

"I don't believe you," he croaked.

In reply, Natasha gazed openly at his throbbing erection. "Oh, Daddy, what a huge dong you've got."

"Just wait till we're off this plane."

Sitting cross-legged on the floor of Rudy Gioberti's black limousine as it glided away from the airport, Natasha just could not wait a moment more to discover the nature of her punishment.

"You know I got her juices all over my face and in my hair. It was like being under the shower, but I still managed to swallow most of her stuff. It was wild, Rudy, really wild."

That did it. She watched as he lifted the false bottom out of his case, and wondered what was going to happen. She licked her dry lips, then gasped in surprise at the length and thickness of the black rubber dildo he had produced. It would split her in two. She felt her juices flowing as her body prepared for the painful assault. He gave the signal and she got onto her knees, hitched up her skirt, and bent over. Gioberti rammed the head of the fake penis into her vagina. Natasha squealed. With both hands he pushed it between her slim, tanned thighs as far as it would go. Despite the exquisite pain the girl was very close to orgasm, but she knew she had to hang on. Then she felt his own rampant tumescence penetrating her rectal passage, and, violated from both ways, she achieved a tremendously sustained, awesome, racking climax.

Sabrina Cary Howard Woodville was fast asleep in bed in her Hampstead hideaway home when the doorbell rang. And then the phone. Constantly. It was almost two in the afternoon but Sabrina had not got to bed until six that morning, because of Joy Joy.

Finally rousing herself from her slumbers, Sabrina covered her nude form with a silk robe and stumbled to the door.

"Joy Joy? What a time to call round. You know very well what time I got home last night. This morning, rather. Well, you'd better come in while I get that bloody phone."

"Don't."

Something in the earnest tone of Joy Joy's voice and the gaunt expression on her face made Sabrina pause and turn.

"There's been a plane crash," said Joy Joy. "In Turkey."

"Robin?"

"Darling, I'm so very sorry..."

Badyr Al Hussein was tired, and not just because Sabrina was sexually insatiable. Not just because he had been out gambling until dawn in the casino at Monte Carlo. Not just because of the traffic on the long morning drive from Antibes to Nice airport. His was a fatigue of the soul; a weariness without end, unless he so chose to end it by ending his own life. For that was the source. He was a man who was sick of the life he was living. Only his sense of humour kept him sane.

But this morning as the hum of the massive jet's four engines lulled him back to sleep, his sense of humour had deserted him. He looked down at the Princess as she dozed on, her black hair tumbling over the pillow, the silk sheets clinging to her perfect body. She was a Princess because he had wanted her to be. Badyr was that powerful, just as he had brought Roxanne Duparier Adonisthenes, the world's most beautiful widow, and his employer and cousin, King Rashid, together in an affair which scandalised the whole world.

After her eventful flight to Florida, Roxanne booked into the Breakers Hotel on the Florida Keys south of Miami. And waited. And waited. It was seven the next evening when she answered the door to him.

"Twenty four hours you've kept me waiting, Your Majesty. I hope you're worth it."

"Why don't I show you?"

They dined at his private villa together with other members of his staff and entourage. After dinner they were finally alone, sitting on the beach hand in hand. They talked about each other and how each came to be where they were at that moment.

"The important thing is you are here because you want to be, and so am I. Truly." The King took her in his arms and kissed her, and they sank back slowly onto the sand and kissed for a long time, her arms wrapped tightly round him.

They stopped. He raised his head and looked at Roxanne. Their breaths caught as their eyes met. His hand caressed her blonde hair.

"I want you to make love to me," she murmured.

They got to their feet and brushed off the sand, laughing. They walked slowly up the beach to the patio and in through the French windows to her bedroom. She turned to face him. His hands went to her dress, undoing the buttons all the way down the front. After each button they kissed hungrily. She reached for his belt, undid it, unclipped the waistband, eased the zip down, then slipped her hand inside to feel his huge erection.

"My God," she gasped, "you're hung like a horse." She giggled. "That's what you are. My Arab stallion."

She held his hard, throbbing penis for a moment, shivering with pleasure as his hands stroked her breasts, teasing her nipples into hard points. Now their need for each other could be denied no longer. In only a matter of a very few seconds they were naked and lying on the bed together. They both gasped as their bodies touched, it was like a small but sharp electric shock, and they embraced passionately, hands and tongues, lips and fingers and even toes, in happy exploration. She fellated him till he moaned, then she rolled over onto her back and opened her legs.

"Now, my stallion. I want to be mounted. I want to ride."

He knelt between her spread thighs and slid his rampant phallus slowly, very slowly, so she could almost howl with delight, into her wet, wide-open vulva. She groaned, her head thrashing from side to side, her back arching in her need to take all of him into her, and she came, flooding him with her warm juices.

He knelt back on his heels, waiting for her to come down, then entered her again. She gasped. She licked her dry lips and flung her arms round his neck as he began to move, pulling out and pushing in. Her legs went up and around him, her ankles crossing above his thrusting buttocks. His long shaft touched her deep, deep inside, and every penetration raised her up to that extreme level of feeling she had already experienced once that evening. But once was never enough for Roxanne Duparier Adonisthenes.

He speeded up. Her eyes glazed, her mouth opened in a soundless scream of ecstasy as his jism spurted into her in spasm after racking spasm, six in all.

A long time later they stirred a little and kissed and opened their eyes. They caressed each other's bodies and cuddled tight. In the morning they made love again and it was just as good. The soothing sound of the waves lapping on the shore floated in to them. The King gave in to sleep as Roxanne wrapped herself in a towel and gathered up her clothes.

They were happy all that summer.

Central America was, thought Lyssette Cromwell, a very seductive, exotic and frightening place. When she wasn't needed on the film set, Lyssette would go to the main square of the town and wander through the large open markets, where piles of golden mangoes and fish still wet from the sea were on sale, where old women sold gnarled roots. Everything was for sale in San Vincente, including human life. There were bandits in the hills. Corruption hung heavy in the air like dust on the stillness of late afternoon, but from the north came the promise of cool, clean tomorrows. There was revolution on the wind.

Everyone in the film unit, cast, crew, director, lived in one house: the biggest house in the very best neighbourhood of the town. It had once been the home of the Vice-President of El Salvador. Large and spacious, built around an inner courtyard as such houses in the region often are, it had a spectacular view of the coastal town spread out below the hill, and of the Pacific. The sunsets were ripe gold, and the garden within the courtyard was lush with wild orchid and jacaranda, night-blooming jasmine and red and purple bougainvillaea.

Making movies is an extremely boring way of making a living. Lyssette felt herself suffocating in a luxurious prison and to relieve the boredom she toyed with the idea of an affair with the director. But he was more interested in the leading man. Lyssette made do with her favourite dildo she had brought with her from London. The replica phallus was fully ten inches long and very detailed and lifelike. She had bought it one summer in Bangkok, and been shown the full potential of its use by Joy Joy de Ferrare.

Consumed by hatred and loathing, Susie and Roman abandoned themselves to the act of love, copulating like dogs in heat. Sensation overwhelmed them. They surrendered themselves to the warmth that was welcome even in the oppressiveness of the hot Cairo night, and to a wetness that stimulated even in the suffocating humidity.

Roman wanted to kill her; to make her come and come and then blow her brains out with the gun he had bought to kill himself with. But now he felt stronger, more of a man than he had felt for two years, since the shocking discovery that the woman he was in love with was Jacqueline Duparier, his step-mother. Now, once again, his father had stepped in to spoil things. To avoid a scandal, Jacqueline had been exiled to the family estates outside Paris, where she remained, shunned by the rest of the family. Well, thought Roman, the great Jean-Claude Duparier was going to pay.

Susie had her first orgasm on top. Then he was on top and thrusting himself into her, harder and harder, violent and harsh, punishing her until she strained for and achieved a second climax. Only then did Roman allow himself to let go. Susie felt the searing hot rush of his semen melt her loins and knew that now was the moment.

His jerking body forcing her down into the bed, she nevertheless got an arm free and reached for the gun where it lay on the night table beside the bed.

THE SAMURAI

Simon Barnes was wide awake, but he wished to reverse the situation if at all possible. Waking up in such a state was no new thing to Simon, and it did not get any easier with age. He kept his eyes tight shut. The main reason for this had less to do with keeping the light out of his eyes than with the identity of the unknown woman lying beside him. Drink did something to the critical faculties, as far as his appreciation of female attractiveness was concerned, but then perhaps she was also wondering just what it was she was in the sack with.

Simon had a long, aristocratic, but tough face, the chin firm, the mouth hinting at sensuality and just a touch cruel. His well-proportioned body, hard-muscled and superfit, was over six-foot-long and deeply tanned all over. His eyes were grey, his beautifully-cut short hair a rich, golden brown.

An incoming round of high-calibre ordinance detonated inside Simon's skull. He had tried to move. Now he knew better; he would lie still. There was just one problem with doing that. The taste in his mouth compared unfavourably with the tactile sensations to be garnered in a camel's arsehole. What he needed was water, in great quantities, to drink and to shower in, but that meant moving.

At this point Simon felt a hand on his belly. Slowly it moved downward to his crotch. His hangover subsided as his penis sprang to life in the girl's hand. He felt the girl change position. In a moment her warm breath was on his balls, and he opened his eyes and buried his face between her sleek thighs as her lips closed round the swollen crown of his organ and began to suck.

They climaxed together and fell apart. Simon threw the sheet back.

"Good morning," said the girl, brightly. "How's your hangover?"

"Better, thanks to you." He looked her over. She was obviously a model, very slim, very young, very sleek and stylish. A little too angular for his taste, if he was being perfectly honest, and not the sort of girl for a lifetime commitment, but fine as a companion for the evening.

"Forgive me, but my memory of last night isn't clear."

She laughed. "I picked you up in Tramp. You were dancing with Susie Watkins until I butted in." She looked at her watch. "Christ, I've got a photocall in half an hour." She wriggled into her tight dress and combed her fingers through her black mane. "If you find my knickers, you will give me a call, won't you? The name's Natasha Landi."

He watched her go with some regret.

Simon leant heavily in with the left shoulder. The pony responded to his command instantly, nostrils flared, the animal's coat steaming in the sultry heat. Rico Manzetti was so effectively ridden off the ball that it looked as if he had never intended to approach it in the first place.

Simon kept his shoulder in the American's face for just long enough to make his point, and it was not lost on Manzetti.

Polo was a game for gentlemen and Simon Barnes was considered by many as the best player in England, but despite his acknowledged brilliance he had a reputation for erratic play. This, together with his taste for a social life that was well and truly in the fast lane, meant that his appearances for the national team were less frequent than was desirable.

Simon had good reason to be grateful for the Prince of Wales' friendly advice about playing polo in Florida. Dehydration should be avoided at all cost. The Americans, using a spot of gamesmanship, had set the start late in the afternoon when the sun would be unmercifully hot and the air so sticky and humid it was almost wet enough to drink. In such conditions the player's skin can not lose heat because sweat will not evaporate. On his old friend's advice, Simon had avoided lunch and alcohol and instead between chukkas drank a lot of cool water. He had also taken the further precaution of having Locks of St James' design a special lightweight helmet. When the bell went at the end of the final chukka the score in favour of the English team was ten goals to four.

So now it was definitely time for something stronger than water. He made for the drinks tent and ordered a huge jug of Pimms Number One. He was soon joined at his table by two pneumatic, peroxide blondes who introduced themselves. Beverly, "call me Beaver", spoke with a Texas drawl. She wore green hot-pants and a see-through blouse. Her thighs were short and heavy, her ass large but well-shaped, but her breasts were by far her best feature: perfect, girlie-magazine-style beach balls of superbly constructed flesh that defied gravity. Her companion's name was Cindy. She was taller, thinner, and prettier than Beaver.

"And who do I have to thank for your delightful company?"

"We're a peace offering from Mr Manzetti," said Beaver.

"Ah, the tooth fairy."

The girls' laughter was a trifle hesitant.

"You're not afraid of him, are you?" asked Cindy.

"Should I be?"

The girls looked at each other. And said nothing. Simon ordered a magnum of Dom Perignon. After it and the Pimms had been consumed by the trio, the Englishman had a suggestion to make.

"If you enjoyed the champagne I have another bottle in my room."

"We thought you'd never ask," said Beaver...

They never did get around to that second magnum of Dom Perignon, for in moments of arriving in his hotel suite on Miami Beach, Beaver had freed Simon's erection from one confinement, in his pants, to another, in her mouth. Like a paper chase, various items of clothing were scattered enroute to the bedroom.

Once there, Simon swiftly penetrated each girl in turn, always withdrawing before climax. The three snorted some good smack and then the two hookers got into 69 while Simon watched. Finally he rammed himself up Beaver's fat ass. The slippery warmth of her bowels plus the acute tightness of the anal opening was just too much. He came noisily.

Beaver retired hurt shortly after, leaving Simon and Cindy to really get to know each other.

"Jeezz, oh, Jeezz, oh, ohhh, baby, baby, baby, baby."

"Cindy, you're wonderful, ahhhhhh, wonderful."

"Oh, keep doing it to me, ohhh, ohhhhhh, eeeooh, oh."

"Ahhhhhh, yes ... yes."

''I love, it."

"Cindy, darling."

"Baby, baby, ohhhhhhhhh."

Simon was wide awake. Some warning bell had sounded deep in his sleeping mind. He lay still, listening for the cause. Then he heard it. Two men were quietly approaching along the corridor, and it was their very stealth which had alerted him. He looked at the girl. She was lying close beside him with her beautiful, sexy back towards him. She had not stirred. Otherwise motionless, he reached out slowly to the bedside table, where his hand closed about the hilt of his Italian diving knife that since his Army years had been a constant companion, especially at night.

Simon was the youngest son of the Earl of Strathmoor. After Harrow and Sandhurst he joined the Scots Guards, but life in the peacetime Regular Army quickly palled so he volunteered for the Special Air Service Regiment. This crack unit had been formed in the North African desert during World War Two to operate secretly behind enemy lines. By 1966, when Simon was accepted by the SAS, the war in Vietnam was in full swing. The 9th Marine Expeditionary Force had arrived the previous year, and the Air Mobile Division was about to join it. America's Special Forces unit, the Green Berets, had been in Indochina for three years as advisers, and there were units from Australia, New Zealand, South Korea and Thailand fighting alongside the Americans and the South Vietnamese. Officially, there were no British forces involved in the war, despite the presence of two Commonwealth allies, but in actuality a token unit of SAS volunteers were attached as advisers to the South Vietnamese Army.

So it was that for two years Old Harrovian Simon Barnes stalked the dank and dark and sinister rain forests of South East Asia in search of the "enemy": the Viet Cong. He and the team of ARVN Rangers he commanded lived off the land, holing-up in the daytime, moving and killing at night. They soon became more like the Cong than the Cong. Simon came home the youngest lieutenant colonel in the British Army at that time.

Now, twenty years later, lying in a dark hotel bedroom in Miami, he felt akin to his young self of long ago and far away. He got out of bed without waking Cindy, wondering who the two intruders were. From Rico Manzetti no doubt, he thought. Bare-assed naked, he crouched down in a shadow-filled corner of the room and waited.

But not for long...

The morning after his return from Miami, Simon Barnes drove his matt black Targa Porsche from his Belgravia apartment to the RAC Club in Pall Mall. For the rest of that morning he got himself together with the help of the hot room and the morning newspapers, followed by the steam room and cold plunge, and then finally, when his reflexes were once again alive and kicking, he did twenty lengths of the pool. Still he brooded over the deaths of Manzetti's two hoods, and he was still brooding when he met Edwina Lawrence for lunch at the Cafe Royal some time later:

There was a centre to his life that was missing. He had glimpsed it briefly in the jungles of Vietnam, but that was so long ago. Now he was merely drifting. Polo took him all over the globe, and his skill at the game, plus his charm, good looks, and aristocratic heritage, meant that he knew a circle of people to make Viviane Ventura green with envy. He lived, ate, and slept with the rich, beautiful, and infamous celebrities whose exploits in the gossip columns and scandal sheets brightened the lives of many ordinary people too dull and stupid to aspire to such antics themselves. Villas in the South of France, chalets in Gstaad, and holiday homes on Mustique were always at his disposal. And yet...And yet.

"Darling Simon, why so gloomy?"

"Oh, dear Edwina, hello," he said, standing up. They shook hands. "Please sit down and tell me all the latest news. I'm a little out of touch."

"Is that all you want of me? I am disappointed."

He gazed at her large breasts, the outline of which was clearly visible through her silk dress. She was not wearing a bra. He looked down at her lap where her long legs flowed from the demure skirt. He had a sudden, sharp stab of need to part those pale, flabby thighs and ram himself into her, squeezing her pendulous, heavy boobs and twisting them till she screamed.

"Perhaps you have a couple of hours to spare after lunch?"

"Indeed I do," she gasped, smiling broadly. Her newly-stiff nipples, pushing aggressively against the silk fabric, sent him an unmistakable signal. The bonk was fixed.

"So what's been happening while I've been away in the colonies?"

"Well, Fraser Karl had his trip to the Palace. Now he's setting up a film to star his black mistress, Monique Starr. Sabrina Howard has been a very busy girl since she hit town, partying and dating like mad. Rumour says she's just got married to Badyr Al Hussein and Joanne Layde and Veronica Capital are both said to be livid. If the rumour is true, Sabrina must have had a quick and very quiet divorce from you-know-who." She paused.

"Do go on."

"Well, I don't want to put you off your lunch but there's been a mass murder at the North London home of Jon Revere, the photographer. He and his wife, Linzi Baker, the nude model, and five friends were stabbed to death."

"Good God. How awful. When was this?"

"Two days ago."

"I don't suppose the police have any idea who it was?"

"My dear, it was Michael Cord. He just went berserk. God knows why."

As Edwina continued to talk, giving him all the gory details so far released to the media, plus the about-town speculation that what had been described as a quiet dinner with friends was in fact a boozed-up, spaced-out sex and drugs orgy which went wrong, Simon got that tingle of excitement at the back of his neck he always felt at the scent of danger.

"Ram it in, ram it in, ram it in, ram it in." The voice, hoarse, gasping, belonged to Edwina Lawrence in coitus dementia: love mad/mad love in truth, thought Simon, who was having difficulty keeping pace with her. But he did as he was commanded.

Her response was to groan and shudder, pulling taut the silken bonds by which her wrists were secured to the bedposts. This was Edwina's idea as was the large fake phallus strapped to his belly. Folded under him with her legs over his shoulders she could thus be penetrated in both places at once, and Simon was only too eager to oblige and turn her favourite wet dream into a very sweaty reality. While the dildo occupied her over-used vulva, his true erection was well-sheathed in the tight hole between her slack buttocks. Or at least it should have been tight, but Edwina had obviously been to one orgy too many.

"Oh, Simon." There were tears in her eyes. "You're wonderful."

"So are you," he lied.

Her orgasm boiled over him in a welter of cries and gasps, flailing limbs and jerking hips, and followed by loud declarations of her love for him. In among all this activity his own ejaculation passed almost unnoticed, even by himself.

It was Edwina who invited Simon to a housewarming party in

Sussex the following weekend, and it was there he met the tall, dark-haired, strikingly sensuous Beth Blackshaw.

For the trustees of Dartington Hall, one of the most progressive and famous independent schools in England, it had been the kind of week only to be found in their worst nightmares. And the sort of scandalous exclusive Fleet Street editors only dream about: HEAD AND WIFE POSED FOR PORN MAG. Day by day the tabloid press disclosed the singular hobby of the headmaster, Dr Lyn Blackshaw and his attractive wife, Beth.

At a traditional public school the damage might have been confined to embarrassing the governors who hired him.

At Dartington it proved much more difficult to prevent the mud from sticking to the school. For although the Blackshaws posed for photographs of simulated copulation in the magazine New QT several years before joining the school in April 1983, the incident became hopelessly confused in the minds of many people with Dartington's style of progressive education.

The first weeks of the summer term passed smoothly enough despite the threat of opposition when the new head extended the compulsory part of the school syllabus. The real trouble, when it came, was over discipline. At half term, Dr Blackshaw summoned four boys to his office and expelled them without warning. Two of the pupils had stolen textbooks from the school.

All the children at Dartington were furious at the manner of the expulsions and parents were divided as to whether it was right to expel them, but everyone was agreed that it had been handled badly. Dr Blackshaw resented the criticism and his relations with both staff and students rapidly turned sour. By the end of term there was open hostility. This culminated in an incident at the school dance when Blackshaw had to be separated from a teenage boy who was wearing a Mayfair magazine pin-up of the nude Beth Blackshaw on the back of his leather jacket.

For the increasingly isolated headmaster the issue was the criminal acts of some of the children, but for the talented, capable teachers, the pupils, and many of the parents who had become involved in the situation, the issue was Blackshaw's unwillingness to deal with the problems in the tradition of a progressive school. This was highlighted when he called in the police to investigate drug abuse and pointed out two boys in the quad. Their rooms were searched, cannabis found, and a total of three boys charged with possession.

By this time the staff were worried not just about the damage to the school's ideals but also to their own professional reputations. At least one member of the staff was close to a breakdown. A staff meeting in July recorded two votes of no confidence in Blackshaw and in August, after term ended, four of the staff resigned. A few days later Blackshaw sent out a printed circular to all parents which detailed drink, drugs, burglary, and under-age sex offences at the school.

The letter was leaked to the national press, and the interest of a part of Fleet Street in the more sensational areas of news led inevitably to the disclosure of the sexy photos. On that Sunday in September Rupert Murdoch's News of the World stunned the townspeople of Totnes by reprinting a Mayfair photo of the pneumatic Mrs Blackshaw. This was followed in Wednesday's Sun by a much riper selection of pictures, not on Page Three, but across the centre pages. Finally, on the Friday of that week, the Sun published New QT's study of the Blackshaws in coitus delecti. Blackshaw resigned.

But this was far from being the end of the affair. Ravishing Beth had become an instant celebrity, much in the same manner as big-breasted Erika Roe did the previous year. What's more, Beth was unrepentant. Interviewed by a Sunday newspaper at the end of the week about the sensational pictures and her sexpot image she declared: "I'm no scarlet woman." Talking at their home in Totnes, Devon, in the school grounds, she also spoke frankly of the situation at Dartington.

"I'm not ashamed of the photographs. I'm not ashamed of anything I've ever done in my life. But I am ashamed of the depths some of the people at the school have sunk to. I am talking about a small group who had it in for us."

Beth had no regrets over the magazine pictures and smiled as she said: "That was a long time ago. We often celebrate our marriage together. We are a loving couple."

She said she had been overwhelmed by messages of support she had received from parents, school staff, and pupils since her husband's resignation. Gazing from the detached house to the school buildings across a meadow she said: "I don't know what the future holds for us now. Everything has happened so very quickly. But my husband and I are still very much in love. This won't harm our relationship. We need constant stimulation and new experiences to keep life exciting."

As if to prove her words, the following Sunday in the centre pages of the same newspaper, appeared a photographic spread of Beth by David Bailey. One topless shot depicted the thirty-seven-year-old Mrs Blackshaw proudly showing off a pair of breasts any teenage starlet would sell her soul for.

After stripping off for her picture session Beth was not slow to bare all about her unconventional love life:

"The whole world thinks my husband and I are a kinky, swinging couple prepared to try anything. The only thing we are guilty of is being in love, deeply in love. But now we feel we have to open our hearts to explain everything. We want to tell everyone that there was nothing dirty or sordid about those pictures. Honestly, we are proud of them and don't regret a thing. Not a single thing."

Of posing for Bailey's camera in sexy undies and going topless Beth, 36-24-36, speaking at a London hotel after the storm over the nude photos had forced her and her family to leave their home in Totnes, Devon, and go into hiding, said:

"David Bailey is such an easy man to relax with and pose for. There I was, wearing beautiful sexy undies, with the world's most famous photographer taking pictures of me as a real woman. It was all so natural, wonderful."

However, at this point, Beth wanted to put her naughty image behind her and become a serious sex therapist, with her husband, in order to help other people with their sex problems.

"Working together we believe we could help people overcome their hang-ups," she said.

Simon was immediately attracted to Beth Blackshaw. This was more than the physical appeal of her body; he thought her a bright, witty, stylish, down-to-earth, determined, ambitious lady with lots of sparkle. She found him equally congenial as a dinner party companion, and being without her husband she was glad of the company.

They talked of India, which Simon knew and Beth and her husband had planned to visit.

"Why do I come, I always wonder," said Simon. "Why am I here?

At that first fatigued moment in the steaming Indian dawn, why must I continually return to that tormented, confused, corrupt, futile and exasperating land as though I loved it, needed it, as though I had to be forever reminded of its sorrow and the splendour of its hopelessness? Every time I return my heart sinks, but each time I say good-bye to India I know there is some part of me I have left behind, some final question yet to be asked."

"And answered?" said Beth.

He smiled. "India never answers your questions."

"Oh, I do wish we were still going, but this thing came up for Lyn. I could still go. I haven't cancelled the tickets and reservations as yet, but I'd need a protector." She grinned. "Are you free for the next two months?"

Some days later, Beth decided to confide in Simon and tell him her side of the story.

"You don't have to. There's no need."

"But I do, and there is a need. Just because I'm the wife of a public school headmaster, it doesn't mean I'm not a real woman. All I was ever guilty of was being a real woman and in love. Someone who is proud of her body, someone with feelings and desires, someone who believes it is not sordid to enjoy being admired by men. Especially a man like you." She winked.

Simon laughed.

Beth went on: "The most important ingredient in a modern marriage is, of course, love. That's why Lyn was delighted to see those so-called saucy photos of me in a girlie magazine. He was pleased for me, knowing that something I wanted had been achieved. Other men might admire my body but Lyn knows it is definitely not for other men to share. Our deep feelings for each other enable us to beat the evil gossips who did their best to destroy us. Together, Lyn and I can climb mountains and scale the peaks of passion and pleasure, and nothing will drive a wedge between us. We have worked hard to build a tender, loving relationship, and that means sharing the joy of exploring all the sexual experiences, of breaking down the barriers of inhibitions, and of being totally open and honest with each other."

"I'm very glad to hear that, Beth."

"Lyn and I hide nothing. That includes our feelings, our emotions, and our fantasies. Our own relationship is, I think, absolutely wonderful, and not just the physical side. We have a meeting of minds as well as bodies. Every morning that we are together Lyn brings me breakfast in bed and always wakes me with kisses. I'm conscious of his warm, tender embrace before I'm even aware of the sun streaming through the bedroom window, and purring like a contented kitten I lie naked between the sheets. What more could a woman possibly want?"

"Modesty forbids me from answering," said Simon, smiling.

"Indeed? Well Lyn's a great romantic. He tells me constantly how good I look, and I always do look good because I feel good. We turn each other on all the time. With Lyn that involves many different things, including food. We often eat in the bedroom instead of the dining room. Sometimes we sit like a teenage couple feeding each other, naked, on the floor of our bedroom with a bottle of champagne between us, peeling prawns or prising open oysters and eating from each other's hands. Our enjoyment of Bollinger, Krug, Moet and Chandon had led us to working out our very own aperitif to lovemaking."

"Do tell."

"I gently pour champagne on a bed of creme de menthe. The colour effect is out of this world. I call the concoction: 'Arise my love'."

"And does it have the desired result?"

"Every time."

"Must try it sometime."

Beth laughed. "Not too many long-established couples behave like that I suppose. We're also very fond of bathing together and all-over body massage. Sometimes I will give Lyn a massage just to revive him after a tiring day, but then on other occasions I will manipulate him in a more sensual way. His hands know how to turn me on at any time of the day or night. We are a very sexy twosome, on occasion really wild, and at other moments very romantic. We've always made love anytime, anywhere. In the open air, sex can be an explosive experience. Indoors it can be an intense personal joy. Even at Dartington we had our moments, on the flat roof of the schoolhouse."

"I bet you did."

"How well I remember that first time. It was a warm, wonderful, starry summer night. It must have been about two in the morning when we decided to go outside. We had been lying in bed when we just thought it would be a shame to waste such a beautiful night. We walked naked through the French windows from our bedroom onto the stone-floored roof area. I clearly remember lying there on a blanket watching the stars, and just being naked under such a beautiful sky added to the pleasure. It gave a whole new dimension to our lovemaking. As on the day we took time off from the troubles at Dartington Hall to enjoy a country walk together and the sudden appearance of a rainbow over a bend in the river turned our thoughts to love. I can still recall the damp grass beneath our bodies."

"Your husband is a very lucky man."

"Oh, I'm the lucky one. I met Lyn on holiday in Spain. My family were making plans for my marriage to a childhood sweetheart before we set off, but the courier on the coach tour just happened to be a young man called Lyn Blackshaw, and he was the target for every love-hungry girl on the trip, including me. I took off my engagement ring and gave it to my mother. Eventually Lyn turned up at my hotel bedroom door clutching a bunch of flowers and asked me if I would go for a midnight swim with him. We made love on the beach. That was twenty years ago."

"You make me very envious."

"How?"

"Your happiness. The way you and Lyn feel about each other, and are able to show it without reservation. Nothing false, no pretence."

"Have you never felt that way about someone?"

"No."

Beth Blackshaw smiled. "You will. It happens to everybody at least once in a lifetime. I found mine early but there's still plenty of time for you, and you do have one or two advantages over the average guy."

Simon was astonished to discover that he was blushing. No woman had been able to do that to him since he was fourteen. Perhaps that was part of the problem.

"Sorry," she said, "I didn't mean to embarrass you."

"I didn't think I could be anymore. It's a rather refreshing feeling. I bet you make Lyn blush all the time."

Beth tapped a finger against her pursed lips. "Perhaps you two should meet."

"That would seem to be a good idea. Especially if I'm escorting you to the other side of the world."

So the very next night Simon had dinner with the Blackshaws, knowing full well that Lyn would take the opportunity to check him out, and not minding in the least. In fact they got on very well. Beth talked more about the photographs.

"Let me set the record straight. It all started twelve years ago when I worked in a Kent village at a junior school. I discovered from the other wives that most of their men folk were bringing home girlie magazines. I was shocked. Lyn had never been interested in such things and I couldn't understand why young men should waste money on nude pictures of women. My friends and I were just as attractive as those women, so I decided to prove the point by getting my pictures in one of these magazines. Lyn and I decided on Mayfair after going through a whole pile of girlie mags. Some of the others were a bit near the knuckle.

"Anyway we agreed that on the next sunny day we would take the plunge. It turned out to be a weekend when we picked up our camera and walked half a mile to a roadside orchard. I was wearing a wrap-around Indian-style dress that was easy to whip off. We'd taken nude pictures of each other indoors before but had never been bold enough to try it outdoors. Soon I was cavorting naked around the orchard with Lyn happily snapping away. Later I turned up unannounced at the Mayfair offices, stood before the picture editor and said: 'I know this is a hell of a cheek but are these good enough to be published?' Well he must have seen something to his liking because later their photographer Roy came down for dinner, and a picture session was arranged.

"What a day that turned out to be, totally enjoyable. There were some full frontals, straight topless, and delightful shots of me in skimpy white outfits. One set showed me outside the local church wearing tight shorts and carrying a hockey stick. Then the photographer suggested that Lyn and I posed naked together. The idea was harmless so we did. They were not porno pictures. We did not make love in front of the camera. In fact it was one of the few times in our marriage when Lyn failed to find me sexually exciting. At one point we were laughing so much the photographer had to stop the session."

"Those were the photos that appeared in New QT?" asked Simon.

"Yes. They weren't meant for publication but we were not annoyed when we saw them in the magazine because they were such nice pictures."

Many nations and peoples have affinities and historical bonds with Asia, but nothing compared with the elusive, and indissoluble relationship that exists between the British and the Indians. Europeans go to India either from curiosity or addiction. You are either into the package tour of the Taj Mahal and Kashmir, with a few sample curries on the way, or else you are led spiritually to some fashionable ashram where you can spend much money learning how to be poor. Each group feels nothing but contempt for the other, yet they are looking for much the same thing. For India is exactly what you want from it, so long as you do not seek comfortable compromise, but some people never come to terms with its extremes. Most visitors make the great mistake of thinking of India as one country, one nation. Today it is an independent republic but it remains what it always was: a collection of different and differing states, each with an individual culture and language. Everything is contrast. The dusty emptiness of the heartland against the thronging masses of Calcutta, the frozen snows of the high Himalayan north against the baking beaches of the Madrasi south; the dense rain forests of Coorg and Mysore against the arid deserts of Rajputana. There are many Indias, too many to know.

The desk clerk in the Palace Hotel, Mysore, said with a mournful sigh: "Madam, it is all exhausted." There was not, in other words, a stamp to be had for a postcard to England, so Beth pushed the card to the bottom of her holdall. That infectious Indian fatalism was at work again.

Mysore, in the south, is an elegant city of princely design. The Maharaja's Palace had white columns and cool shades of pistachio, gold-tipped fly whisks and marble lamps shaped like lotus flowers. Even the Town Hall looks regal, thought Beth. In the courtyard among the bougainvillaea blossom she found the daily town bulletin. It read: 'Births 63, Deaths 17' and there were blanks against 'Plague, Cholera, Influenza, Smallpox, Typhoid, Diptheria'. When Beth told Simon about it later he said: "A good day."

At the top of Chamundi Hill there is the two-thousand year-old temple with its garish gods and goddesses. In the white heat Beth was glad to be led into the cool courtyard by a young boy.

"Please, twenty- five paise for a holy coconut," he said.

The money was for the holy man who proceeded to smash the coconut. He looked at the remains and shook his head.

"This one no good," said the boy. "Please, you buy another?"

Families of chattering peasants, having rice picnics, had flopped in the gods' courtyard. A pushy guide reached for Beth's camera.

"I will clic you."

"No thanks."

The priest daubed the red tilak on her forehead and then ordered her to drink from a small brass water pot. She lifted the pot to her lips while the grey monkeys played in the temple grounds, chasing each other and squeaking. She wondered if she might soon be a new statistic on the Town Hall notice board.

Cochnin, on the Malabar coast, smells of cloves and spices. The island of Willingdon has a village green, large mock Tudor houses, and is like a Chobham-by-Sea with its decaying colonial atmosphere. This is strangely in contrast to the great cantilevered Chinese fishing nets along the beach, relics of the court of Kublai Khan, and looking at dusk like a design in tin at the Tate Gallery.

Simon took Beth to Jew Town. Here the last of a colony of White Jews eke out their days playing cards in the narrow street where once their ancestors lived in houses with bleached blue shutters and names like Mandalay and Sassoon Hall. There are about fifty White Jews left, pale, with only a hint of dark in their skins, and many more women than men. Beth thought the place unutterably sad and depressing, with its goats chewing at banana skins in dusty doorways, and pillaged statues with gaudy red hearts and virgins in blue, sold by sad-faced Jews. Perhaps, thought Beth, it was a fitting if small revenge for their persecution by the early Portuguese settlers. Only the 1568 synagogue made any money.

They were staying in the Malabar Hotel. With its white pillars and verandas overlooking the harbour it was once the best hotel in Cochnin. Now run down and gone to seed. There was a curious Somerset Maugham atmosphere about the place still, Beth felt, and about Simon too. One dusk she emerged onto the lawn after dressing for dinner to find her escort clad in a beautifully tailored white suit, sipping gin and tonic. They ate in the smaller and less pretentious Casino Hotel which served a memorable fish masala.

On the cruise ship from Cochnin to Makshadweep they drank fenni, a very powerful mixture of spirit and coconut juice, and were taught to levitate, a skill which seemed to disappear with the onslaught of an extreme hangover. But for a pound each Beth and Simon sampled the hangover cure of a coconut oil massage, shampoo and pedicure. Beth had her eyebrows plucked the Eastern way, while a girl with a piece of thread between her teeth removed the hairs from Simon's nose.

Lakshadweep was a string of undeveloped coral islands in the Arabian Sea where there was nothing to do except search for coral, swim, and eat fresh fish cooked on a fire of driftwood. One could stay in a tent at Kavarthy and Banagram, or in a Dak bungalow, or in the guest house, which was a hut selling old soap and Horlicks. Beth and Simon spent a week on the islands, cut off from the world, though the fisherman praying to Mecca, bowing on his wooden boat at sunset, did once have a letter for Beth from the mainland beneath his fishing nets.

Back at the Malabar Hotel, Simon found a letter waiting for him.

"It's from Jackie. He's invited us to stay for the weekend."

"Lovely. What does Jackie do?"

"Not a lot. He used to be a maharaja."

So it was on to Gujarat. At Ahmedabad Airport they were told: "His Highness is waiting for you", and so he was, bearded and chuckling. His full name was Fateshingh Gaekawad of Baroda, but to his staff he was Highness, to his family he was Fateh, and to his Western friends he was Jackie. He greeted them warmly and Simon introduced Beth to him.

"Madam, this is a great pleasure."

The chauffeur loaded their bags into the boot of the red Fiat, but it was Jackie who pulled on the driving gloves. On the way to Baroda they stopped under a banyan tree, ate sardine sandwiches and drank pink gin, watching the goats with their curly fantails, and the sure-footed camels. Girls in their purple and orange saris, delicate and straight-backed, went about their road-building tasks, hatching huge boulders.

The palace was all Arabian Nights balconies, portraits of sad-eyed maharanees, Aubusson carpets frayed by age, stuffed squirrels and bats, tiger heads mounted over Limoges bowls and chaises longues. There used to be six hundred servants in the good old days, before 1947.

They spent the afternoon under a canopy watching cricket, a game, said Jackie, invented by the British because "not being spiritual people, they had to think of something to give them a concept of eternity". That night at dinner they met his mother, who wore the white homespun material worn by Gandhi as a protest against the importation of English cloth. She was only fifteen years older than Jackie.

For those susceptible to past palatial glories, the Palace on Wheels, a train made up of saloons once used by maharajahs, steamed through the best of Rajasthan and to the desert of Jaisalmer. For some railway enthusiasts it was bliss to be on such a train for seven days. At every stop they would jump off, men in shorts displaying knobbly white knees, to study the bogies. For Beth the Palace on Wheels was an engaging adventure, though it had been rather unwisely marketed as a 'railway cruise', causing some of the Americans aboard to complain about the lack of baths and bidets.

In Simla they are very proud of the old maharaja's palace, a summer home which is now a hotel. It is full of narcissus bloom, has two pink stone sentry boxes, and white cherubs with jet black hair perched on the lawns. Down in the woods, as Beth and Simon discovered, there is a wooden cottage for Indian newly-weds which is decorated in what Beth considered to be appalling taste: red candlewick, satin hearts with purple flowers and pictures from the Karma Sutra.

"There is," said Simon, "a tea garden in Darjeeling called Lingia, in the foothills of the Himalayas. The air smells of jasmine and through the red of the poinsettias you can see tips of snow. When you taste Darjeeling tea, with its evergreen shiny leaf and camellia blossom, you'll never use a teabag again."

"Well, what are we waiting for?"

After all she had seen, Beth found Heathrow Airport very dull.

"You know, I'm beginning to understand India. At least about the way it takes hold of the imagination of everyone who goes there. I'll see it in my dreams for a very long time."

"And do you want to go back?"
"Oh, yes."

Simon returned to his apartment. He turned the key in the lock
and opened the door.
"Had a pleasant vacation?" said Rico Manzetti.
Simon Barnes closed his apartment door and leant his back
casually against it. Rico Manzetti smiled.
"Ain't you even gonna ask how I got in yer pad, ya schmuck?"
"Go fuck yourself, Manzetti, and take these goons," he said,
indicating the two solidly-built gentlemen behind the armchair the
huge flabby bulk of the American gangster was occupying.
"You wasted two of my boys. They were good boys."
"Not good enough. Are these the replacements? They don't appear
to be good enough either," said Barnes.
"We're gonna find out right now, yer limey faggot."
Simon laughed. "This is not Miami, and you, sir, are no Al
Capone."
Manzetti turned purple. "Kill the bastard."

The sudden death of a loved one is always a traumatic experience
for those left behind, especially when that loved one was brutally
murdered. The crazed monster who stabbed Cherie Halvinne to death
brought such a trauma to Scott Brinkley. He went through the media
circus surrounding the funeral in a daze, totally numb. It took him a
month to sort things out in his mind.
Now he decided that it was time he paid a visit to his home town
of London and looked up some of his old East End mates. There was
one lad, called Chris Crowther, who had been his best friend at school
and who he had not seen or heard from in many, many years. But as
chance would have it, he was flicking through the pages of a magazine
called 'Panache' when he read the following blurb:

'Chris Crowther, one of Britain's leading young stage designers, is
one modest man, as Edwina Lawrence discovered when she talked to
him about his work. So to find out more she met four actresses who
know his clothes at first hand. Jenni Assetor, Sian Phillack, Sarah
Humpelman and Alison Fuchs are in no doubt about the importance of
Crowther's designs, and are not prepared to be modest on his behalf.'

Edwina Lawrence found Chris Crowther to be extremely shy and modest and therefore difficult to interview. He was polite about it, but he was always trying to switch the conversation away from his own efforts in order to praise those of the directors and actors he had worked with. His recent sets for King Lear and Measure for Measure for the RSC had a triumphant reception from the critics. His clothes for King Lear were chosen to represent Britain in an exhibition in Paris. Famous rock star Wing Wangher, lead singer of the group Big Log, commissioned Crowther to do the costumes for their recent video.

"Just how important is costume to your performance?" asked Edwina of the beautiful Jenni Assetor.

"Oh, costume is everything. It affects the way you walk on stage; it affects the way you speak your lines; it affects the way you feel. If the costume is not right, it prevents you from discovering the true character you are attempting to play."

The other actresses were equally strong in their praise for Crowther's work and talent.

"You could just eat him," said Alison Fuchs, famous amongst the London night-club set as an expert in fellatio. "He's just an absolute pet to work with."

Alison Fuchs was one of the topics of conversation between Crowther and Scott Brinkley when they finally got together over a pint in an East End pub one lunch time.

"Here, Chris, what's that Alison bird like in real life?"

He laughed. "You mean, in the flesh?"

"Yeah. I saw her in that horror film, 'Witch Story'. Bloody hell, she's got a pair of nipples on her like organ stops."

Crowther nearly fell off his bar stool, laughing. "Now I know why you became an actor. You wanted to share a bathtub with Alison Fuchs."

"Okay, okay. So tell me what she's like."

"Ravishing. And she does have rather prominent nipples."

"So how can I meet her?"

"Well, I could invite her to one of my parties."

Scott grinned. "Great. Terrific. You're a real mate."

"Speaking of mates," said Crowther, "you should really wear a condom to bonk little Alison. After all, you don't know where she's

been, but I do. Or at least, I've heard the gossip about her."
Scott made a face.

"Chris, darling. Lovely party."
"Alison, dear heart. Have you met Scott Brinkley?"

"Ooooooooo, Ohhhhhhhrrr-oooooooooohhh, yes, yes, yes, punish me, ahhhrr, oooohh-oooo, your dong, ahhh, so deep in me, ohhhhh, yes, yes, hurt me, please, ahhhhhhh, ahhhh, I'm coming, ahhhhhhhhh-ohhhhhrrrr-oooooooo."

"I was born in Kashmir," said Alison, quietly, some time later. It was almost four in the morning and the pre-dawn glow in the eastern sky threw some much needed illumination into the gloom of Scott Brinkley's hotel bedroom.
"Do you go back?"
"As often as I can, which is not very often at all." She paused. "I had made plans to go there next month with my boyfriend, then we broke up. I don't really know what to do now."
"Don't you? I do."
They made love again. And again. Finally, Alison came up with the right idea.
"Why don't you come with me?"
"I thought you'd never ask," said Scott.

Manzetti's two paid assassins drew knives Jim Bowie would have been proud of and advanced, grinning. Obviously people who enjoyed their work, thought Simon Barnes, who had met such creatures on numerous occasions in his hectic past. He dove into a falling roll, ending up at the feet of the negro thug, who didn't even have time to be startled before the heel of Simon's left foot pumped upward in a swift punching motion, and the negro staggered back, the knife falling to the carpeted floor, both hands clutching his groin.
Manzetti made a headlong dash for the door as Simon sprang to his feet and whirled to face his second attacker, offering only his left-side body profile for the on-coming blade. The second thug was white. Manzetti was nothing if not an equal opportunities employer, thought Simon, and laughed out loud. The thug blinked in surprise and got the sole of his opponent's left foot square in the middle of his chest. The

next kick tore the knife from his grasp and fractured his wrist. Howling in pain, he fled, the black one close on his heels.

So much for the black and white minstrel show. Simon looked around. The living room was a wreck but at least he had acquired a pair of great knives. He would have to have a talk with the night porter about letting strange men into his rooms.

The nursing home in Gupkar Road was still there, still the same. The chinars were taller now and thick, shady plane trees surrounding the wood and brick house, with its painted verandas and quiet gardens. Behind it, nearly one thousand feet up, the Shankacharya dome crowns the Takht-i-Suleiman, a Hindu temple on a Muslim hill.

"I was born here," said Alison Fuchs to Scott Brinkley, outside the nursing home. "Hairy as a monkey I was too. The doctor who delivered me was pleased at my prompt arrival as he was going to dinner with his parents and didn't want to be late. A year later we left Kashmir and India for good. In dreams I remember a cot in a sunny garden, high fir trees and distant mountains, butterflies in the tall flowers round the town of Gulmarg. Of course, I was far too small to have really taken all that in. These were dreams created from tiny black and white photos. I caught whooping cough at six weeks and almost died."

Scott looked her pointedly up and down. "It would have been a tragedy."

Kashmir, at India's northern tip and ringed by the Karakoram and the Himalayan mountain ranges, is sometimes said to be this globe's most pretty plot. The capital is Srinagar, sprawling comfortably among the Dal and Nagin lakes, criss-crossed with treelined canals and surrounded by paddy fields. The Jhelum river loops through the city.

From the upper deck of their houseboat, Scott and Alison could see the two hills that dominate Srinagar: Takht-i-Suleiman, Solomon's Throne, thickly wooded and deceptively steep and Hari Parbat, the Green Hill, its face turned south to the city and its tail trailing into the lotus fields. The Mogul king, Akhbar the Great, built a fort on it which was virtually impregnable.

The three royal gardens, Cheshmashahi, Nishat, and Shalimar, are spread almost side by side. Above the Cheshmashahi, the Royal Spring, stands Pari Mahal, the ruins of a palace built centuries ago for a royal astrologer.

"It used to be full of snakes."

Scott glanced at the floor around them. "Used to be?"

"Used to be."

She knelt down in front of him. "See, it's perfectly clean and tidy now." She unzipped his fly.

"You're incredible," he moaned, thrusting his erection into her mouth.

Alison was right. It had been cleaned, restored, and the gardens planted. But few people went there anymore, making it the perfect semi-public place for a little fellatio.

With a sharp jab - jab - jab of his hips, Scott spurted his jism into her snug throat, knowing it wouldn't stay there. She turned her head away and spat out the offending material. It was a source of wonder to Scott that someone who so enjoyed giving head was unwilling to swallow come. As he watched her hawk and spit, he promised himself one day to make her swallow it, one day very soon. The flash fantasy renewed his hard-on.

Alison giggled. "What a dirty mind you have," she said, in such a way that it seemed she had just read his thoughts. In Kashmir that didn't seem such a crazy idea. Scott blushed.

"Well, now," she said, stroking the underside of the purple glans with one provocative fingertip, "we can't have you walking around Srinagar like that, and it's far too big to tuck away in your pants."

He laughed. "It's a problem, isn't it? Why don't you stand up?"

Alison felt her flesh twitching behind the crotch of her knickers as she obeyed him. He took hold of her hand and pulled her across the room. Her legs went weak. She felt Scott's mouth on hers. Her lips parted. At that moment she felt his hand come up beneath her cotton frock, heard the rasp of the material giving way, and then the warmth of his large hand between her thighs, tearing apart the white cotton briefs to stroke her mound of Venus.

She put her arms round his neck. He placed both his hands beneath her bare buttocks and lifted. She gave a little hop and wrapped her long legs about his waist. His tongue was in her mouth and she sucked it. He gave a sharp jerk of his hips and Alison felt something hot and hard slide against her upper leg. She let her left hand drop from his neck, reaching down to guide him into her wide-open, juiced-up vulva. Unable to see it, she imagined that the pole of hard muscle her hand had just closed around was even more enormous and blood gorged than she knew it to be. It pulsed in her hand like a living animal, and almost weeping in her need she pushed the swollen triangular crown up against the entrance to her vaginal passage.

Scott thrust himself inside with a grunt of pleasure, answered by her with a shuddering gasp. Now they rested for a moment, panting, leaning on the wall, until Alison murmured in his ear: "Ram your thing into me, darling, ram it right up. Hurt me a little, make me cry."

He did just that. He pounded her into the wall with a whole quiver-full of arrow-sharp thrusts that brought her to the arm-flailing, heel-drumming, mewling, hair-tearing edge of orgasm, needing only the scalding rush of his ejaculation to send her over. He knew that and held back for as long as he possibly could.

"Come, you bastard," she shrieked.

Scott surrendered to the inevitable with a heave of his loins that would have thrown her off his organ but for the wall. Alison felt like a salmon swimming against a floodtide as his seed fountained into her womb.

"OOOOOOOOHHHHHHHRRRRRRRRRAAAAAAAAAAAAAA"

They clung together in silence, shuddering, for several minutes before Alison gently broke the spell:

"Oh, darling, that was wonderful." She unlocked her legs from the vice-like grip her taut thigh and calf muscles had held his waist in and lowered her feet to the floor. She kissed his cheek. "My feet may be on the ground but my head is definitely in the clouds. I'm tingling all over." She kissed him again.

Scott nuzzled her ear, capturing the delicate lobe between his teeth. "I love you, Alison."

"I love you."

They hugged, then set about tidying themselves up.

"My God," she cried, mock-serious, "just look at the state I'm in. I bet I'll be bruised black and blue by tomorrow."

He laughed.

"You beast, you absolute beast," she declaimed grandly. "How dare you laugh at the poor innocent maiden you have just this moment ravished in the most brutal way." She picked up her torn panties off the floor. "Look, look. You animal, sir! You vile, debauched cad."

Scott, getting into the spirit of things, assumed the bored, limp-wristed pose of a Regency dandy, flicking a handkerchief at the dust motes hanging motionless in the still air.

"My dear girl. Flattery will get you nowhere."

"Oh, yeah? What if I said you should take up acting again?"

He smiled bleakly. "Bad dreams. Too many bad dreams."

"You're thinking of Cherie Halvinne. I'm sorry."

"No matter."

The setting sun had turned the plaster colonnades to apricot. From the king's turret they could see Gulmarg in the Pir Panjal. The room was like a gazebo, octagonal, with windows to the floor. Outside, the sheer walls fell away to the valley where the lights were coming on in the city. Almost at their feet, one thousand feet below, the candles were being lit in the Jama Masjid mosque, the biggest in Kashmir, and the muezzin called the faithful to evening prayers.

From the five terraces of Pari Mahal you can see the Nagin lake and the floating gardens, the Dal lake, its edges stapled with houseboats, and the Char Chinar, a tiny square island with the four plane trees which give it its name at each corner.

"Let's go back. Anya will be waiting."

Beautiful, copper-skinned Anya was almost sixteen and soon to be wed. She was the adopted daughter of Abdul Qadir, the owner of the houseboat Scott and Alison were renting.

It was called the Flower of Asia and was one of the oldest and grandest of the many houseboats on the Dal lake. It was moored behind Nehru Park, a small pleasure garden, in a bed of water lilies. The boats were wedged into position with long poles, and only very seldom could one feel the slightest motion of the lake.

Every flat surface, every corner, every handle, rail and frame of the Flower of Asia was carved. The ceilings were cut in a traditional geometric pattern of interlocking circles and stars. The chests and tables were walnut, carved with lilies, lotus blossom, birds and Chinar leaves.

Anya's main function was as cook and general servant, but whenever Scott or Alison were feeling sexually jaded, Anya would be invited to join them in the bedroom. She was a virgin so Scott used her only orally and anally, and Alison was careful when touching-up Anya not to puncture the girl's hymen.

And the girl went to the temple with her husband-to-be, still a 'virgin'.

And Alison and Scott went home.

Susie Watkins Duparier got away with the murder of her husband, Roman. There was, officially, no crime committed, and, therefore, no need for any punishment. There was no trial, no public scandal. Jean-Claude had seen to that.

Thirty-six hours after Roman's death, his body was on the Duparier Learjet bound for New York. His father sat alone with the coffin in the curtained-off section, drafting a new will in longhand on a yellow legal pad. Everything Jean-Claude now owned or ever would own was to go to his beloved Roxanne. It was bad enough that his daughter should think that Roman had killed himself. How much worse would her pain be should she ever discover that her father had conspired to keep the full horror from her?

Susie sat alone beyond the curtain. Jean-Claude wondered if he would ever be free of her, or ever want to be.

"So Michael Cord wasn't acting alone."

William Darrow looked up from the report at the grim face of Simon Barnes.

"No, sir. I'm convinced the real targets were Lyssette and myself."

"Then Raoul Julian is still alive."

Barnes nodded. "The explosion at Bogota Airport that destroyed Julian's private Learjet on the tarmac must have been a real eyebrow sizzler."

"Extensive plastic surgery?"

"Very. I was as close to him as I am to you, and never realised. He has a whole new identity to go with his new face. Raoul Julian is now Rico Manzetti."

CARIBBEAN RETURN

Two days after reporting to Darrow on the Cord killings, Barnes woke in his room at the St. Regis hotel. It was the morning after his arrival in New York. He shook the woolliness of jet-lag out of his head and jumped impatiently out of bed.

Simon walked over to the window and pulled back the curtains. His room faced north, towards Harlem. He gazed for a moment towards the northern horizon. It was going to be a beautiful day. He smiled to himself and shrugged his shoulders, walking quickly to the telephone.

"St. Regis Hotel. Good morning," said a female voice.

"Room service," said Barnes.

"Room service? I'd like to order breakfast. An ice-cold carafe of freshly-squeezed orange juice, two eggs, over-easy, with ham, wheat toast, and lots of black coffee."

He gave himself a freezing cold shower while he waited for it to arrive. When it did, he sat down to it at a table by the window. He was ravenous. Over the coffee, he pulled out a book William Darrow had given him to study, in particular the section on Haiti. The book was The Travellers Tree by Patrick Leigh Fermor.

"It's by a guy who knows what he's talking about," Darrow had told him, back in London. "And don't forget that he was writing about what was happening in Haiti in 1950. This isn't medieval tall tales. Voodoo is real. It works."

'The next step,' he read, 'is the invocation of evil denizens of the Voodoo pantheon, such as Don Pedro, Kitta, Mondongue, Bakalou and Zandor, for harmful purposes: for the reputed practice of turning people into zombies in order to use them as slaves; the casting of maleficent spells and the destruction of enemies. The effects of the spell, of which the outward form may be an image of the separate use of poison... These secret societies of wizards are the mysterious groups whose gods demand, instead of a chicken, pigeon, goat, dog or pig, as in the normal rites of Voodoo, the sacrifice of a "cabrit sans cornes". This hornless goat, of course, means a human being...'

Simon turned over the pages, occasional passages combining to form an extra-ordinary picture in his mind of a dark religion and its terrible rites.

'...Slowly, out of the turmoil and the smoke and the shattering noise of the drums, which, for a time, drove everything except their impact from the mind, the details began to detach themselves... Backwards and forwards, very slowly, the dancers shuffled, and at each step their chins shot out and their buttocks jerked upwards, while their shoulders shook in double time. Their eyes were half-closed and from their mouths came again and again the same incomprehensible words, the same short line of chanted song, repeated after each iteration, half an octave lower. At a change in the beat of the drums, they straightened their bodies, and flinging their arms in the air while their eyes rolled upwards, spun round and round...

'...At the edge of the crowd we came upon a little hut, scarcely larger than a dog kennel: "Le caye Zombi". The beam of a torch revealed a black cross inside and some rags and chains and shackles and whips: adjuncts used at the Ghede ceremonies, which Haitian ethnologists connect with the rejuvenation rites of Osiris recorded in the Book of the Dead...'

As Simon continued to read, he could not help but remember, like a tolling bell, one particular fact from Darrow's briefing in London: that Aubrey Caligari, a top OSS agent in Occupied France during the War, and one of the founding fathers of the CIA, was born in Port-au-Prince, the dingy capital of Haiti.

'...A fire was burning, in which two sabres and a large pair of pincers were standing, their lower parts red with the heat: "le Feu Marinette", dedicated to a goddess who is the evil obverse of the bland and amorous Maitresse Erzulie Freda Dahomin, the Goddess of Love. Beyond, with its base held fast in a socket of stone stood a large black wooden cross. A white death's head was painted near the base, and over the crossbar were pulled the sleeves of a very old morning coat. Here also rested the brim of a battered bowler hat, through the torn crown of which the top of the cross projected. This totem, with which every peristyle must be equipped, is not a lampoon of the central event of the Christian faith, but represents the God of the Cemeteries and the Chief of the Legion of the Dead, Baron Samedi. The Baron is paramount in all matters immediately beyond the grave. He is Cerberus and Charon as well as Aeacus, Rhadamanthus and Pluto...

'...The drums changed and the Houngenikon came dancing onto

the floor, holding a vessel filled with some burning liquid from which sprang blue and yellow flames. As he circled the pillar and spilt three flaming libations, his steps began to falter. Then, lurching backwards with the same symptoms of delirium that had manifested themselves in his forerunner, he flung down the whole blazing mess. The houncis caught him as he reeled, and removed his sandals and rolled his trousers up, while the kerchief fell from his head and laid bare his young woolly skull. The other houncis knelt to put their hands in the flaming mud, and rub it over their hands and elbows and faces. The Houngan's bell and "acon" rattled officiously and the young priest was left by himself, reeling and colliding against the pillar, helplessly catapulting across the floor, and falling among the drums. His eyes were shut, his forehead screwed up and his chin hung loose. Then, as though an invisible fist had dealt him a heavy blow, he fell to the ground and lay there, with his head stretching backwards in a rictus of anguish until the tendons of his neck and shoulders projected like roots. One hand clutched at the other elbow behind his hollowed back as though he were striving to break his own arm, and his whole body, from which the sweat was streaming, trembled and shuddered like a dog in a dream. Only the whites of his eyes were visible as, although his eye-sockets were now wide open, the pupils had vanished under the lids. Foam collected on his lips...

'...Now the Houngan, dancing a slow step and brandishing a cutlass, advanced from the fireside, flinging the weapon again and again into the air, and catching it by the hilt. In a few minutes he was holding it by the blunted end of the blade. Dancing slowly towards him, the Houngenikon reached out and grasped the hilt. The priest retired, and the young man, twirling and leaping, spun from side to side of the "tonnelle". The ring of spectators rocked backwards as he bore down upon them whirling the blade over his head, with the gaps in his bared teeth lending to his mandrill face a still more feral aspect. The "tonnelle" was filled for a few seconds with genuine and unmitigated terror. The singing had turned to a universal howl and the drummers, rolling and lolling with the furious and invisible motion of their hands, were lost in a transport of noise. Flinging back his head, the novice drove the blunt end of the cutlass into his stomach. His knees sagged, and his head fell forward...'

Simon stopped reading. He shuddered. He had had quite enough of that, thank you. His breakfast finished, he dressed and went out.

He spent the morning on Fifth Avenue and Broadway, wandering aimlessly like a typical tourist, gazing into the store windows and watching the passing crowds. He had a typical American meal at a diner on Lexington Avenue and then took a cab downtown to police headquarters, where he was due to meet UNSIS agent Roger Black at 2.30.

Together they went over the reports of the US Coastguard Service, the US Customs Service, the FBI, Naval Intelligence, the CIA and the United Nations Secret Intelligence Service, on the Caribbean operations of Aubrey Caligari's criminal organisation, SPEAR, the Special Program for Extortion, Anarchy and Revenge.

As a long-time resident of Jamaica, Simon was amazed to read the full extent of the criminal activities that had been going on under his very nose. It was like some monstrous octopus, extending its tentacles from Haiti to all the islands of the region.

"There's so much loose money sloshing around as a result of the trade in heroin and cocaine that even your innocent Jamaicans can't help but be corrupted by it all," said Black.

Simon nodded, silently. Just one more reason to get even with Raoul Julian.

VOODOO

In his life Simon Barnes had, from time to time, found it necessary to re-invent certain details about his past. The scale of invention depended on who was the recipient of the information. The truth, after all, was equally open to interpretation.

His mother was certainly not English, perhaps. At some point in later life she had acquired a title, though whether by marriage or simple affectation was a matter of conjecture to her neighbours in Monte Carlo, where Simon was born. His father was English, which gave Simon both British and Monegasque citizenship. That was all he gave to the new-born baby, having quit the domestic scene some months before Simon's arrival. It was the purest chance that, after leaving the Army, Simon should choose to live in the West Indies and thereby discover his father to be a hotel owner in Haiti. In the few years they had together before his father's murder by the Tonton Macoute, Simon came to love and respect the man. If only he could have got as close to his mother, but he hardly ever saw her, even as a small child, and when he was enrolled in the local Jesuit College years went by without a sighting. At least the austere education provided by the Society of Jesus prepared him for life in the Army. Even on the day of his mother's death, as he stood by the hotel swimming pool, looking up at the fantastic tracery of woodwork against the palms and the inky storm clouds blowing over Kenscoff, he remembered a line of Latin he learnt from the Jesuits: 'Exegi monumentum aere perennius.'

One summer afternoon when he was seventeen, and at a loose end between the finish of college and the start of his army career in the autumn, he managed to bluff his way into the Casino. In the space of an hour and a half he won a thousand pounds and lost his virginity. This latter act took place in a bedroom of the Hotel de Paris, and his seducer was a woman at least fifty years older. They had met in the Casino and seeing his winning streak she had begun to lay her chips on the same numbers. Leaving together, she invited him back to her rooms for tea and he agreed, trying desperately to look and sound older and more sophisticated.

He could now no longer remember the chain of events that led from the tea table to that first adult, open-mouthed kiss on the sofa. She was married to a director of the Banque de l'Indochina. He was in Saigon visiting his Chinese mistress. There was little more conversation after that first long kiss. She soon led him to her small white bedroom and her big white bed with carved pineapple bedposts.

A strange thrill ran through the young Simon. With the overweening hubris of someone so young and inexperienced, he had in theory no desire to fuck a woman of nearly seventy, however beautiful and well-preserved she was. And she was. Her name was Nathalie and she was tall and shapely, with white hair. Yet the beauty of her fine, haughty face was unobscured by age. The wrinkles were scarcely visible. And her wide blue eyes tantalised him as she took his hand and guided him across the thickly-piled white carpet to the bed. He sat down and she started to undress.

He was surprised to discover that she wore no underclothes, apart from a suspender belt to hold up her stockings. Her dress slid to the floor and she stepped out of it to hold herself proud and erect in her nakedness. Her figure had seemed so trim Simon had assumed she was tightly corseted, but now he saw that her muscles were still taut. From a distance it was the body of a woman of forty or so, but up close he could see the small wrinkles and puckers in the skin, which was without the elasticity of youth. Still she had strong ballerina's legs, and the hair under her arms was dark, as was the thick bush between her thighs.

Then she took him in her arms in a long embrace and slowly but expertly undressed him, kissing his shoulders and chest, her hands feeling him all over. They lay down on the bed and he touched her breasts, her belly, finally daring to reach between her legs, letting his hand linger on her cunt. His fingers probed inside, finding her moist, open, willing.

Yet an odd thing happened as they lay on the bed. She was finding it difficult to keep him erect long enough to allow penetration. Her fingers were having no success on him, even her lips and tongue had failed to sustain stiffness in his unused cock, when into the room suddenly, from the harbour below the hill, flew a seagull. Nathalie cried out. It was she who was afraid now. Simon put out a hand to reassure her as the white-winged bird flapped around, and found himself as firm as a man and took her with such ease and confidence it was as though they had been lovers for a long time.

As if in a dream he lay on top of her, feeling his skin against hers, to achieve that final intimacy that only belongs to two naked bodies, his hard prick sinking into a honeyed cunt whose elasticity was undiminished by age, and held him close. With his arms round her, and kissing her full mouth, he fucked her slowly, then fast, and felt her body vibrate with excitement and grow warm in his embrace, until, after what seemed like hours of blissful motion, she came with one loud cry. His own pleasure had been so attached to hers, growing out of it naturally, that when her orgasm was over he came at once with a wet sweetness so overwhelming he thought he would die.

But what had actually happened was the realisation of how good it was to be alive, and soon his cock was hard with mischievous anticipation. When she rolled onto her stomach he was on her again, grasping her hips in both hands and rushing into her. She gasped with surprise, then gave her provocative laugh, while his organ bounded joyously in and out of her wide-open, deep, liquid cunt. Now up on all fours, her long, pendulous, full breasts hung forward at a strange angle. He groped them greedily as he humped away at her, his groin slapping rhythmically against her backside. The heavy smell of musky perfume and sweat which surrounded her swept over him in an intoxicating wave as he slithered back and forth in the silky envelope of her vagina.

Then he was on top of her again, sucking at her nipples while his hands were dug into her fleshy buttocks, and his throbbing prick, with its spade-like glans, burrowed ever deeper into her sweet, earthy garden to plant its seed there. Each thrust of his hips made her thrill and shudder in time to his rhythm, and soon she was panting, her eyes opening wider at the shock of each heaving motion. Her long nails clawed his back while his kisses on her breasts turned to savage bites. She came with a massive, tumultuous shaking beneath him that took hold of his cock and gripped it so tightly that he ejaculated in a violent, totally out of control spasm that splashed over her thighs and filled her cunt full.

It turned out to be the only love affair in his life which ended without pain or regret. It was in another casino, in Port-au-Prince, that he met the wife of the Colombian ambassador and began an affair that would lead to murder...

One night Simon felt that old urge to live dangerously which he thought his time in the Special Air Service had cured him of, so he took himself off to the casino. In those days, before Baby Doc Duvalier was overthrown, there were enough tourists to keep three roulette tables busy. He could hear the music from the night-club below, and occasionally a woman in evening dress, tired of dancing, would bring her partner to the tables. He thought Haitian women were the most beautiful in the world, and there were faces and figures there which would have made a fortune for their owners in any Western capital.

He had been playing for several minutes when he caught the eye of a young European woman across the table. She smiled and began to follow his stakes, saying a word to her companion, a huge man with an enormous cigar, who fed her with playing chips and never played himself. It was as though they were dancing in step, the girl and Simon, as in a Malayan ron-ron, without touching, and he was content that she was pretty. He remembered Monte Carlo. Perhaps the big man was a banker with an Oriental mistress too?

Soon he tired of their dance and left the table to cash his chips. When he turned away from the cashier behind his grille, the girl was standing behind him, smiling.

"Hello, I'm Lyssette Julian," she said lightly, holding out her hand.

"Simon Barnes," he answered, feeling her cool fingers grip his hand.

She went by him to get her money. She was quite tall, voluptuous, blonde, with pale blue eyes and an engaging wiggle. She looked, he thought wrongly, German, and he guessed she belonged to the large German community in South America, for he had noticed her wedding ring and recognised the surname.

"Where's your husband?" he asked.

"In the car outside, waiting for me," she said, pointing.

It was a large black limousine with tinted windows and C.D. plates. The pendant on the bonnet sported the Colombian flag.

"When can I see you again?"

"Here," she said. "Outside in the car park. I can't come to your hotel."

"Tomorrow night?'

"Yes, if you like. At ten." She looked over her shoulder at the car. "Very good. Very good. Now I must go. Raoul is waiting. Good-bye."

He watched her get in the back beside her monstrous husband, and the limo glide away into the darkness of a humid Haitian night. She was driving that same car the next night. He was nearly half an hour late when he spotted the C.D. plate.

"Get in," she whispered, opening the car door for him. "I nearly gave up on you."

"I'm sorry," said Simon. "How long can you stay?"

"I must be back by dawn."

She backed the limo out of the casino parking lot.

"Where are we going?" asked Simon, a little anxiously.

She laughed.

"You do ask a lot of questions. Don't worry, I have done this before."

Ahead of them the port lay in a wash of floodlights. A cargo ship was being unloaded. There was a long procession of bowed figures under sacks. Lyssette spun the steering wheel and the car swung round in a half-circle and pulled up in a patch of deep shadow close to the white statue of Columbus. She switched off the motor and the lights.

"Lyssette."

He put his hand on her knee. The skin felt cold; she wore no stockings.

"And no knickers," she giggled, reading his mind.

She turned to him and they kissed, then she unzipped his fly and went down on him. When he was hard she stopped sucking and took a packet of condoms from her handbag.

"Please don't be offended, Simon. As you know, AIDS is endemic on this island, and besides, I don't want to get pregnant."

"Would that be such a bad thing?"

She smiled.

"It would be difficult to convince my husband the child was his."

"Because it wouldn't be black?"

She fitted the condom over his straining erection and said nothing.

"Well?" he asked.

"No."

"You use condoms with your husband?"

"He hates the things."

"I'm not too keen on them myself," said Simon.

"You don't understand how it is between Raoul and me," she said quietly.

166

"Tell me, Lyssette."

"The English are so naive. The condom is to protect you, not me. Raoul is into sodomy in a big way. Men, women, children, animals, He's a madman. He thinks he's the reincarnation of Baron Samedi."

"Good God, you mean he buggers you. His wife?"

She gave him an icy smile.

"It must be wonderful to be so innocent. Buggery is the least of the things he's done to me and made me do."

She glanced at his jutting, rubber-sheathed cock and gave a bitter little laugh, devoid of genuine humour.

"Look, Simon, it's waving at me."

He pulled her body out from under the steering wheel and thrust her across his thighs, scraping her leg on the dashboard so that she gave a cry of pain.

"Sorry."

"Don't be," she murmured, her lips against his neck.

Hunching her skirt up around her waist and exposing her bare arse, she squatted over his cock, and holding it steady in one hand, lowered herself onto it, fitting her ripe buttocks into his groin, the back of her neck against his mouth now and her bare legs spread-eagled, one across the dashboard, the other out the window. When she came, she shivered and her hand shot out and fell on the car horn, setting it wailing. The noise disturbed Simon. He didn't come.

He realised he had slept a moment, woken, and discovered her sleeping. They were still sitting in the same cramped position. He looked at his watch. It was not yet midnight. His leg hurt. Moving it woke her. They fucked a second time, while the cranes swung over the cargo ship in the harbour, and the long procession of workers passed from boat to warehouse, bent under their cowls of sacks like monks. This time the friction of their awkward copulation was enough to make him ejaculate into the sheath, and this time she gave a little squeal and thrust her fist against her mouth to smother it. Her body lost its tenseness. She was like a tired child resting on his knees.

"What is it?" she asked, after a long silence.

"I was just wondering when I shall see you again."

"Why, tomorrow, of course. Same time, same place."

She was suddenly cheerful, and brisk, showing well-practised skill in removing the condom without spilling a drop of his jism, and carefully wrapping it in a tissue before dropping it out the window, then using other tissues to wipe him and herself clean.

"It wasn't exactly an ideal bed," said Simon.

"We'll get in the back of the car tomorrow."

So the affair began, and continued, with minor variations. During her period she would treat him to a succession of blow and hand jobs, still using a condom, and once offered him the choice of buggery as an alternative, which he refused. For fucking, the back seat was better, but Simon still longed to make love with her in a bed. He kept badgering Lyssette until, with the help of a trusted woman-friend and the convenient absence of Raoul, in Colombia for consultations with his masters, they spent a weekend of frantic, ecstatic lovemaking at the woman's villa at Cap Haitien.

It was there that Simon finally persuaded her to dispense with the condoms and go on the Pill.

"But what if I do have AIDS?" she asked.

"I'll take that chance," he said. "Damn it, Lyssette, sex has always been dangerous. That's why it's so exciting. There's never been a time when sex and death haven't gone hand in hand. Now it's AIDS. This time last century syphilis was the great killer, and throughout history women have died because of back street abortions. So-called, simple, childbirth, has been the biggest killer of all. Has all that ever stopped men and women falling in love?"

"You fool," she said with a sad smile, shaking her head in resignation.

"What greater gift can I give you than my life? Fuck AIDS. T.S. Eliot said it best: 'The awful daring of a moment's surrender. By this, and only this, we have existed'."

Lyssette wiped away a tear.

"Bastard. I bet you say that to all the girls."

She lay on the edge of the bed and pulled him towards her, drawing up her knees.

"Let's do it," she gasped. "Let's do it quickly."

The sun had not yet risen as they drove back to Port-au-Prince from their love-nest at Cap Haitien. The lightning began to play over the slopes of Petionville. Sometimes a fork would quiver in the ground long enough to carve out of the dark the shape of a palm tree or the corner of a roof. The air was full of the coming rainstorm, and the low hum sounded to Simon like voices chanting.

LADY ELIZABETH GOES TO HOLLYWOOD

Malibu is a section of beach-front and backup property not very different from many other such developments along the vast and contrasting coastline of the United States. Malibu's houses, at least the ones on the beach, looked rather shabby from the outside; closed, as they were, against the Pacific Coast Highway's heavy traffic, by solid walls and thick front doors, their wood and paint work weathered within a year by the action of salt spray and wind off the ocean. Malibu had far more impressive houses in the Colony, on the cliffs, and back in the hills, where the views of the ocean were panoramic.

Malibu is also a millionaire ghetto, though the laid-back style of the place might fool the unwary. To own a strip of prime Southern Californian beach cost the proverbial arm and a leg, but the undisclosed refund of kudos from the movers and shakers of the LA-by-the-seaside-elite always made the purchase worthwhile.

Brett Sagan owned his piece of beach, on which the joggers could cross near the tide-line and lovers could stroll on hand in hand, but no one could make camp, or make love, on the warm white sand rising back up to what was the true front of his house, he felt, the deep redwood sun deck. Not that he had ever chased any walker or jogger or lover off his private beach in the thirteen years he had owned the property.

Sagan was fifty-nine; fifty-five with the aid of a long-ago doctored birth certificate. He was in pretty good shape, though he wore a 'rug' on his balding dome and personality lifts in his shoes. He had been a star since the sword and sandal epic, 'Prince of the Barbarians', in which he had played the Emperor Hadrian, with the help of considerable make-up since he had only been nineteen at the time.

He was a matinee idol in the days when that meant two majors a year, and the popularity he earned then had carried him over into today's industry where television and TV stars dominated Hollywood, where most of the movies that got made had 'pre-sold' to HBO, or some other cable channel or video offshoot, stamped all over them. Most of these pictures featured the TV-transfers: women like life-size Barbie dolls, and just as plastic, and leading men with narrow waists and careful hairdos, who ran around a lot and said things like: "Yeah" and "Right". There were only two or three major films out of Hollywood each year for all the stars to compete for. The other pictures were oriented to the needs of the sex, drugs and rock-n-roll audience; full of teen-mag idols no one had ever heard of and would never hear of again.

In this new Hollywood, Brett Sagan was slipping badly. The few really big, old-style features were being packaged by agents or indeed producers with tax shelter money, and they all thought him a bad risk because of the poor response to his last two films, which he had directed as well as starred in.

It should have been three films. Back in '84, Robert Gideon had offered him an incredible comeback opportunity: Hollywood's first major-studio, big-budget, big-name hard-core-porno-flick. Based on a literary novel, and with a screenplay authored by an Academy-Award-winner, this audacious project couldn't fail, said Gideon. Everyone concerned with the movie would be seen as pioneers for the future and not pornographers, he assured Sagan. Hadn't all the taboos over explicit violence in the movies been broken down in recent years? What was left but the sexual taboos?

So the screw was tightened, the weight of argument built up, and Sagan soon exhausted his list of objections. Look at how much money 'Deep Throat' made. That was Gideon's killer punch. With double his normal salary as star and director, plus a percentage of the gross, Sagan could make upwards of ten million dollars.

There were two things necessary to the success of the project: a leading actress who was willing, and getting the hard-core scenes in the can as quickly as possible and locked away from prying eyes.

But Sagan now considered that there had been a jinx on the production from the start. Getting the two fuck and suck scenes he had with Madelaine Sale done was as far as the film went before everything fell apart. Madelaine told him later that some friends of hers had recovered the unedited footage from the studio's vaults at the height of the confusion following Gideon's arrest, and that it had been destroyed.

Now Sandor Michaels, the last survivor of the old administration, had convinced the new head honcho at Sparta to revive the project. Sagan knew it was madness to hit that old dirt road again, but the money they were offering him this time out was twice what he had been promised before. And he did need a big hit, even one like this...

Cap Camerat was a rocky outcrop on the French Riviera, a headland half an hour by road from St. Tropez. A white-painted lighthouse clung to the tip of the cliff. Further along the coast, and clinging to the steep hillside, was a cluster of villas constructed of brick, concrete and wood. It was to one of these that the former Lady Elizabeth Karl repaired in the late spring of that year, to recover from a traumatic divorce.

She was a long-legged blonde with green eyes, a thin, hollow-cheeked face, and a very wide, thin-lipped, sensual mouth. She claimed to be thirty. She had been saying that for several years. Her best features were her boobs, two taut, perfect orbs of tanned flesh set high on her ribcage, and her buttocks, tight round buns with a deep, inviting cleft.

Elizabeth had had little contact with ordinary people. Her kind of celebrity only attracted gawpers, con men, sexual exploiters. Women were always on their guard against Elizabeth. They distrusted her, and they were jealous of the effect she had on their men, so she had no close girlfriends to jolly her out of her blue funk. Fraser Karl had tried everything to keep her. He had soothed and flattered the cock sucking bitch, promising to give up Monique, but nothing worked.

At Nice airport Elizabeth went to the Hertz stand and hired a car with Fraser's gold American Express card. Soon she was driving beyond the palm trees of the airport and out under the Mediterranean sun.

The villa was also being paid for by Fraser. From inside the house the view of the Med was all but obscured by the mass of greenery hanging over the glass doors from the roof. They made the sunlight that filtered in green. But outside on the balcony it was a different story. The brilliant Provencal sun beat down on her as she watched the white-sailed yachts glide over the calm azure surface of the sea. It was the first moment for a very long time that Elizabeth had felt at peace.

Only a few of the neighbouring villas were occupied so she was free to come and go in a wonderfully new world of near solitude she had never known before. Every morning she would sunbathe nude on her private section of the sand in front of the villa, but the sea was still too cold to swim in.

The days passed, her tan deepened, the memories faded, the wounds began to heal over. She even felt a little guilty about the ease of it, which was a new sensation in itself.

Then she had an idea. She would go to Hollywood and try her luck in the movies. She had contacts there to help her get started, and one in particular, Veronica Capital, who was now a big name in Tinseltown. Of course, they had not seen each other in years, but Veronica would be sure to help out, give Elizabeth the introductions an eager starlet needed to get on.

It was raining in Paradise, the first for many weeks. To celebrate, if that was the right word, Jackson LeMay got in his BMW and drove down the canyon road onto Sunset and turned west towards Beverly Hills. He had decided to pay a visit to Rudy Gioberti, the boss of Sparta Studios in Burbank, to view his extensive collection of porno flicks and listen to more of Rudy's ramblings about making a "frigging fortune" from the latest of Jackson's novels.

He leaned on the brake as the rush of traffic suddenly slowed in front, backing up for two blocks from San Vicente. Then the traffic moved off again and he moved with it, a little more cautiously this time. He had only been in LA for eighteen months and was not used to driving slowly in rain, as most of the Angelinos did.

It was always nice to get out of that snarl-up into Beverly Hills, and even more with the rain on the palm trees, the shrubs, the flower beds and the manicured lawns. Rain or no, the sprinklers kept on working, so did the Mex and Jap gardeners. Beverly Hills, in the flat-lands between Sunset and Santa Monica Boulevards, was a sweet-smelling, peaceful oasis where the rich felt safe.

He turned onto Bedford, going south, and saw her, a voluptuous figure in a bright-crimson slicker, even before he had straightened the BMW's wheels. She was almost at the end of the long, downward-sloping, palm-lined street.

He felt the quick tingle of desire he always felt whenever he set eyes on her, but the pleasure this time was mingled with pain. What the fuck was the cunt doing on the street where Rudy lived? She had never met him, Jackson had seen to that, but she did not look up, only pulled the matching crimson rain hat low against the driving spray. He went shooting by and in the mirror saw her cross the street to where she had parked her Jag. At the corner he did a U-turn and came back up the street. He looked across from her car to Rudi's incredible brick castle with its pro-standard tennis court in back, and its swimming pool, jacuzzi, hot tub and other cunt bait, and he knew, with a sick feeling in the pit of his stomach, that Veronica Capital had gone for the bait. He had a flash of Gioberti's infamous ten-inch prick sliding into her from behind, and Veronica wriggling, loving it.

No, no, no. There must be some innocent reason for his Ronnie to be on this street. He laid into the horn, stopping beside the Jag. She turned, saw him, smiled her big, wide, happy-to-see-you-my-darling smile through the glass at him, and he knew she would have a simple explanation.

She got out of her car and into his. She kissed him, her pretty face all shiny and flushed with the rain, her full, pink lips parted, pushing the hat back off her head, and into the back of the BMW without caring, shaking out her long, dark, almost-black hair and laughing, saying: "We've got to stop meeting like this honey."

Laughing, she peeled off the crimson slicker like someone peeling the skin off some lush, bursting-with-sweetness fruit. Her melon-sized breasts, of course, but his lusting gaze also took in the belly and thighs pushing against the clinging satin cloth of her tight skirt, and the long legs encased in shiny pantyhose. He could smell her perfume, it was strong, but underneath was the other smell, the sex smell, the smell of a woman who had just been well and truly fucked.

He couldn't understand what she thought she was playing at. It was as if the last eight years of her life had never happened. Sure, he realised what a shock it had been to be written out of the top prime-time soap, 'Houston', at the end of last season, but this was madness. He had been glad when she dropped her Little-Miss-Perfect, butter-wouldn't-melt-in-her-mouth act, which he had always thought was silly, considering what her pre-'Houston' reputation in Sin City had been. She was getting that rep again.

"Want to eat?" he asked, with no appetite.

She checked her watch. Nodded.

"There's a cattle call in Burbank I was supposed to go to. I'll give it a miss. Yes, let's have lunch, honey."

"Who's running this cattle call?"

"A guy called Dickey."

"Walter Dickey? With the jail bait daughter?"

"I guess so, honey. You seem to know more about the guy than I do."

"By reputation only. I hear he casts small parts on his office couch."

She giggled sexily. "Who doesn't in this town?"

"Well, if you take that attitude, why not hit the orgy scene, regain the anytime, anywhere, anyhow rep you used to have. Become a party girl and you'll soon find yourself giving head for a walk-on in a daytime drama."

Her smile faltered. "What's the matter?"

He jerked a thumb at Gioberti's house.

"You don't seriously believe I've been screwing Rudy?"

"I don't want to."

"Then that's all right then," she chirped, smiling brightly.

Grimly he worked the gearshift and steered the BMW back along Bedford, feeling the anger welling up in him. The bitch was going to bluff it out.

After the two roast beef on whole wheat at a ritzy delicatessen they often visited, she took his hand. The delicate fingers circled his wrist, stroked it sensually. He felt the erotic power in those fingers that had done so many wild, orgasmic things to him, and he knew he was beaten. He knew Gioberti had just had her but he still wanted her himself.

"Got an hour for Veronica?" she purred.

"Yes."

"You're a god-damned bull for your age."

She stood up, gave him a salacious wink, and turned. He followed her out to his car. Even behind the crimson slicker her ass was spectacular, the cheeks pushing out, shouting for attention.

Gioberti rang her next morning.

"That was LeMay who picked you up outside my house?"

"Yeah."

"Yeah?" he shouted into the mouthpiece. "I've got a deal going with him. I stand to lose half a million dollars. Cut the fucking crap and tell me what he wanted."

"The same as you. My cunt."

"Okay. Take it easy, girl. I just want to know what happened between you and him."

"I've got delicate eardrums, Rudy."

"Delicate everything," he laughed, harshly, knowing he could make her come round. Like the way he had got her into his bed.

"Tacky, very tacky. Now you want to know if Jack knows what I was doing on Bedford. Right? Well, he does."

"Jesus Fucking Christ. You should never have come around here."

"Well, you asked me, didn't you? And you've been asking a dozen times or more this last year. So I finally decided to find out if the ten inches was a reality or no. And there it was. So I satisfied my curiosity and you certainly satisfied yours, you bastard. Private parts very sore, I said good-bye. I meant it. I still do. It was our first fuck session and our last. Just you bloody well remember our deal when the time comes to cast the movie and Jack suggests me for the second female lead."

"Don't worry, I never renege on a deal, Veronica. What's he call you? Ronnie?"

"Oh, he calls me lots of different names," she purred: "Cock sucker, Ball breaker, Come-freak, Tight-ass. You go ahead and package the movie and who knows what the future might hold."

He began warming to the toughness of her, to the smoky sexuality of her, in her carnality so like a man, the need for many different partners.

"Can you handle Jack?"

She laughed. "What do you think, Rudy?"

One week later, after both Veronica and Gioberti had worked on LeMay, the trades carried the following piece:

'A production company has been formed by Saudi financier Badyr Al Hussein, in association with Sparta Studios chief Rudi Gioberti, Brett Sagan Productions, and Jackson LeMay Enterprises, to film LeMay's novel "Tender Falls the Rain."

'Veteran Sagan will co-star with the untried Veronica Capital, best known for her role in the prime-time continuing drama "Houston", in what is being described as an uncompromisingly realistic and powerful espionage-romance.

'Heavyweight hyphenate Burke Carr has joined the production to author the screenplay and take on line-producer chores as well. A supporting cast of Academy Award winners and nominees is being sought, according to Gioberti.'

REVENGE

Port-au-Prince was a very different place a few years ago. It was, Simon supposed, just as corrupt; it was even dirtier, he remembered; it contained as many beggars, but at least the beggars had some hope, for the tourists were there, despite, or because of, the tyrannical rule of Papa Doc Duvalier and his private army of thugs called the Tonton Macoute.

Not wishing to announce his arrival in advance, Simon had flown from New York to Miami, and on to Kingston, Jamaica, with three different airlines and under three different names, making a detour to New Orleans on the way to satisfy himself he was not being tailed. Finally, at Kingston, he boarded a Panamanian cargo steamer bound for Haiti and Port-au-Prince.

There is a point of no return unremarked at the time in most lives. When he thought of all the grey memorials erected in London to equestrian generals, the heroes of old colonial wars, and to frock-coated politicians who are even more deeply forgotten, Simon Barnes could find no reason to mock the modest stone that commemorated his father on the far side of the international road which he failed to cross in a country so far from the country of his birth. At least his father had paid for the monument, however unwillingly, with his life, unlike the generals and politicians. Should his business with Raoul Julian take him north to Monte Cristi and the frontier with the Dominican Republic, Simon promised himself to seek it out.

His father had been killed sending the young Simon to safety but his elderly mother still lived on in Port-au-Prince as housekeeper of the run-down, near-empty hotel his father had once owned. He had been back a few times since. What a wonderful place the city was to leave; the last time in a plane that was pitching and tossing in the thunderstorm which loomed as usual over Kenscoff volcano. Looking down through the free and lucid air, the port had seemed tiny compared with the vast, wrinkled wasteland behind; the dry, uninhabited mountains, like the broken backbone of an ancient beast excavated from the clay, stretched off into the haze towards Cap Haitien and the Dominican border.

Ostensibly, Simon Barnes was returning to this country of fear to visit his mother. As the steamer drew in to the harbour it was late in the afternoon, and the huge mass of Kenscoff volcano leaning over the town was half in deep shadow. The stone Columbus, under which he and Lyssette used to make love in her husband's car, had been destroyed by rioters in the intervening years.

Disembarking, he found there was no message waiting for him from the British Consul, so he assumed that at the moment all was well. There was the usual confusion at immigration and customs. They were the only boat, but the shed was full of porters, taxi-drivers, police and beggars, lots of beggars. Forcing her way through the crush, a familiar face smiled at him. It was a pretty face, belonging to a sexy little negress with a touch of white blood in her. Her jet-black hair, as sleek as the finest permanent wave, framed a sweet, almond-shaped face with rather slanting eyes under finely-drawn eyebrows. The deep purple of her parted, sensual lips was thrilling against her bronze skin. All Simon could see of her clothes was the bodice of a black satin evening dress, tight and revealing across her firm, small breasts. She wore a plain chain of gold round her neck and a gold band round each thin wrist. Gigi was an old friend. Gigi was a whore.

They embraced. Gigi giggled.

"I'm glad to see you, Simon."

"Not surprised to see me here?" he asked, a little tensely.

"Well..." she paused, a teasing half-smile playing on her lips. Finally she gave a little nod and laughed. "I heard there was a tourist ship coming in. Don't worry, Simon. Baron Samedi doesn't know you're here."

"I wish I could be so sure, Gigi."

"Want to stay at Madame's?"

"Yes."

"You'll find everything just the same."

"Including you?"

"Of course," she giggled. "I'm still the best piece of rumpy-pumpy you ever dipped your dong into. Right?"

"Right," agreed Simon, laughing with her as she squeezed his crotch.

"I have Madame's car outside."

"I have to see my mother first," said Simon. "Do you mind?"

"Of course not. A man should respect his mother."

The car was an old Peugeot. They got in the back while the driver loaded Simon's luggage in the boot.

"Hotel Racine, George," said Gigi to the driver when he got behind the wheel.

"How are things here?" asked Simon.

"All as usual. All quiet," said George.

"No curfew?" Simon asked, turning to Gigi as the car pulled away.

"Why should there be?"

"The papers reported rebels in the north."

Gigi shrugged her slim shoulders and smiled.

"There are road-blocks now between Port-au-Prince and Petionville," George murmured, as much to himself as his passengers.

They passed the remains of the Columbus statue; the dark was rapidly falling. Lights were burning in the exhibition building, while in the public park the musical fountain stood black, waterless, unplaying. They passed the blackened beams of the house destroyed in the riots that led to the overthrow of Baby Doc, and mounted the hill towards Petionville. Halfway up there was a road-block. A man in a torn shirt and a grey pair of trousers and an old soft hat which someone must have thrown away came trailing his rifle by its muzzle to the door. He told them to get out of the car to be searched.

"I'll get out," said Simon, "but the lady stays put."

"Darling, don't make a fuss," said Gigi, whispering. "There are no such things as white man's privileges here." She squeezed his arm. "Besides, darling, I'm only a working girl."

She led the way to the roadside, putting her hands above her head and giving the militiaman a smile Simon hated. Simon watched as the man squeezed her breasts and ran his hands down over her thighs and buttocks and up between her legs. He grinned and said something to her to which she nodded. While the second man kept his rifle trained on Simon and the driver, the first militiaman unbuckled his pants and let them pool around his ankles. Gigi went quickly down on her knees in front of him and took his stubby erection in her mouth. He came quickly. She turned her face away and spat out the offending matter. The man pulled his trousers up and said something else to her. She hitched her tight skirt up her sleek thighs and bent right over to expose her bare buttocks, resting her head on the ground. The two militiamen exchanged a few words before the second man went over to Gigi and dropped his trousers, kneeling down behind her. Simon clearly heard her grunt as the man entered her anus. The sodomy was as quick as the fellatio had been. Afterwards, Simon was allowed to go over and help Gigi to her feet. She said nothing as they got back in the car and drove away. There was a closed expression on her face that looked like it had been set in stone.

Suddenly, all around them, above and below, the lights went out. Only a glow around the harbour and the government buildings remained. It was then that Gigi burst into tears and Simon held her in his arms.

The car entered the steep drive lined with palm trees and bougainvillaea. He always wondered why the original owner had called the hotel the Racine. No name could have been less apt. The architecture of the hotel was neither classical in the eighteenth-century manner nor luxurious in the twentieth-century fashion. With its towers and balconies and wooden fretwork decorations it had the air at night of the set of a haunted house movie. But in the sunlight, or when the lights went on among the palms, it seemed fragile and period and pretty and absurd. Simon had grown to love the place, and was glad in a way that it had found no buyer. There were certainly ghosts in it: in the voices calling from the bathing-pool, in the rattle of ice from the bar where Vincent made his famous rum punches, in the arrival of taxis from the town, in the hubbub of lunch on the veranda, and at night, the Voodoo drummer and the dancers, with Baron Samedi a grotesque figure in a ballet, stepping it delicately in his top-hat under the lighted palms. He had known for a short time all of this.

They drew up in the darkness. Everything was just as before. Simon left the car and walked up the steps in the dark. At the top he nearly stumbled. He called out: "Vincent, Vincent," but no one replied. The veranda stretched on either side of him, but no table was laid for dinner. Through the open door of the hotel he could see the bar by the light of a tiny oil-lamp. This had been once his father's dream of a luxury hotel; a circle of light which barely touched a half-empty bottle of rum, two stools, a syphon of soda crouched in the shadow like a bird with a long beak. He called out again: "Vincent, Vincent," and again nobody answered.

He felt under the bar and found an electric torch. He went through the lounge to what had been his father's office, the desk covered with old bills and receipts. He had not expected a client, but even Vincent was not there. What a homecoming this was turning out to be, thought Simon. He remembered his mother's appeal. It had come in the shape of a picture-postcard which showed the ruined citadel of the Emperor Christophe at Cap Haitien. On the back was written, in a scrawled hand, 'If you come this way, please visit another old ruin. Your loving Maman.' The last time he had seen his mother was in Paris in 1974, and there had been no letters. This was the nearest to a maternal approach she had ever made.

Below the office was the bathing-pool. About this hour the cocktail guests should have been arriving from other hotels in the town. Few in the good old days drank anywhere else but the Racine. The Americans always drank dry Martinis. By midnight some of them would be swimming in the pool naked. Once, as a boy, he had looked out of his window at two in the morning to see a couple fucking in the pool below. There was a great yellow moon overhead and he could see that the woman had her tits pressed against the side of the pool as the man took her from behind. He could clearly see the passion on their faces. The man was the French ambassador. The woman was Simon's loving Maman. She didn't notice him watching her fornicate while father slept; she didn't notice anything that night but the man who was pushing, pushing into her.

Simon heard steps in the garden coming up from the direction of the swimming pool. The broken steps of a man limping. Vincent had always limped since his beating by the Tonton Macoute. He went out onto the veranda to meet him.

"Is that you, Monsieur Barnes?" the old man called up nervously, his oil-lamp casting a corkscrewing light along the curved path from the pool.

"Yes, Vincent, it's me. How are you?"

He stood below Simon looking up with a sick expression on his black face. He did not reply.

"I have come to see Madame la Comtesse, Vincent."

At that he nodded and brightened. "You have come from England?"

"Yes."

"From London?"

"Yes, Vincent."

"London was very cold?"

"It was raining when I left," said Simon. He began to feel a little awkward. He had expected a warmer welcome in his mother's house. He waited for Vincent to negotiate the steps up to the balcony, and together they went into the bar. Vincent was a tall, elderly negro with a Roman face blackened by the soot of cities, and with hair dusted by stone.

"Is my mother well, Vincent?'

"No, Monsieur Barnes."

"What is it?"

"Her heart."

"Then I'll come back in the morning."

"The afternoon would be better, monsieur."

"Very well, Vincent. Goodnight."

Simon went back out onto the veranda and down the steps to the waiting car. Far off in the mountains beyond Kenscoff a drum beat, marking the spot of a Voodoo tonnelle. It was not often one heard the drums now that Baby Doc had been deposed. Something padded through the dark, and Simon turned to see a thin, starved dog at the bottom of the steps. He got in the back of the Peugeot beside Gigi.

"Let's go, George," said Gigi.

Simon looked back at the fantastic tracery of woodwork against the palms and the inky storm-clouds blowing over Kenscoff.

"Anything there for you, Simon?" she asked as they drove away.

"Not anymore," he murmured. "Not anymore."

The long, long day was not over yet; midnight was an hour and an eternity away, thought Simon, as George drove the old Peugeot along the edge of the sea, the road pitted with holes. This was George's idea, to avoid the roadblock on the return journey, and though it was the long way round no one was going to argue with his choice of route.

There were very few people about. Perhaps they had not realised the curfew had been lifted, or they feared a trap similar to the one George had driven into on the way to Petionville, where all the foreign hotels clustered together on the hillside as if for safety. On Simon's right were a line of wooden huts in little fenced saucers of earth where a few palm trees grew and slithers of water gleamed between like scrap-iron on a dump. An occasional candle burned over a little group bowed above their rum like mourners over a coffin. Sometimes there were furtive sounds of music.

Just before Madame Olga's, the road branched, the tarmac came to an abrupt end. To the left was the main southern highway, which, because of the lack of tarmac, was almost impassable except by jeep.

It was two years or more since Simon had last been to the brothel, and he was surprised to see a road-block on the highway. Gigi groaned at the sight of the advancing militiamen.

"Get us out of here, George," said Simon.

The driver needed no further prompting to swing the car quickly onto the right fork towards the brothel compound. A shot was fired in the air by one of the men at the road-block, but there was no sign of any pursuit.

"Are they following?" asked Gigi, not daring to look herself.

"No," said Simon, holding her in his arms as they sped towards the long, low stable-like hut divided into stalls, which was the quarters where love was for sale, or at least rented by the hour, from Madame Olga's harem of very young, very beautiful girls.

Madame Olga herself was from Thailand, and Simon now realised that she was probably a SPEAR agent. She dressed her girls in white muslin with balloon skirts to show off their slender legs the colour of young deer. She pretended that her girls were from good families, that she was only helping them to earn some pocket money, and it was a lie easy to believe, for she had taught them perfect manners, in public. Till they reached the fucking stalls her customers too had to behave with decorum, and to watch the couples dancing it was possible to think it was an end-of-term celebration at a convent school. Madame Olga had a sweet, kindly face and a tiny delicate body which must once have been beautiful. She had heard their approach, plus the gunshot, and was standing on the threshold, holding up an oil-lamp as George brought the car to a stop.

Simon was no longer in the mood for sex but Madame Olga remembered him and was grateful for the way he had tried to protect Gigi from the attentions of the rapacious militia. Not only did she allow him to stay, but she sternly refused to accept any money from him. He smiled and shrugged, knowing it was a brave man who would willingly incur the wrath of this little old woman. On one occasion some six years earlier he had seen her go in to rescue one of her girls from a brutal customer, taking a hatchet from the kitchen and charging an opponent who was armed with a knife and twice her size. He turned and fled.

Madame Olga and Gigi disappeared inside together and George took Simon's bags to his room as Simon himself went into the bar. At a table by the wall with his gaze fixed intently on Simon as though he had never once escaped from it was the police officer Simon had seen watching him at the customs shed. The black opaque lenses shielding the policeman's eyes seemed even more ridiculous in the gloom of Madame Olga's salon. But Simon wasn't about to laugh.

He ordered a rum and soda and took it to a table as far from the cop as was possible in the small room with its makeshift stage at one end. Simon had just sat down when a single white spotlight came on to reveal four grinning negroes on stage in flame-coloured shirts and peg-top white trousers, squatting astride four tapering barrels with rawhide membranes.

"Voodoo drummers, Mr. Simon Barnes," said a voice. The policeman sat down beside him.

"What do you want?" asked Simon.

"Later, Mr. Englishman. Let's enjoy the show first."

A tiny figure, swathed completely in black ostrich feathers, stepped into the light in front of the drummers.

"You'll like her," said the cop. "She sucks like a vacuum cleaner and fucks like a bitch in heat."

The girl put her hand up to her throat and the cloak of black feathers came away from the front of her body and spread out into a five-foot black fan. There was absolute silence among the watchers save for the soft thud of the drums behind her, and the groans and yelps of those of Madame Olga's customers being entertained elsewhere in the house.

The girl swirled the cloak slowly behind her until it stood up like a peacock's tail. She was naked except for a brief V of black lace and a black sequinned star in the centre of each breast, and the thin black domino across her eyes. Her body was small, hard, bronzed and beautiful. It was slightly oiled and glinted in the white light.

The audience was silent. The drums began to step up the tempo. The bass drum kept its beat dead on the timing of the human pulse. The girl's naked stomach started slowly to revolve in time with the rhythm. She swept the black feathers across and behind her again, and her hips started to grind in time with the bass drum. The upper part of her body was motionless. The black feathers swirled again, and now her feet were shifting and her shoulders too. The drums beat louder. Each part of her body seemed to be keeping a different time. Her lips were bared slightly from her teeth. Her nostrils began to flare. Her eyes glinted hotly through the diamond slits. It was a sexy, pug-like face; chienne was the only word Simon could think of to describe it.

The drums thudded faster in a complexity of interlaced rhythms. The girl tossed the big fan off the floor, holding her arms up above her head. Her whole body began to shiver. Her belly moved faster; round and round, in and out. Her legs were now spread wide as if straddling an imaginary lover. Her hips began to revolve in a wide circle.

Suddenly she plucked the sequinned star off her right breast and threw it into the audience. The first noise came from the spectators: a quiet growl. Then they were silent again. She plucked off the other star. Again the growl and then silence. The drums began to crash and roll. Sweat poured off the drummers. Their hands fluttered like grey flannel on the pale membranes. Their eyes were bulging, distant. Their heads were slightly bent to one side as if they were listening. They hardly glanced at the girl. The audience panted softly, liquid eyes bulging and rolling.

The sweat was shining all over the girl now. Her boobs and belly glistened with it. She broke into great shuddering jerks. Her mouth opened and she screamed softly. Her hands snaked down to her sides and suddenly she had torn away the strip of lace. She threw it into the audience. There was nothing now but a single black G-string covering her vagina.

Now the drums went into a hurricane of sexual rhythm. The girl screamed softly again and then, her arms stretched before her as a balance, she started to lower her body down to the floor and up again. Faster and faster she went. Simon could hear the audience around him panting and grunting like pigs at the trough. He felt the palms of his own hands become sweaty. His mouth was dry.

Two huge negroes, naked except for gold lame jockstraps, appeared on either side of the gyrating girl. They untied her G-string, revealing her ripe, shaven pubic mound. The girl sank to her knees and removed the jockstraps of the two men.

"These nigger bastards are always so well hung," sneered the cop, who was a mulatto.

The girl squealed as she was penetrated fore and aft simultaneously. There was a delighted howl from the audience. Harsh obscenities were shouted from different corners of the room. Then, without warning, the whole room was plunged into total darkness and

Simon's senses were suddenly alert to danger.

"Don't move, Mr. Englishman," said the cop. "I have a gun pointed at your chest. Just sit back and enjoy the ride."

The howling of the mob was disappearing rapidly. At the same time Simon felt cold air on his face. He felt as if he was sinking. Something snapped shut above his head. He put his hand out behind him. It touched a moving wall a foot from his back.

"Lights," said another voice, quietly.

Simon found himself in a tiny square cell. To right and left were two more mulattos in dark glasses with guns trained on him. There was the sharp hiss of a hydraulic garage lift and the table settled quietly to the floor. Simon glanced up. There was the faint join of a broad trap-door a few feet above their heads. No sound came through it. One of the mulattos grinned.

"Hi, there, captain," he said to the cop. "This the honky?"

"Yes, Yaphet. This is the one."

Yaphet seemed to be in charge. The pistol he held trained lazily on Simon's heart was very fancy. There was a glint of mother-of-pearl between the dark fingers on the stock and the long octagonal barrel was finely chased. He was a paunchy man in a chocolate shirt and lavender-coloured peg-top trousers. He came round the corner of the table and shoved the muzzle of his gun into Simon's stomach. The hammer was back.

"You shouldn't miss at that range," said Simon.

"Shut the fuck up, honky," the mulatto growled. He frisked Simon expertly with his left hand; legs, thighs, back, sides. He dug out Simon's gun and handed it to the cop, then he turned back to Simon.

"The Baron wants to see you, honky."

He was hauled to his feet by the cop and the other mulatto. He was shoved against a section of wall which opened on a pivot into a long bare passage. The man called Yaphet pushed passed them and led the way. The door swung to behind them as their footsteps echoed down the stone passage. At the end was a door. They went through into another long passage lit by an occasional bare bulb in the roof. Another door and they found themselves in a large warehouse. Cases and bales were stacked in neat piles. There were runways for overhead cranes. From the markings on the crates it seemed to be a liquor storehouse. They followed an aisle across to an iron door. The man called Yaphet rang a bell. There was absolute silence. Simon guessed they must have walked at least a hundred yards away from the brothel.

There was a clang of bolts and the door opened. A mulatto in evening dress with a gun in his hand stepped aside and they went through into a carpeted hallway. Yaphet knocked on a door facing them, opened it and led the way through. In a high-backed chair, behind an expensive desk, the Baron sat looking quietly at them...

Raoul Julian, aka Rico Manzetti, smiled at Simon Barnes' shocked reaction to the former's appearance. The ambassador sat back, his huge head resting against the back of the tall chair. It was a great football of a head, twice the normal size and very nearly round. The skin was grey-black, taut and shining like the face of a week-old corpse in the river. It was hairless, except for some greyish brown fluff above the ears. There were no eyebrows and no eyelashes, and the eyes were extraordinarily far apart, so that one could not focus on them both, but only on one at a time. Their gaze was very steady and penetrating, as Barnes remembered from Miami and London. When they rested on something, they seemed to devour it, to encompass the whole of it, as the cancerous tumour was devouring Julian's brain.

"I see," said Julian, adopting the American intonation of his alter ego, Manzetti, "ya wonderin' how I did it, eh schmuck?" He laughed, his flabby bulk shaking with mirth. The thought of this hideous monster copulating with Lyssette revolted Simon, especially as Lyssette had described Raoul's cock as a good eight inches long in repose and more than twice that erect. She had once joked that she would be able to get a job as a sword swallower should Raoul ever divorce her, after all the years she had spent deep-throating her husband's huge dong.

"Amazing what a good wig and a Hollywood make-up artist can do," sneered Simon in reply to Julian's taunts. "You were never much to look at, even before the explosion."

Julian was wearing a dinner jacket on his six-foot-six, twenty stone frame. There was a hint of vanity in the diamonds that blazed on the man's shirtfront and at his cuffs. The wide, short neck and broad shoulders just about carried the huge head. There were few wrinkles or creases on the dead face, while the forehead bulged before merging with the polished, hairless crown. The large hands rested half-curled on the table in front of him. There was nothing else on the desk save a large intercom with about twenty switches, and a very slim ivory riding crop with a long, thin white lash.

"I was fucking Lyssette after she met you, every-which-way, right up to the day I agreed to the divorce, Mr. Barnes."

Simon glanced round the room. It was full of books, spacious and restful and very quiet, like the library of a millionaire. There was one high window above the monster's head, but otherwise the walls were solid with bookshelves. Simon turned round in his chair. More bookshelves packed with tomes. There was no sign of a door, but there might have been any number of doors faced with dummy books. The two mulattos who had come in with Yaphet stood rather uneasily against the wall. The whites of their eyes showed. They were not looking at Julian but at a curious effigy which stood on a table in an open space of the floor to the right, and slightly behind, the seated Julian.

A five-foot white wooden cross on a raised white dais. The arms of the cross were thrust into the sleeves of a dusty black frock-coat whose tails hung down behind the table to the floor. Above the neck of the coat a battered bowler hat gaped at Simon, its crown pierced by the vertical bar of the cross. A few inches below the rim, round the neck of the cross, resting on the cross-bar, was a deep, starched clergyman's collar.

At the base of the white dais, on the table, lay an old pair of lemon-coloured gloves. A short malacca stick with a gold knob, its ferrule resting beside the gloves, rose against the left shoulder of the effigy. Also on the table was a battered black top hat.

This evil scarecrow gazed sightlessly out across the room: God of the Cemeteries and Chief of the Legion of the Dead, Baron Samedi. Simon shivered and looked away, back to the great grey-black face of Raoul Julian, SPEAR's Chief of Operations in the Caribbean and South America. He noticed now that though Julian's eyes rested on him, they had become slightly opaque. He had the impression that the brain behind them was occupied elsewhere.

Julian spoke.

"You stay, Yaphet." His eyes shifted. "You two can go." Then, to Simon: "You may smoke, Mr. Barnes."

Simon reached for his cigarette case and lighter, a matching set in gold and platinum from Tiffanys of New York.

Julian pressed down a switch on the intercom panel.

"Send in Ms. Annalise," he said, and centred the switch again.

There was a moment's pause and then a section of the bookcase to the right of the desk swung open.

One of the most beautiful women Simon had ever seen came slowly into the room and closed the door behind her. She stood just inside the room and looked at him, taking him in slowly inch by inch, from his head to his feet. When she had completed her detailed inspection, she turned to Julian.

"Yes?" she inquired flatly.

Julian had not moved his head. He addressed Barnes.

"This is an extraordinary woman, Mr. Englishman, as well as being a great piece of ass. For both reasons I intend to marry her. I found her in a cabaret in Port-au-Prince. She was doing a telepathic act which I could not understand. I looked into it and I still could not understand. But there was nothing to understand. It was magic."

He paused. Turning away from Simon, he gazed impassively at the girl.

"For the time being she is proving difficult for me to overcome. She is a virgin in her cunt. She believes she will lose her powers once her hymen is broken by a man. She does not like oral sex and will only allow me to fuck her in the ass sometimes. That is why she is called Annalise."

The girl said nothing but took a chair similar to Simon's from beside the far wall and pushed it towards him. She sat down almost touching his right knee. She looked into his eyes.

Her face was pale, with the pallor of white families that have lived too long in the tropics. But her face contained none of the usual exhaustion which the tropics impart to the skin and hair of white people. Her eyes were blue, fiery and disdainful, but, as they gazed into his with a touch of humour, he realised they contained some message for him personally. The look in her eyes quickly vanished as his own answered.

The girl's hair was blue-black and fell heavily to her shoulders. She had high cheekbones and a wide, sensual mouth which held a hint of cruelty. Her jawline was delicate and finely cut. It showed decision and an iron will which were repeated in the straight, pointed nose. Part of her beauty lay in the lack of compromise. It was a face born to command. The face of the granddaughter of a French Colonial slave-owner.

She wore a long evening dress of heavy white matt silk whose classical lines were broken by the deep folds which fell from her shoulders and revealed the upper half of her breasts. She wore diamond earrings, square-cut in broken bands, and a thin diamond bracelet on her left wrist. She wore no rings. Her nails were long and pointed, with crimson enamel.

She watched Simon's eyes on her and nonchalantly drew her forearms together in her lap so that the valley between her ripe, full breasts deepened. The message was unmistakable and an answering warmth must have shown on his cold, drawn face, for, suddenly, Julian picked up the ivory whip from the desk beside him and lashed across at her, the white leather thong whistling through the air and landing with a cruel bite across her bare shoulders.

Simon winced even more than she did. Her eyes blazed for an instant and then went opaque. She slowly sat more upright. He felt a glow of excitement and a quickening of the pulse. He had a friend in the enemy camp.

"Annalise is my inquisitor, Mr. Englishman," said Julian. "Torture is very messy and people tell you what will stop the pain. But this girl can divine the truth in people." He turned to her. "Are you ready, Annalise?"

She had a pack of cards in her hands and she started to shuffle them. After a moment or two she paused. She looked up.

"Yes, the cards are ready."

"Look into her eyes," said Raoul Julian to Simon.

Barnes did so. This time there was no discernible message in Annalise's gaze. Her eyes were unfocused. They looked through him.

"Now, Mr. Englishman," said Julian, "I believe you are a British Secret Service agent. Is that true?"

"No."

"Then why are you in Haiti?"

"To see my mother. She is ill."

Simon felt an uncanny chill run up his spine. For a moment there was dead silence in the room. He could hear Yaphet's rasping breath just behind him. The mulatto was probably pointing his pearl-handled gun at Simon's skull. Would the girl betray him to Julian? Could she even tell if he had lied? Simon tried to look indifferent. He gazed up at the ceiling, then back at her.

Her eyes came back into focus. She turned away from him and looked across at Julian.

"He speaks the truth, Raoul," she said coldly.

Julian was visibly surprised at such an outcome. He reflected for a moment. Then he decided.

"Yaphet, break the little finger of Mr. Barnes' left hand."

Outwardly, Simon feigned horror, but inside he was elated. This was his big chance. Yaphet would have to put his gun away. As the mulatto walked jauntily over to him, Simon clutched madly at the arms of his chair.

"No, you can't," he cried. "Please don't."

The girl's eyes were wide upon him, her red lips slightly parted. His coward act was going down well. He sensed the presence of Yaphet at his shoulder and, in one swift movement, was on his feet and whipping his right hand, straight and flat as a board, round and inwards. He felt it connect with a thud. The mulatto cried shrilly like a wounded rabbit. Simon reached inside Yaphet's jacket and pulled out the pearl-handled gun.

"Good-bye, Julian," he cried, calmly shooting the monster between the eyes.

The girl screamed as her tormentor's huge skull exploded under the impact of the bullet, punching the body backwards off the chair. The mulatto, meanwhile, was bent double, his hands between his legs, uttering little panting screams. Simon whipped the gun down hard on the back of Yaphet's head. It gave back a dull klonk as if he had hammered on a door, but the mulatto groaned and fell forward onto his knees, throwing out his hands for support. Simon hit him a third time, and there was a satisfying crunch of bone and a final short scream was driven out of the man before he slumped to the floor.

Simon spun round to face the shocked Annalise.

"How do we get out of here, girl?"

She walked towards him, her heavy breasts rising and falling with her quickened breathing. She put her arms around his shoulders. Her black hair fell away from her head in a dark cascade. She took his face between her two hands and held him away from her lips, panting. Her eyes were bright and hot. Then she brought his lips against hers and kissed him long and lasciviously, as if she were the man and he the woman.

They parted finally, Simon gasping for breath. She laughed. She took a handkerchief from her purse and wiped the lipstick off his mouth. Then she brushed the hair away from his forehead, her fingers touching the edge of the scar.

"One day you must tell me how you got that," Annalise murmured, kissing him again, lightly and tenderly.

"I want to make love to you," he said, thickly.

She laughed again.

"I don't need the cards to tell me that."

"You kiss more wonderfully than any girl I've ever known, Annalise."

She put her hands on her wide hips and grinned at him.

"I have waited a long time to meet the man I would give my virginity to," she said. "And when I first saw you, I knew it would be you."

He stepped forward and put his left hand on her breasts, feeling the firm roundness of each and the hard nipple. He kissed her white throat, catching her flesh between his teeth and giving her a sharp nip.

She gasped, pushing him away and rubbing her neck.

"Simon Barnes, you sadist," she murmured. "I'm going to work you down to the bone."

She pressed him up against the wall, her arms went round his neck and they kissed passionately. He slipped his hands down her back until they came to the cleft at the base of her spine, holding the centre of her body hard against him. He could feel the heat in her loins. She was open to him, ready for him. Then she reached over his shoulder and pressed on one of the books in the serried shelves. A large section of the wall opened on a central pivot.

"You wanted a way out, didn't you?" she said, escaping from his embrace with a giggle. Simon followed her into a short, carpeted passage ending in some stairs that led downwards. He groaned in frustration.

"You little cocktease."

She turned round and gently placed her fingertips against his lips.

"Allumeuse is the nice word for it, Simon. It is fun for me to be able to tease such a man as you, but it's a game I know I don't have long to play, for soon, because of you, I shall finally be free of this life in the underworld. My virginity will be your reward, but not just yet. You will need my psychic powers intact if you are to defeat the zombie legions of Baron Samedi."

She paused. She licked her dry lips.

"None of the mulattos would dare enter Raoul's inner sanctum uninvited. It will be many hours before the bodies are discovered. We have time. The stairs go down to my bedroom. If you so desire it, you can use my body."

He sighed.

"Oh, yes, Annalise, I want you. Anyway you'll let me."

She put out a hand and touched his sleeve. Her eyes had the faraway look that he had seen before.

"Come on, then," she murmured, leading the way down the stairs.

The bedroom was stark, containing nothing but a huge, circular bed and a small bedside cabinet in white wood. She hitched up her dress and lay face down on the bed, displaying two gloriously round, white buttocks. He grasped her hips in both hands and impaled her on his shaft...

Simon Barnes awoke suddenly and with the sick certainty that his mother was dead.

"Annalise, wake up. We have to get back to the hotel. My mother..."

She put her hand on his arm.

"I know."

They dressed hurriedly and Annalise led him to safety along the maze of underground passages until they emerged from some disused mine workings on the lower slopes of the mountains above Kenscoff. It was almost noon. By the time they were walking up the gravel drive of the Hotel Racine, the sun was about to set behind the great hump of the extinct volcano. Simon couldn't help noticing that the bougainvillaea needed cutting back and there was more grass than gravel on the drive.

They entered the hotel by the balcony and went upstairs. The walls were hung with paintings of scenes from Haitian life: forms caught in wooden gestures among bright and heavy colours; a cock-fight; a Voodoo ceremony; vicious black clouds over Kenscoff; banana trees of stormy green; the blue spears of the sugar cane; golden maize. Vincent opened the door and Simon went in to the shock of his mother's hair spread over the pillow; a Haitian red which had never existed in nature. It flowed abundantly on either side of her across the great double bed. It was a shameless bed, built for one purpose only, with a gilt, curlicued foot board more suitable for a courtesan of old than an old woman, newly dead.

There were tears in Vincent's eyes, and Simon divined the truth of it at the last. The old negro had been his mother's lover; here, in this gaudy boudoir, in that obscene, leering bed. He could see Vincent's ebony buttocks straining between Maman's slack, pale thighs. He could hear his mother's rasping voice transformed into an animal grunt. He felt Annalise squeezing his hand hard and thought he could hear her soothing voice in his head. He looked at Annalise, then back at Vincent.

"I'm sorry," said Simon. "I know you loved her."

"Thank you, Monsieur Barnes."

Simon walked over to the bed. She, even in death, might have passed anywhere for a woman in her late forties, and he could see nothing of the invalid about her. A doctor was called, and the formalities completed, and an ambulance took the corpse down to the mortuary in Port-au-Prince. As it disappeared down the drive, Annalise went to speak with Simon, who was intently watching the tail-lights of the vehicle moving down the hill.

"Vincent very much wants us to go with him to a voodoo ceremony tonight, on the mountains above Kenscoff."

Simon looked at her.

"Why the hell not. Sure."

It was after midnight when they set off. They drove some twelve miles, and when they left the car on the road behind Kenscoff they could hear the drums beating very gently like a labouring pulse. It was as though some huge creature out in the humid night was out of breath. Ahead was a thatched hut open to the winds; the whitewashed interior illuminated by guttering candlelight.

The ceremony inside the hut went on for a couple of hours before the climax. The first thing Simon saw as he went in was the choir of negro girls in white who were beating the drums softly, clandestinely, insistently. Annalise grasped his hand. They stood on one side of the tonnelle, while Vincent stood directly opposite. Between them stood the pole of the temple, stuck up like an aerial to catch the passage of the gods. A whip hung from it in memory of the island's slavery past. On the earth floor, around a small brazier, a design had been drawn in ashes; the summons to a god. Was it a summons to Legba, the seducer of women, to Erzulie the sweet virgin of love, to Ogoun Ferraille, the patron of warriors, or to Baron Samedi in his black clothes and his black Tonton glasses, hungry for the dead?

The priest came in from his inner room swinging a censer, but the censer he was swinging in their faces was a trussed fowl. When he had completed the circle of the tonnelle the houngan put the head of the black chicken in his mouth and crunched it cleanly off; the wings continuing to flap while the head lay on the dirt floor. Then the priest bent down and squeezed the neck like a tube of toothpaste, and added the rusty colour of blood to the ash-grey patterns on the floor.

The dancers became more reckless as the night advanced. They swayed and chanted and clapped along to the beating drums. Now Simon saw Vincent move into the ring, his eyes turned so far up into his head that only the whites showed, his hands held out as though he were begging. He lurched upon his wounded hip and seemed on the point of falling as he moved in a circle. The drums were silent now, the singing faded away to nothing; only the houngan spoke in some language older than Creole, perhaps older than Latin, and Vincent paused and listened, staring up at the wooden pillar. Then the houngan went over to Vincent and placed the red scarf of Ogoun Ferraille across the elderly negro's shoulders. The warrior god had been recognised.

A machete was put in Vincent's hand, and he raised it slowly, swinging the machete in a wide arc that made the onlookers duck. The next moment there was chaos in the tonnelle as Vincent went into a wild dervish dance, the machete flashing and cutting, people screaming and falling over each other to get away. Vincent's face ran with sweat, his eyes were unseeing. He spun round and round, then fell down on the floor in a dead faint. The drums beat, the girls chanted. Ogoun Ferraille had come and gone.

The unconscious negro was carried into the inner room and the crowd began to leave. The show was over. It was then that Simon noticed that Annalise had put her hands over her face and was swaying gently from side to side. Pulling her hands away, he saw the expression of great sweetness on her face. Erzulie had come too. She ran outside, and Simon followed.

The predicted thunderstorm had at last arrived, and before they had crossed the clearing they were both soaking wet and laughing excitedly as the lightning flashed above them. As they plunged into the undergrowth, Annalise caught her skirt. She stopped, turned to Simon, and began to undress. Soon they were both naked, the warm rain sluicing down over their exulting bodies.

"Isn't this marvellous?" she yelled above the storm.

"Wonderful," he answered.

They clasped each other, hugging tight, wet skin to wet skin, then she slipped from his arms like an eel, giggling, and ran into the trees, Simon fast on her heels. She led him beneath a hanging vine, where the grass was almost dry, and they began to make love. Her hands wandered all over his body, teasing his flesh with agile fingers. He pushed her up against the bole of the tree and pressed himself onto her urgently, kissing her wet face all over before fastening his hungry lips to her mouth and sucking and biting her full lips, snaking his tongue between them to meet hers. Then he bent down, nuzzling at the damp patch of pubic hair between her sleek thighs like a puppy. She groaned and parted her legs so he could get his tongue further into her cunt, while her fingers tousled his hair.

Now he stood up, eager to fuck her. She leant back against the rough trunk. The lips of her cunt were gorged with blood and parted willingly to welcome his jutting cock, which was soon in her warm, slanting passage. When he entered her, she gave a little gasp and was still for just a second, and then, with a powerful forward thrust of her pelvis, she locked her satiny legs around his hips. Perhaps because she was so young, and a virgin, the mouth of her vagina was deliciously tight, and its walls so elastic that they gripped his cock incessantly, bringing him almost to the point of climax every time he moved inside her.

"Ah, so nice, so big," she moaned. "I've often wondered what it would be like the real way, with a real man. Oh..." she caught her breath. "I'm glad, you know, when you bummed me, you didn't come. Ah... I knew then you were the right man to take my virginity."

Locked together in such a stand-up fuck, his every movement produced a relentless friction against her clitoris, and soon she was moaning constantly with gratification and clasped his shoulders in an animal need to be closer to him. Her boobs were squashed against his chest, damp, bulbous flesh with sharpened nipples which sent thrills through his straining muscles.

"I want to lie down," Simon said at last, dying to feel the full length of his prick sink into her, to reach her soft womb, a luxury which was impossible while they stood against the tree.

"Yes, oh, yes," she murmured, as he lowered her off his shaft and her feet touched the wet grass. "But out here, in the rain. Fuck me in the rain, on the wet ground."

She lay face down on the sodden, earth-scented grass, her body silvered by the transient moon. Bending over her, he pulled up her haunches until her plump, voluptuous arse was hard up against his belly, and drove his cock into her cunt from behind, able, at last, to bury himself to the very root of his prick and feel her cunt yield to the ardent invader.

At first, he stayed there without moving, so sweet was the sensation of being held tight in that dark cavern. Then he fucked her like a dog, mounting her, pawing her back as he panted and pushed himself into that sheath-like passage. Each time he went in, he felt as if his shaft was being eaten up. The laboriousness only added to his growing excitement, and hers; each movement was so much longer and heavier than when a cunt is wide and wet. He could not see her face and expression but he heard her call out in delight as he went in ever deeper.

At last he could hold back no longer.

"I shall explode," he cried. "Come with me."

The words acted like a trigger, and she came like a wild thing. In that tight enclosure he felt every spasm that shook her, and she squeezed his come out of him with overwhelming force, as he let himself go and cried to the moon. Straining against each other, they were reluctant to stop, and together rolled over and over on the grass, forgetful of wetness and mud. When they finally parted, the falling away was like dying.

By the time they had recovered sufficient strength to stand up, the rain had eased considerably. Retrieving their sodden clothes they stumbled back to where they had left the car, and drove back to the hotel. The tyres were crunching on the gravel driveway before either of them spoke.

"I know this sounds silly," said Annalise, hesitantly, "but thank you."

He pulled the car up in front of the veranda steps and switched off the engine.

"The pleasure was all mine," he said, trying to keep a straight face.

"No it wasn't," she answered, with mock indignance, and they both laughed. Their eyes met and agreed that they must have another fuck. With a squeal, she jumped from the car and ran up the steps into the hotel...

It was nearly four in the morning, and after a night of passionate love-making with Annalise, Simon was too exhausted to sleep, so he was wide-awake and watching her sleep beside him when the Tontons drove up to the veranda and shouted to him to come down.

The captain from the brothel was the leader of the group, and he held Simon at gun-point while his men searched the kitchen and the servants' quarters. Simon could hear the bang of cupboards and doors and the chilling sound of breaking glass.

"What are you looking for?" Simon asked, as calmly as he could with a gun on him.

The captain lay on a wicker chaise longue opposite the hard upright chair his captive was on. The sun had not yet risen but the mulatto wore his dark glasses all the same.

"Where is the girl, Monsieur Barnes?"

"What girl?"

The policeman changed the position of his gun. The sky reddened over his shoulder and the palm trees turned black and distinct. Simon, dressed only in a silk robe, was sitting on a straight dining-room chair, and the mosquitoes were biting his ankles. The gun had been pointing at his stomach, but now it pointed at his chest.

"What do you know about the death of the ambassador?"

"Which ambassador is that, Captain?" said Simon.

"I could shoot you very easily, Monsieur Englishman. It would be a pleasure for me. Resisting arrest, you know."

"I very much doubt the British Consulate would accept such a ridiculous story."

The mulatto grinned.

"I don't give a flying fuck. Now tell me where the girl is or I will kill you."

"I am here," said Annalise, standing at the foot of the stairs, totally nude.

"Come here," the policeman barked, sitting up.

"Of course, Captain," she cooed.

Her hands behind her back to expose her breasts and pubis, she moved suggestively forward across the lobby to the veranda. Behind her back she was holding Simon's Ingram machine-pistol; a full clip rammed home and the safety catch off.

"Raoul always said I gave great head," she murmured huskily.

"Now that he's dead I need to find another powerful man to love. Would you let me be your lover, Captain? Please? I want to lick your whole body, every inch."

The obscene litany had had its effect on the mulatto. Simon noted both the hard-on bulging against the crotch of the policeman's trousers, and the fact that the gun barrel was no longer pointing at him.

"Now," yelled Simon.

He kicked backwards, overturning his chair and rolling clear as Annalise produced the Ingram, triggering a burst of 9mm steel-jacketed slugs that cut the captain in two. Simon scooped up the dropped automatic and blew away the solitary Tonton standing beside the black sedan. Then he took the Ingram off Annalise and killed the remaining thugs as they came charging out of the hotel kitchen.

"Are they all dead?" she asked.

"Yes."

She hugged herself. "I think I should get dressed. You too."

He nodded. "The roads will be quiet now. We'll take their car," indicating the sedan, "and make for the border. Shouldn't be too tricky." He smiled. "If there's any trouble, you can have another go with the Ingram."

She did not laugh.

"Don't be sad, Annalise. I have a place in Jamaica. You can stay there as long as you want."

"But not with you?"

"I have a wife waiting for me in England."

"You love her very much?"

"I've killed for her."

EXECUTIVE ACTION

January 20th, 1997

"I, Clark Marley Reynolds, do solemnly swear that I will faithfully execute the office of the President of the United States, and will, to the best of my ability, preserve, protect and defend the Constitution of the United States. So help me God."

The United States had, for the first time, produced a black President for the Oval Office. The Rev. Jesse Jackson had come close in '88, but now, at last, Black America could see that it was equally possible for one of their sons to reach the highest office in the land.

His hand still resting on the bible, the Forty-third President smiled at his beautiful young wife. It had to be admitted, even by his staunchest supporters, that Reynolds was not typical of his fellow blacks, even in the America of the Nineties. A former star athlete and Senator for Virginia, he was the only child of a formidable set of parents, father a doctor, mother a lawyer, and both seriously plugged into the power network of Washington DC. Such an upbringing gave him the drive, ambition and positive self-image necessary for an individual's success in any field of endeavour, in any country, but still, sadly, not the norm for the descendants of those Africans stolen from their homes two hundred years ago and transported thousands of miles to service the white man's empire.

There was another way in which he differed from other blacks. His white wife. Valerie Elaine Sinclair was the epitome of the Wasp Princess. Her family were always referred to as the Hyannisport Sinclairs, as if where they had their summer retreat was somehow part of their name. But they had been around a long time in American politics, supplying Congressmen and senators to oil the political machine long before the Kennedys emigrated from Ireland.

Getting the future First Lady into bed had not been much of a struggle for the handsome, virile, charismatic Senator from Virginia, but getting her to the altar had been. Her family were kind to his face but less than happy behind his back, so Clark Marley Reynolds, upper-middle-class achiever though he was, had had a taste of the bile of prejudice, and knew struggle.

After a fierce primary campaign, he had narrowly beaten President

Gary Hart on the third ballot at the Democratic Party National Convention in Miami. In November of 1996, he had survived an even fiercer contest with the Republican candidate, former President Robert Dole, who had won in '88 but lost to Hart in '92. Now Reynolds had become President with one of the smallest margins of the popular vote, a mere two per cent, in American political history.

Outgoing President Hart shook hands vigorously, for the benefit of the TV cameras, with the man who had humiliated him in Miami. They smiled warmly at each other. The next person to shake Reynolds' hand was ex-First Lady Nancy Reagan, widow of Ronald Reagan. There were rumours already on the Washington cocktail party circuit that Nancy would be a candidate herself in the year 2000.

While the applause died down, the new President of the United States waited for the twenty-one-gun salute to come to an end. Clark Marley Reynolds carefully cleared his throat off-mike and faced fifty thousand spectators on the Capitol Plaza and many hundreds of millions watching the world-wide television hook-up. In the bitter, wintry air, his breath fogged in front of his face as he spoke.

"Vice-President Cuomo, Ms. Chief Justice, President Hart, Vice-President Ferraro, Reverend clergy, and my fellow Americans of whatever colour or creed..."

The First Lady looked on, smiling occasionally to herself as she recognised some of the words and phrases she had contributed to her husband's speech. As she listened, she couldn't help casting a glance at the equally beautiful woman sitting beside her, the outgoing First Lady Donna Hart. Valerie knew that in American politics nobody could be written off. Even Nixon had been a candidate in '88, but in '87, Hart's Presidential hopes had been dashed with the news of his extra-marital affair with the bit-part actress and nude model Donna Rice; the woman Valerie was now sitting beside; the same woman who had been First Lady of the nation for the past four years.

"Good speech," murmured Donna, as the President finished his eleven-minute address and sat down, and everyone else, including Donna, stood up and clapped.

"Thank you," said Valerie, sweetly.

1997

Clark Marley Reynolds, the first black President of the United states, woke as usual at 5.30 am that Friday morning. He showered, shaved, and dressed, then chaired a 6.00 am working breakfast with his aides and advisers, which lasted an hour. By this time Valerie, his wife, would be awake and having her breakfast in bed, and it was part of the daily routine of their life at the White House that Clark would spend the next hour with his wife. Sometimes they would make love, but that was an activity they usually reserved for the evenings. Often they would just talk and read the morning papers together. Even so, it was a special part of their day, and each looked forward to it.

Clark, at forty-seven, was the second youngest inhabitant of the Oval Office in the country's history. He was a tall man, over six foot, with an athletic, muscular frame that some men found intimidating and many women found extremely attractive. He was also very black, which seemed to have a similarly divisive effect on the sexes, though his handsome face, in particular his patrician nose and thin lips, betrayed the fact that his East African heritage had been diluted somewhat over the centuries. But what really got Washington high society in a lather was simply that his wife was white.

The former Valerie Elaine Sinclair of Hyannisport was a lithe, long-legged, blue-eyed honey blonde with the well-bred good looks of Grace Kelly or Candice Bergen and the body of Bo Derek. Vassar and a Swiss finishing school had turned a precocious girl into a well-mannered, well-read young woman, intelligent, witty, and charming, but politically naive. A year at the Sorbonne changed that. She rebelled against the life of indolence her parents had planned for her by working for Ted's election campaign in 1988. That was where she met Clark. Eight years later she returned to the White House, not as a campaign worker this time but as First Lady. She was twenty-nine.

"Good morning, darling," he said, as he entered the bedroom. The April sunlight spilled into the room through the bullet-proof glass in the windows, and made a dazzling halo of Valerie's hair.

"Clark, have you seen what they're saying about you in the Post?"

"No. Is it bad?"

"Awful. I suppose the honeymoon is over."

"Guess so, Val."

He took the paper from her hands and dropped it on the floor. She looked up at him and smiled.

"Isn't it supposed to last a hundred days?"

He sat down beside her on the bed. They kissed.

"Mmmmm ... Nice," she murmured, caressing the nape of his neck. "Can't you tell me anything about this trip?"

"I wish I could, honey. It's just impossible at the moment, but when I get back on Monday you'll be... almost... the first to know."

"After the man from the Washington Post."

He laughed with her. "God, I hope not. It's supposed to be a secret."

"Baby," said Joy Joy de Ferrare, brushing a stray chestnut curl off her cheek with an impatient hand, as the Lincoln Continental purred smoothly along the main boulevard of Springfield, Missouri, "I've been thinking. About us. We really can't go on like this any longer."

Chuck shifted his rangy frame in the driving seat. Beneath his shirt the sunbronzed skin stretched taut across the bunched and sinewy muscles, broken only by a dark cloud of curling chest hair.

"But, Joy, honey," he said, drawing up the black, glittering limousine by the sidewalk, "I thought you wanted it this way. I thought when we sold our controlling interest in the oil consortium to buy the mobile home, that you wanted to be footloose and fancy free."

Their mobile home was a thirty-seven foot Silver Streak trailer with bedroom, studio lounge, two televisions, and five walk-in closets for maximum storage.

Joy Joy gazed moodily out at the oleanders heavy with blossom. "I know what we decided, but it's been a long time. I guess I want to be ordinary again. I guess I want to back up the trailer and settle down." She was small and pretty, with waist-length coal-black hair and deep green-brown eyes whose lustre was scarcely dimmed by a huge pair of horn rimmed glasses. Her voice held a tipsy huskiness that sent Chuck's blood coursing through his body like the dark turbulence of a millstream.

"I suppose I always knew it would come to this," he said, brokenly. "All those years we were working, you and me, eighteen hours a day, seven days a week, to build up the construction company, I knew your thoughts, your heart, were somewhere else ... Okay, sweetheart, it's your move."

Joy Joy wrenched her body round to face him, the thin silk of her blouse clinging to her firm, round, long-nippled breasts, her eyes alight.

"Oh, Chuck," she breathed, "I knew you'd understand, I knew..." But her words were lost as his mouth sought and found hers, bruising it with passion unchecked. Fiercely yet tenderly his arms enfolded her, crushing her body in a fusion of mutual desire, and as his mouth continued to ravish her eager lips Joy Joy was caught in a powerful undertow of erotic excitement ...

So the diplomat's daughter, who was born in Bangkok and spent her early years in Paris, settled down with her husband on an unspoilt three hundred and fifty acre ranch near Branston, Missouri, which they proceeded to develop into a one hundred million dollar theme park complete with hotel, conference centre, sports complex, and three thousand seat opera house. On that Friday morning in April 1997, they could look forward to the park's grand opening on July 4.

The United States Air Force call it a VC-137C stratoliner, which is their term for a Boeing 707 commercial long-distance airliner, but when the President of the United States is on board, the four-engined jet becomes Air Force One.

The Boeing had been converted to include an office and apartment-style suite for the President between the forward and centre passenger compartments. Nobody but the Chief Executive and the First Lady ever used that suite; there was plenty of room elsewhere on the plane for other passengers. When carrying other VIPs, she would be designated Air Force Two, but whatever her name the plane was always crewed by members of the USAF's 89th Military Wing, stationed at Andrews Air Force Base, Washington DC.

At the underground headquarters of UNSIS, the United Nations Secret Intelligence Service, situated in a huge bunker deep beneath the UN Building in New York, the Director, William Darrow, was briefing Agent Simon Barnes.

"What do you know about Aubrey Caligari?"

"No more than anyone else," replied Simon. "Caligari is very rich, a recluse, no photos exist of him. Politically, he's on the ultra Right-Wing."

The dour, craggy features of Darrow's face composed themselves into something approaching a smile.

"If that were all, Caligari would be no more of a problem than the John Birch Society or the Minutemen."

Barnes stayed silent, waiting.

"Tell me about SPEAR, Simon."

"An international crime syndicate, sir. The initials stand for Special Program for Extortion, Anarchy, and Revenge. Members are drawn from top criminal organisations around the world like the Mafia or the Yakuza from Japan. The ruling council is made up of twelve people, one of whom is voted in by the others as chairman. In 1984, SPEAR suffered a major setback with the deaths of Nikos Adonisthenes, Tran Phan Lon and Curtis Brown, all council members. The last-named was being considered as the next chairman. It's taken SPEAR several years to recover."

Darrow nodded. "Yes, good, but there is one point you've left out. The new chairman of SPEAR is Aubrey Caligari." He let the news sink in. "The President leaves Andrews Air Force Base for the western White House at 10 am EST. I'm assigning you to the Secret Service team aboard Air Force One."

"Then," said Simon, "there is a real threat to the President's safety?"

"Yes."

Joy Joy de Ferrare hadn't always been her name. More than thirty years had gone by yet she thought about those 'lost' months of her fifteenth year almost every day. It was 1965, and she was on vacation in Southern California with her best friend, Kelly, and the girl's parents. They did the usual things that tourists do in LA: the Universal Studios tour, a day-trip to Disneyland, examining the famous foot and hand prints in the cement outside Grauman's Chinese Theater. One evening, Kelly's parents were invited to a party, leaving the girls alone in the hotel suite. It was the first time during the whole of the vacation that they were free of Kelly's parents, and Joy Joy needed little persuasion to make the most of the opportunity.

So it was that in a singles bar in downtown LA, the young Joy Joy met Curtis Brown. He was much older, not handsome, but with an animal attraction she found hard to resist. When he smiled, she felt as if someone had poured cold water down her spine. It was a good feeling. He opened a small packet of white powder and dropped a pinch into her soft drink. Coke, he told her. So was the drink, she replied. They both laughed.

Kelly had disappeared by this time, so when Curtis offered to show her his 'movie-star' house in Laurel Canyon, a happily high Joy Joy could not refuse, but as they left the parking lot behind the bar, the headlights of Brown's Mercedes illuminated a couple joined in frantic copulation in the front passenger seat of another car. The girl was kneeling astride the man's lap, facing him. She was naked from the waist down, her pale boyish buttocks were being roughly fondled and grasped by the man, whose face was in shadow. The girl's face, however, could clearly be seen. Her head was thrown back, the eyes half-shut, the mouth open in an O of mingled pleasure and pain. It was Kelly.

Simon was met at Andrews by Fred Marsden, head of the secret Service detachment travelling with the President.

"Hello, Barnes. Glad to have you along."

"Hi." Simon showed his identification to the perimeter guard and they went through.

"Something must be up when you boys at UNSIS take an interest in a routine flight like this."

They looked at each other.

"You're angling, Fred."

He grinned. "Guess so. Let's get aboard. The President likes to leave on time."

At the top of the aircraft steps, trim and fresh in her uniform, the stewardess smiled and welcomed them aboard. "Good morning, gentlemen." She was a very pretty young woman, whose voice was as cool and pleasant as the candid look of interest her deep blue eyes conveyed to Barnes. Her black hair was cropped very short, the jagged fringe providing a dark, uneven frame for the pale beauty of her face, with its high cheek-bones and firm jaw, strong, straight nose and sensuous, not-too-wide mouth.

Once inside, they took their seats and fastened their seatbelts, and the aircraft took off. The gleaming white and silver bird roared into the western sky, climbing rapidly to twenty thousand feet. The seatbelt sign went out and the stewardess came round with the drinks trolley.

"Thanks, honey," said Marsden, accepting a scotch and water. Barnes had the same. The girl gave Simon a deep, searching stare which he frankly returned. She said: "My name's Kelly," and sauntered off up the aisle, swinging her hips suggestively.

Marsden laughed. "What do they see in you?"

"That is something I have often wondered about myself."

Never having suffered from migraine, Simon was surprised by the blinding pain that overtook him as he finished his drink. There was an acute burning sensation behind his eyes, and his vision misted up like condensation on a windscreen, before failing altogether. Darkness enclosed him...

From the age of eight in her native town of Dark Oaks, Maine, Kelly Gordon had been a thief. Her career began with the theft of a diamond broach from the mother of a classmate. She got ten dollars for it, which was itself a steal, but the young Kelly had failed to recognise the stones as real gems. It was a mistake she would not make again.

Ten years later she left home and Dark Oaks and, as far as she could see, would never need to return to either. She had amassed a fifty-thousand-dollar bank account in the meantime, which was kept for her by an admiring professional fence who was also her lover. This little nest-egg was effectively doubled, when, to celebrate her eighteenth birthday, she carried out a daring hotel raid which the police considered had to be the work of a squad of acrobatic commandos.

For that was Kelly Gordon's forte: she channelled her astonishing degree of physical fitness, her sporting prowess, her breath-taking beauty and very considerable intellect into becoming one of the world's best cat burglars. And she used her skills to steal diamonds; her abiding passion, apart from men. It was in trusting a greedy lover that she made her second mistake, and William Darrow snatched her from the clutches of New York's finest to enrol her as an agent of UNSIS.

She was sitting in the foyer of the Watergate Hotel when Simon Barnes came in. He spotted her immediately, for she was wearing the uniform of an Airperson First Class, USAF. He had been heading for the reception desk but changed direction when he saw Kelly. As he got closer his stride faltered and he blinked. Kelly Gordon had that effect on men.

"You must be Sally's replacement?" he said, managing to stay in character; not knowing the girl was another player in the game.

"Yes, sir."

Kelly arched her back, holding her legs apart, her hands behind her bent knees, the soles of her feet caressing his chest, as his penis entered her. The bed groaned as he plunged rhythmically back and forth...

When UNSIS agent Simon Barnes recovered from the drug Kelly Gordon had given him in his drink aboard Air Force One, and found himself looking down the barrel of the 9mm automatic pistol she was holding, he, of course, had no idea that she too was an agent of UNSIS. Indeed, his thoughts were quite the reverse, especially when he saw the body of Fred Marsden slumped in the aisle, a six-pointed Ninja death star embedded between his eyes.

"I'm so sorry about your friend, Simon," whispered the girl.

"Are you?" he growled, his eyes blazing hate. "Are you really? And after everything we did together, what, only hours ago. You cold-blooded bitch."

"Don't, Simon. Please don't."

"Is the President safe?"

"Of course. He would be no use to Caligari and SPEAR any other way."

"Is Caligari on board?"

"No."

"So why am I still alive?"

"Good question," she murmured, drawing closer until he could smell her perfume. She gave him a grim little smile. "Let's just say I enjoyed our spot of monkey business."

They exchanged a long, silent glance, broken only by the lumbering approach of one of the team of hijackers. He was one of the late and unlamented Tran Phan Lon's army of Ninja thugs, trained in Thailand. Ten to one that was where Aubrey Caligari was holed up, thought Barnes.

"Now do you understand?" whispered Kelly.

"What you do?" the thug snarled in fractured English to the girl.

"Don't be jealous, Chung-Li," she said lightly, smiling her brightest smile at the bestial killer. "I was just telling him what a lousy fuck he was."

Chung-Li laughed, and laughed again as she winked at him, rolling her hips as she walked away down the aisle. The Ninja took his eyes off Simon for just long enough. The UNSIS agent braced himself against the back of his seat and kicked out suddenly, catching the Thai in the groin with the heel of his right foot.

"AHHHHHHHHH."

At the sound of the man's scream, Kelly spun round and raised her gun in both hands. "Don't move, Chung-Li."

The gentleman in question was doubled-up in the companionway, his hands between his legs. When he straightened up, the action was a blur in Simon's eyes, like the blade of a flick knife appearing, and in Chung-Li's right fist glinted a six-pointed Ninja throwing star.

"Kill him," he screamed at Kelly.

In the one second it took Simon to shout that order, and the three seconds it took the girl to register the meaning of his words, and Chung-Li's lightning-like movements, the glittering star of death had covered three-quarters of its flight.

She pulled the trigger of the 9mm Luger. The bullet made a soft, squelching thud as it contacted the Ninja's fat gut. He flopped back across two seats. At the same moment the throwing star struck Kelly in the windpipe. She staggered back, choking, firing wildly. One bullet punched a neat hole in the perspex of a window opposite the slumped form of Chung-Li.

Instantly, there was a tremendous howl, almost a scream of rushing air as the cabin depressurised. Simon strapped himself in quickly and looked for Kelly. Alive or dead he knew not, but her body was wedged between a seat and a partition wall at the far end of the compartment. He watched in horror as the still-living fat man was sucked screaming out through the small window and into the stratosphere, thirty thousand feet above Missouri.

After that, all hell was let loose. With an appalling crash of crockery from the galley, the huge plane stood on its nose and dived. The last thing he knew before he blacked out was the high-pitched whine of the jet engines from the open window, and a hallucinatory vision of pillows and rugs shooting out into space all around him. The pain in his lungs was unbearable.

He came to with the captain of Air Force One leaning over him, shaking him by the shoulder and saying something.

"Are we down?" mumbled Simon. His head cleared. "The President?"

"Is okay. Bit of a hairy landing. When everything went haywire we managed to disarm the other hijackers."

"And Kelly?"

"In a bad way, but she'll live to stand trial for high treason."

"No, she won't, Captain," Barnes said with a smile, getting slowly to his feet and surveying the damage around him. Fred Marsden's body was missing.

"Must have gone out the window," said the captain, following Simon's gaze. "Still think the girl shouldn't stand trial?"

"She's an agent of UNSIS. She works for William Darrow."

"How do you know?"

"Monkey business," said Simon Barnes, remembering Clarence Darrow and the famous 'monkey' trial of the 1920s. "A spot of monkey business."

ENDINGS AND BEGINNINGS

The Hotel du Cap is more than a hotel; it is a legend. A serene white and blue shuttered Second Empire building, it is set on a hill overlooking twenty-two acres of scented pine woods and rose gardens on the tip of Cap d'Antibes, and its elegant paths wind down toward the Mediterranean and the Eden Roc, the world's most exclusive beach.

The guest list is a who's who not of the year or of the decade but of the century: F. Scott Fitzgerald wrote about it; Chagall and Picasso strolled through its gardens; the Prince and Princess of Lithuania honeymooned in adjoining suites numbers 33 and 34; Joanna Jerome and Lyssette Cromwell were among its great beauties and Porfirio Rubirosa and Nikos Adonisthenes among its great playboys, and it was there one day in June, 1987 that Susie Watkins married Paul Ashley.

Jean-Claude Duparier, the bride's lover and former father-in-law, gave Susie away, and Roxanne Duparier Adonisthenes, the bride's former sister-in-law, was the first to wish the couple well after the vows had been exchanged.

Two hundred guests swirled around the ground floor and the gardens and out onto the pebbled, curved drive. Among them was Simon Barnes. When Jean-Claude had announced the appointment of Roxanne to the vice-presidency of Duparier/Europe one week before the wedding, a new life insurance policy was negotiated reflecting Roxanne's value to the company. As part of the terms of the policy, the company required that Roxanne be attended at all times by a personal bodyguard.

Jean-Claude had not hesitated to select Michael Cord for the job. In a well-tailored dark suit, Cord blended in perfectly with the other guests and unobtrusively hovered close to Roxanne, never taking his eyes off her.

Many of the guests knew some of the story, but the one person who did know the whole story was the one person to turn down an invitation. In London, Joy Joy de Ferrare lay on her couch, a Charvet robe the texture of heavy cream against her bare skin, and while Susie and Paul exchanged vows in Cap d'Antibes, she dictated the first line of her new book into a tape recorder: "Theirs was not a marriage made in heaven, but a coupling conceived in hell."

Jean-Claude Duparier, everyone at the wedding had remarked, must have discovered the elixir of youth. He had never looked better or seemed happier; never more charming and charismatic. As the host at the wedding, he appeared to enjoy it more than anyone, including the bride and groom, and was among the last to leave. His Learjet waited in his private hangar at Nice/Cote d'Azur airport.

As the gleaming limousine glided along the high Corniche road, with the lights of Monte Carlo reflecting off the dark mirror of the Mediterranean, Jean-Claude thought about the new hotel and leisure complex he was going to build at Bodrum, on the Turquoise coast of Turkey. Called Halicarnassus in antiquity, it was one of the few ideal and still-unspoilt tourist areas in the world. The harbour was ideal for yachts and motor cruisers; the site had ancient ruins, pine forests, white beaches, picturesque local markets, and a Crusaders' castle guarding the harbour. Across the narrow inlet lay the Greek island of Kos. Jean-Claude looked forward to telling Roxanne about it.

Since Roman's death they had become more than father and daughter, and much more than business partners. At lunch in the Paris Ritz a week before the wedding, they became not just allies but accomplices...

"Twenty million dollars should be enough, Father," said Roxanne, adding, with a smile, "Even for her."

"I don't know."

For the first time in his life, Jean-Claude doubted the power of money.

"She'll jump at it."

"Susie Watkins isn't our only problem," said Jean-Claude. "Felix Krug is reluctant to have you named vice-president of Duparier/Europe."

For several months Jean-Claude had wanted the announcement made. Roxanne had worked at the London offices of the company for more than a year, and it had still not been officially announced that she was being groomed to succeed her father as chief operating officer in Europe.

"So Felix isn't keen, is he?" said Roxanne. "Well, fuck him."

Jean-Claude and Roxanne looked at each other, a deep look, a look they both understood, a look that no one else could have interpreted.

"Fuck them both," said Jean-Claude.

As Roxanne and her father crossed the ornate lobby of the Ritz Hotel, they had become the principal players in a drama invisible to onlookers.

Jean-Claude was consumed by thoughts of revenge, money and death. His obsession with Susie Watkins was destroying his life. The guilt he felt over his son's death was eating at his soul. By saving Susie from a murder charge he had condoned her crime. There had to be a way to break free. He looked at Roxanne, walking next to him, matching him stride for stride, and wondered how to put his feelings into words.

"I think," he began, "there should be conditions."

"That's why we hire lawyers, Daddy."

As Roxanne listened to her father, she thought of what she had learnt in the past few days: that Susie had killed Roman and bound her father to her in an unholy guilty secret; a secret that had led Roxanne to think that Roman had taken his own life.

Jean-Claude and his daughter left the Ritz lobby and stepped into the Place Vendome. Suddenly, he stopped and turned, looking back.

"The Ritz has always been one of my favourite hotels."

"Don't tell me," Roxanne laughed. "You'd like to buy it."

"Why not?" answered her father, also laughing.

They linked arms. For the first time in her adult life, Roxanne Duparier Adonisthenes felt really rich.